SNAKES CAN'T RUN

SNAKES CAN'T RUN

ED LIN

MINOTAUR BOOKS
A THOMAS DUNNE BOOK
NEW YORK

A THOMAS DUNNE BOOK FOR MINOTAUR BOOKS.
An imprint of St. Martin's Publishing Group.

SNAKES CAN'T RUN. Copyright © 2010 by Ed Lin. All rights reserved. Printed in the United States of America. For information, address St. Martin's Press, 175 Fifth Avenue, New York, N.Y. 10010.

www.thomasdunnebooks.com
www.minotaurbooks.com

Book design by Jonathan Bennett

Library of Congress Cataloging-in-Publication Data

Lin, Ed.
    Snakes can't run / Ed Lin.—1st ed.
        p. cm.
    "A Thomas Dunne book."
    ISBN 978-0-312-56988-4
    1. Chinese Americans—New York (State)—New York—Fiction.   2. Detectives—
New York (State)—New York—Fiction.   3. Human trafficking—Fiction.
4. Family secrets—Fiction.   5. Triads (Gangs)—Fiction.   6. Chinatown
(New York, N.Y.)—Fiction.   I. Title.
    PS3562.I4677S63 2010
    813'.54—dc22

                                                            2009041524

First Edition: April 2010

10 9 8 7 6 5 4 3 2 1

For my grandparents

Man's nature is evil; goodness is the result of conscious activity.

—Xunzi (c. 312 B.C.E.–?)

SNAKES CAN'T RUN

1

August 1, 1976

TO THE NOTICE OF NOBODY IN CHINATOWN, MY PARTNER AND I climbed out of a manhole on Bayard Street close to the intersection with Mulberry. It was the third storm drain section we had checked out that day.

I sat on the back bumper of our Con Ed truck and Vandyne joined me there after pulling out two cold cans of Coke from the cooler in the front seat. I wiped off the Tiger Balm from my upper lip and nose onto my sleeve. We were smelly and exhausted. Ghosts swam by in the humidity.

We pulled the tabs off our Cokes and flipped them into the open manhole.

"I feel like I just climbed out of the *Poseidon,*" I said.

"I remember seeing white girls in shorts climbing ladders, but I don't remember any of the Chinese people making it out," said Vandyne.

"I would have followed Gene Hackman. He was in *The French Connection.* He knew his stuff."

"That was an okay movie. But considering the number of shafts there were in *The Poseidon Adventure,* how come Shaft wasn't in it?"

"I'm sure he was holed up somewhere with some lady."

I wiped my forehead with the cold soda can. I pointed to the open manhole.

"What do you think?" I asked Vandyne.

He shrugged. "How about we close up and take the truck back? We'll talk in the truck."

"Let's do that."

We finished our sodas and chucked the cans into the open manhole. They made no sound.

"Hey, Chow, can you get that cover back on?" Vandyne asked.

"Why me?"

"Because you're good at it and I have seniority."

"Is this in my job description?"

"Just remember one thing, partner. You signed yourself up for these assignments. You wanted it."

I folded up the orange gate that had blocked off traffic and put it in the truck. Then I grabbed a crowbar and dragged the manhole cover back on. The late-summer sun reflected off a windshield directly into my eyes and I had to keep my head down.

I threw the crowbar into the back of the truck and slammed the door shut. Vandyne started up the engine before I jumped in on the passenger side. I reached over and cranked up the AC.

"That starts blowing cool pretty quick," said Vandyne. We wound our windows up.

"There were people down there," I said. "Maybe like a week ago, judging by the footprints and other garbage."

"You're right. Probably twenty people."

We both had field experience in Vietnam. Even though we had been back to the World for four years, our memories were still fresh. Too fresh.

"But no shells, no bodies, no blood," I said.

"The tourists said they heard gunshots and yelling coming from the gutter."

"Maybe it was kids who were lighting up firecrackers and dropping them down there."

"Personally," said Vandyne slowly, "the worst thing I saw down there was all the congealed grease lying around. Made me think about fat clogging arteries."

"All those Chinatown restaurants have to pour their crap out somewhere. Why not down the gutter? It's right there and you don't even have to pay someone to dispose of it."

There was a loud honking behind us. A noodle truck didn't have enough room to squeeze by. The guy in the passenger seat stuck his head out and saw in my side mirror that I was Chinese. He jumped out and charged up to my window.

I cranked the window down so he could yell at me.

"You guys are the worst!" he started. "Lazy! Stupid! Greedy! You keep raising your rates and now you want to take over the streets, too! Get out of my way, already, or is the black boy too stupid to know how to drive?"

I looked down at my reflective orange vest and my Con Ed patch. I pushed back my hard hat and said, "Eat shit, fuckface."

Vandyne eased the truck away from the curb. "What happened?" he asked me.

"He lost his cat. I told him where to find it."

Vandyne smirked.

We went through a police checkpoint before getting onto the Brooklyn Bridge. A cop came up to the window. He looked in at both of us, nodded, and waved us through.

I leaned back in the passenger's seat and turned to Vandyne.

"I never thought New York would see so much terrorism," I said.

"Me and you both."

The latest bombing by the group FALN, which sought independence for Puerto Rico from the United States, had blown up a phone booth outside of 1 Police Plaza. Two people were lightly injured, but the indignity of having a bomb go off right under our headquarters lit a fire under the ass of the NYPD in general and the Fifth Precinct in particular, because it happened inside our boundaries. All precinct detectives were dispatched full-time on destroying the FALN except for Vandyne, who was the least senior detective, and me, because I was only on detective track. Unlike Vandyne, I didn't have the gold shield yet. I was Encyclopedia Brown with a gun.

"Terrorists only harm their own causes and shame their own people," said Vandyne.

"We'll get those sons of bitches," I said.

I picked up the Chinese papers from the floor.

The Communist-biased newspaper had an editorial about how U.S. Representatives John Young, Wayne Hays, and Allan T. Howe—all recently embroiled in separate sex scandals—were emblematic of a corrupt capitalist society ready to collapse shortly after turning two hundred years old.

The Hong Kong–biased newspaper congratulated Trinidad and Tobago on gaining independence and joining the Commonwealth.

"Anything good?" asked Vandyne.

"Naw," I said. I put an eight-track of *Innervisions* into the player.

"Normally, I don't like synthesizers," Vandyne said. "But this is all right."

"This is what Stevie hears in his head," I said.

For a year, from 1974 to 1975, Vandyne and I were partnered in a sector car for the Fifth Precinct. I could not have asked to be paired up with a better person—a fellow Vietnam vet and someone else who had also killed a little boy there.

Then right before the layoffs and cutbacks from the city's financial crisis kicked in, we lost our car. Vandyne picked up investigative assignments while they had stuck me on a footpost.

They also made me attend community functions in Chinatown so when the pictures came out in the Chinese newspapers there was me in a uniform saying, "See, the NYPD actually hired one of you people!" They were putting the one Chinese cop they had in the most visible position possible.

Sitting at these dinner events depressed me even more because as much as the NYPD was using me to establish legitimacy with the Chinese, the various community leaders were using me to boost their own profiles in Chinatown.

I drank until I forgot everything: frustrations with the job, jealousy that Vandyne was getting ahead, Nam flashbacks. But when I woke up and remembered again, it was always worse.

That was all behind me now, but I still shuddered when I thought about those days.

I folded up the Chinese newspapers and shoved them into my right armpit.

We showered in the Con Ed employee facilities.

"I can't believe how clean this place is," I said. "They give you clean towels, soap, and shampoo."

"We're in the wrong line of work, partner," said Vandyne.

"It's like a country club."

"This is no country club! I bused tables at a country club one summer outside Philly."

"What was it like working for the man?"

"Well, the worst tippers were the Chinese people."

"Chinese people don't join country clubs!"

"I think one of them was named 'Robert Chow.'"

"See, there you go. 'Robert Chow' is not a Chinese name."

"It's not?"

"No. It's an American name."

We got back into our street clothes. Vandyne dressed in khakis, a dark blue buttoned shirt, and a Mets hat. I had on a pair of jeans and a rugby-styled shirt that my girlfriend had paid way too much money for.

We went into the underground parking and got into the unmarked car.

"So very recently there were about twenty people down there," I started.

"The information we got was good."

"The information was old. Where are those people now?"

"The smugglers must have moved them."

"One other possibility," I suggested, "is that those people could have settled their debts all at once and been released. But that's not a likely scenario."

"What else could have happened?"

"The only possibilities are that they paid up, were moved, or were killed."

"Well, they weren't killed. I don't think they've paid up. So where have they been moved to?"

"That's today's bonus question."

"These people who get smuggled in, what keeps them going to work and coming home to the safe house?"

"Chinese people freak out about settling debts. It's shameful to have one, no matter how evil the lender is. Besides, if they tried to run away, they'd probably be killed."

"How much is the smuggling fee?"

"Several thousand dollars."

"Several *thousand!*" exclaimed Vandyne. "That's a lot of money to just see the Statue of Liberty."

"You have to give it to the illegals, they're the huddled masses. From what I've read in the Chinese newspapers, smugglers can even charge ten grand per person."

"How badly could you want in on this country?"

"You know what it's like being stuck in Asia, Vandyne. When you were in Nam, what would you have paid to come back?"

"Wouldn't have paid nothing. A ride back was the very least they owed me. A ride back on a *plane*."

"These people are paying smugglers a thousand-dollar deposit for a ride in a freight container from Hong Kong or Taiwan to San Francisco and then a train across the country and finally a bus or truck to New York City. Then they're basically prisoners until they pay off their debt in a sweatshop, factory, or pross house."

"How long does it take to work off nine thousand dollars?"

"A couple years. More if they lie to you."

We watched two Con Ed trucks drive into the garage and park. The workers shambled out.

"I have a new respect for these guys," said Vandyne. "Who else would be willing to put in forty hours a week down in hell?"

"Yeah, let's think about that when we're writing the monthly check for the next rate hike," I said.

We checked the shields in our wallets and our guns.

"Time to get you to the store, right?" asked Vandyne as he started up the car.

"Highlight of my day," I said.

I kind of meant it, too. Ever since the midget bought the toy store and hired my roommate, Paul, to work there, I had been dropping by informally for the last half hour or so that the store was open. It gave people in the neighborhood a chance to talk to someone in law enforcement without stepping into the police station.

Chinese people are far too superstitious for their own good. They think that if you go see the doctor for a checkup, you'll get cancer. If you buy life insurance, you're going to die. If you visit a police station—for any reason—you'll be thrown in jail.

I'll never understand how people from the great civilization that advanced humankind with the inventions of paper, gunpowder, and chow fun could still harbor so many stupid ideas.

When I walked into the toy store on Mulberry Street, the midget was dealing with a kid who couldn't make up his mind over which kung fu model he wanted. The midget was wearing a collared shirt and had his shirtsleeves rolled up, exposing surprisingly muscular biceps. His combed and side-parted hair was shiny like licked black licorice and he kept his face unshaven, I think to distinguish himself from his customers.

The midget's half-closed eyes regarded the boy at the counter with bemusement and annoyance.

The kid was chubby and you could see that at some point, maybe a few days ago, he had smeared his Fudgsicle-covered fingers across his Shazam! T-shirt. His watery eyes were contemplating two figures in the case behind the cash register. He sucked in his upper lip and spat it out a few times.

"Which one is better?" he asked the midget. "The guy throwing a punch or the guy with one leg up?"

"Honestly, they're both exactly the same, kid," said the midget. He saw me and winked.

"They're doing different things, how can they be the same?"

"They both cost me the same price, they'll cost you the same price, and I'll get the same amount of profit on either one. There's no difference."

"They look different!"

"People look different, too. But they're also all the same."

I went down an aisle that featured paints and balsa-wood sheets and sat on a step stool in the back corner. I nodded to the kid with the broom sweeping up. He grunted something.

I had worked at the toy store after I had come back from Nam and didn't know what the hell I was doing. I was an old friend of the prior owner. But how the midget came to own the store is too complicated to get into now. In other words, it's a story in which I don't come out looking too good.

I tightened my right shoelace and by the time I put my foot down the first person of the night was at my side.

She was an older woman with pinched-in cheeks and a dry crust of a mouth.

"Detective Chow," she started.

"Just call me Robert here," I said. I got tired of explaining that I was only on detective track and not actually a detective yet.

"Yes. I . . . I'm scared. I need my landlord to fix the stairs in my building. It's not safe."

"Mrs. Yung," I said. "You live on the first floor."

"It's just not safe, Robert! There are kids who live in that building!"

I touched her gnarled hand and felt a soft pulse amid the bones.

"You shouldn't be out this late," I told her. "You should be at home."

"Not you, too," she said, moving away.

Two men in their fifties wearing sagging tank tops came up next, looking as glum as the bratty kids they used to be.

"Officer Chow, this guy stole my watch!" the bigger one said.

"Nope," said the other, who had his hands in his pockets past the wrists. "You lost it in a poker game."

"But I need that watch! I can't work properly if I can't keep track of time."

"Should have thought about that before putting it into the pot."

"Can I see the watch?" I asked.

The smaller guy sighed and pulled out his hands. One wrist had on a cheap wristwatch with a fake leather band. His other hand held on to a Timex with a steel stretch band.

"You're keeping his Timex even though it doesn't fit you?" I asked him.

"No, because he's so fat," the smaller guy said.

"I got muscles in my wrists!" said the bigger man.

"Look, how much money are we talking about?" I asked.

"Five dollars," the bigger man said. The other guy nodded.

"Just give him his watch. He'll still pay you the lousy five bucks, all right?"

"It's not right," the smaller man grumbled, although he handed over the watch.

"Hey," said the bigger man. "It's not wound up! It was running when I gave it to you! Officer Chow, make him wind it for me!"

"Wind it yourself!" I said. "You've got muscles in your wrists, right?"

They both walked off muttering and I wondered why I bothered to do this until a young woman walked up.

Her eyebrows were thin and yet incredibly bold above two black satin eyes. She had a pixielike expression that was blissfully unaware of her own beauty, except for her mouth, which was twisted a bit to one side.

"Is the madness over yet?" she asked.

"For tonight, yes, I think," I said. "How was your day, Lonnie?"

"Very, very tiring." She put out an elbow and slumped against a rack of comic books.

"Hey, Sis!" yelled Paul, putting his broom aside. "Don't wrinkle those comic books!"

Lonnie straightened up and held out a paper bag to Paul. "Gee, I guess you don't really want these leftover pastries, then, huh?"

"Aw, I'll take it," said Paul, grabbing it.

"More studying tonight?" I asked Lonnie. I stood up and kissed her on the cheek. Chinese people aren't very affectionate in public. They don't even hold hands in the street, though that's also because the sidewalks in Chinatown are too narrow to go down side by side.

"I still have to finish that book about mass media," she groaned. I didn't know how she worked her day job as a low-level manager at Martha's Bakery and still studied at night. Actually, I never really knew how people studied at all. But hey, I made it through high school without trying too hard.

I got up and walked out with Lonnie, intending to see her to her parents' door. "Paul," I said, "I expect to see you back at the apartment soon."

"Don't worry about me, man!" he said, leaning on his broom. If that kid weren't a genius, I would have straightened him out by now for that attitude of his. I had to face facts, though. That kid was going to be a sophomore in high school and was already way smarter than me. Paul was living with me because his dad, who was also Lonnie's dad, had been beating him. He had also been hanging out with wannabe gangsters in the streets. Lonnie's stepmother was Paul's mom.

The midget had his head down and was writing something on a shipping receipt. "See you two later," he said without looking up.

As soon as we were on the street, a spry old man grabbed my shoulder.

"Robert Chow," he said, "I'm so sorry, I tried to get here sooner."

"Hey, that's all right," I said.

"Do you remember me?" he said. The man was dressed in a tan linen suit and fancy penny loafers that should probably be holding quarters. His beard and mustache were trimmed cleanly. His tan cap was probably covering mostly bare scalp.

"I don't know who you are," I said.

"I'm Mr. Tin. It's 'T'ien' in Mandarin, but you knew me as 'Tin.' You went to school with my son Don."

I felt one of my hands tighten into a fist.

"Sure," I said. "I remember you and Don."

"Well, he's been having problems, Robert. Could you please just go talk to him? Ever since he came back from Vietnam a few years ago, he's had trouble readjusting. We've had him at our home upstate, but things haven't been working out. I got him a place back in Chinatown, hoping that being back in the Cantonese environment would help, but, well, we haven't heard from him in a few weeks."

I looked into Mr. Tin's eyes. I remembered him as the furious dad who pulled me off of Don's moped even though he said I could ride it. Now he looked tired and in need of help.

"You basically want me to check in on him, right?" I asked.

"Yes, that's it."

"Have you gone to the apartment?"

"Yes, just now. I have the keys, but the door is chain-locked. I hear him moving around in there, though. Maybe because of your common experience, he would be more amenable to seeing you."

"Sure, I'll go."

"Here is the address," said Mr. Tin, handing me a card while flashing a look of concern at Lonnie.

"Pardon my manners, Mr. Tin, this is my girlfriend, Lonnie."

"How are you, Mr. Tin?" she asked.

He smiled. "Very, very pretty!" was all he could say.

"This is your phone number on the back?" I asked Mr. Tin.

"Yes. If I'm not there, leave your name with the secretary, but don't say any more."

"I'm on my way," I told him.

He tipped his cap at me and then at Lonnie. A black sedan pulled out from the curb and a rear door opened. Mr. Tin stepped inside and the car tore away.

"Were you friends with his son?" asked Lonnie.

"I was. Sure I was."

"You don't sound like you were."

"The thing about Don was that he was the richest kid in class. He was a nice kid, but he got a lot of breaks in life."

"You sound jealous."

"Yeah, I was." Especially after my first girlfriend, Barbara, left me for him.

"Do you want me to come with you?"

"Oh, no. I've got this one. This is guy talk."

"Did you see him in Vietnam?"

"No, I didn't. He was discharged early for some reason. He wasn't even wounded. I think his father pulled some strings."

"His father is that influential?"

"Lonnie, his dad is officially a representative in the Kuomintang government. You know—the KMT. He flies back to Taiwan to vote a few times every year."

"He doesn't even live in Taiwan. How can he be a representative?"

"He's actually supposed to represent a district in China that the KMT hasn't controlled since they lost the civil war in 1949."

"He lives in America and legislates in Taiwan for a district in China?"

"That's it."

"That doesn't seem to be a real job, then, does it?"

"Anything is a real job if you get paid for it."

A tourist would think that the KMT had won the Chinese civil war by the way their flags flew in most of Chinatown.

When the KMT lost the mainland it retreated to the tiny yam-shaped island Taiwan, also known as "Free China," which was ironic because the people were caught in the grip of martial law. The KMT also held sway over Chinatown.

It was no secret that the KMT backed the Greater China Association, an umbrella group for Chinatown's many smaller family and district associations. Greater China was historically the unofficial government of Chinatown, and mediated between groups and between the Chinese and New York City.

The KMT also owned the largest newspaper in Chinatown and kept a steady drumbeat of anti-Communist features and editorials. Much of the content was aimed at the small but growing community east of Bowery that was loyal to the mainland.

Together Chinese Kinship, a rival umbrella group comprised of Communist affiliates, was growing quickly. After years of enduring KMT dominance in Chinatown, these parties lashed out earlier this year. A bunch of rabble-rousers disrupted Greater China's New Year's Day parade with a protest urging the United States to switch diplomatic recognition to the People's Republic from Taiwan.

The switch was the KMT's greatest nightmare and yet it also seemed inevitable. Nixon merely shook hands with Mao, but Carter—a farmer and therefore a communist—would embrace him like a fellow pinko.

Carter was killing Ford in the polls, too, so the KMT could only root for Mao to die before Carter could be sworn in. Word was Mao was lingering on his deathbed and couldn't last much longer.

I think they needed to consider that the New York Rangers have managed to soldier on in a semiconscious state since 1940.

I walked Lonnie to the apartment where she lived with her dad and stepmother. The building entrance on the south side of Bayard Street was a battered door with sheet metal riveted over it. The ground floor storefront was a souvenir shop that made a lot of money selling cheap ching-chong crap to tourists.

I dropped her off and walked down to the forlorn Park Street address that Don's father had given me. Park Street, which is a long way from Park Avenue, is a steep one-block street between Mott and Columbus Park. Most Chinese people tried to stay off of it not only because it was a bit run-down—even by Chinatown standards—but also because it was right around the corner from three funeral homes by the park.

The ground floor of Don's apartment was the Chinese Longevity funeral home. Through the window all I could see were flowers and closed curtains. Names of the deceased were taped to the glass front door to inform potential mourners without troubling them to actually step into the home and jinx themselves.

Step into a funeral home and you'll die, they think.

I glanced at the names, admiring the calligraphy. It had been a bad week for Lees and Wongs. The building was originally a bank to serve what was then the local Italian immigrant community. The claws of a busty granite eagle clamped the arch above the funeral home's door, its steadfast gaze fixed to a faraway time and place.

Off to the side was the building entrance to the apartments above Chinese Longevity. I pressed the button next to "2R."

I heard a crackle come over the speaker.

"Don?" I asked. "It's Robert. Robert Chow. From Seward Park High. How are you, man?"

Shards of white noise ripped through the speaker. I was about to press the button again when the door lock buzzed. I pushed my way in. The lobby smelled like fried garlic. It was a pleasant note that offset the lobby's smashed tile floor and crumbling plaster walls. Some broken pieces of furniture were neatly stacked at the side of the stairwell.

I walked up to the second floor, wondering why Don's father couldn't have gotten him a better place.

I was about to knock at 2R when Don swung the door open. He was dressed in flannel pajamas and a camouflage jacket. Don's long, lean face dripped with sweat. He obviously hadn't slept in days, yet he managed to look alert enough to drive a trailer truck cross-country.

"Don," I started. "How have you been?"

"Don't you know?" he said.

"No, I don't."

"You haven't heard about my father?"

"No."

"It's in the fucking news every day, Robert!"

I looked into his wild eyes.

"Can I come in, Don?"

"Yeah, it doesn't matter. I don't have anything to hide. Anymore."

I walked in with caution. The apartment seemed to be completely empty except for a sleeping bag on the floor.

"Robert," said Don after he closed the door. "My father is part of a conspiracy."

"What kind?"

"He's trying to use me as the sacrificial lamb to justify invading China."

"Whoa! What do you mean?"

"He's trying to have me kidnapped and murdered to make it look like the Chinese Communists targeted me. They broke the news on the radio."

"Don, you don't seem to have a radio. Or a television."

"I got rid of them. They had microphones hidden in them."

"How come you don't have any furniture, Don?"

"There are men hidden behind the walls. If you listen closely you can hear them talking. They were planning on coming in through a hole and hiding in my furniture. Then they were going to surprise me and take me away."

I looked closely at Don. He believed every single word with all his heart. I briefly considered slapping him.

"There's nobody behind these walls, Don."

"Shhh. Listen."

The only thing I heard was the creaking of the floor as I shifted my weight.

"Hear that?" he asked.

"No."

"One guy just said, 'Robert Chow likes to suck cock.'"

I had to call Don's dad. This man needed help. Professional help.

"Don, I have to go right now. Can I bring you any food or anything else?"

"No," he whispered.

"Are you taking medicine?"

"I'm taking Chinese medicine, but it makes me sleepy. I don't like it. Robert, you have to stop the conspiracy. You have to stop my dad!"

"I will. I promise I will." I walked out of the apartment without turning my back on him, but I didn't go down the stairs until he closed the door and I heard his chain lock rattle into place.

I wanted to do something right away for Don. But I wasn't a doctor, so what could I do but feel anxious? I knew a drink would have calmed me down right away. But I also knew a single drink would send me spiraling off into the abyss. I was an alcoholic on my third month of sobriety, three months into the rest of my life.

I walked east on East Broadway. Apart from Don, it wasn't such a bad day, considering that most of it was spent walking through shit. It was uneventful, so that made it a good day. It's not like we had found bodies or anything.

My apartment was about an eight-minute walk from Bowery, if you walked in the street to avoid the crowded sidewalk. No Chinese people lived where I did, by the southeast corner of Seward Park. It used to be a Jewish neighborhood and plenty of the elderly were still there, mixed in with Spanish-speaking immigrants. Everybody largely avoided me, for a variety of reasons, including my race, my profession, and my past instability due to alcoholism.

The slouching walk-up building that I called home was a lot nicer than anything in Chinatown. The faceless management corporation that ran it and several other buildings had lost a major court battle and made sure to maintain the cleanliness of the stairwells and spray for pests regularly.

I could tell that Paul was home already because my mail wasn't sitting on the radiator. The residents' battered wall-mounted mailboxes, most with the lids torn off, stuck out of the wall like shrapnel from an exploded bomb. They were too daunting for the mailman to deal with. He would simply slap the entire building's mail on the lobby radiator and let us sort it all out. When the heat kicked in, it was probably a major fire hazard.

I went up the four flights to my apartment. I could hear that Paul was watching the 7 P.M. American news with Walter Cronkite. I fished around my pocket change for my door keys.

Then my radio went off with the code for possible dead bodies. Found between the bridges.

I folded my arms over my head and took a deep breath. I had trudged through tunnels all day and had had an extremely disturbing high-school reunion. Didn't that at least call for a mandatory Yoo-Hoo break?

I looked up at the ceiling, a multicolored splatter of cracked and chipped paint with the taped leftovers of torn-down red paper ornaments from Chinese holidays past. A pattern stretched diagonally into the corner—the outline of a lopsided face, sad and bloody.

I turned around and hopped down the stairs. I got on my radio and told Dispatch I was responding now.

2

BY THE TIME I GOT TO HENRY STREET UNDER THE MANHATTAN
Bridge overpass, one black-and-white and one unmarked police car were
already there.

Peepshow was standing at the edge of the crime scene, twirling his
baton, the one thing he could do without fucking up. "Keep moving,
keep moving!" he yelled to the murmuring Chinese people. He touched
his cap when he saw me. I nodded back.

Two bodies, Asian men in their twenties, lay on their sides. Both had
their hands tied behind them with wire. They didn't look fresh, and one
man's tattoo behind his ear stood out in sharp contrast to the white
bloodless flesh of his neck.

I walked up to English, but before I could say anything he put a
hand on my shoulder.

"These fucking bag monkeys won't let me past the tape," he said,
pointing out the forensic team collecting samples around the bodies.

"They're just trying to do their job right."

"I'll do their job for them right now. These guys died from gunshot wounds and the bodies were dumped here. You can analyze for blood type all you want, but you can't find the criminals looking down a microscope."

"I hear you."

"You know what solves crimes?"

"What?"

"Shoe leather. Walking around and asking questions."

"All right."

"Chow," he said, coming in closer. "You see the guy in the crowd in the red knit shirt smoking a cigarette?"

"Yeah," I said, knowing better than to look immediately.

"I don't like his face. Too smug."

"I'll follow him."

"Where's Vandyne?"

"Coming back from Queens."

"How were those drains today?"

"Some people had been down there, but there isn't anything down there now but shit and rats."

"Well, it sure beats having to pose for pictures at the Chinatown Girl Scouts banquet, doesn't it? I'd take shit and rats over that any day. I knew you would, too."

English was referring to my old footpost of walking a tame beat and making with the smiley smiles for the cameras. He used to try to wind me up just for the hell of it. But now that I was on detective track, he was my best friend in the world.

English was the nickname for Detective First Grade Thomas Sanchez. He was a light-skinned Latino who looked Italian. English was as tall as me, but he had a meaty, pockmarked face, like a raw steak after being pounded by a tenderizer. He had gotten his nickname because he didn't know how to speak Spanish despite being the son of immigrants from Puerto Rico.

We walked away from each other without saying anything more. I glanced back at the bodies and rubbed my hands on my legs.

I crossed the street and walked until I was almost in back of the smoking guy in red. I switched my radio off.

I was about ten yards away from him, standing near a stone trestle stained with rust. He looked like he was about my age, mid-twenties, and stood at about five and a half feet. His posture was perfectly straight. That told me something. There wasn't an honest job a man could have in Chinatown that wouldn't crimp his spine by that age.

The man flicked his cigarette away and walked west. I didn't get a good look at his face until we got to Bowery. He had deep-set eyes above a thin nose that bent to his right. The chin was squat and his lower jaw was shifty. He was a hardhead and I could bet that he was packing something to make up for his relatively short stature.

A few steps above the intersection with Pell Street, a taller man peeled off the wall and seemed to cut him off in an unfriendly kind of way. But they were talking and then the smaller man slapped the other guy's back. They laughed a little and then continued north on Bowery together.

I didn't attract as much attention as I used to on this street. My old footpost in uniform included Bowery, and thousands recognized my face from my pictures in the Chinese papers. But sobriety had caused major physical changes, all for the better. My face had slimmed down and my skin reverted to a dirty ivory color. I let my hair grow out, not crazy by seventies standards, but longer than it had ever been.

In my street clothes I looked like another ABC asshole in the neighborhood for some cheap eats.

I put my hands in my pockets, stepped behind a short couple, and continued to follow the two men.

"Oh, no," I groaned to myself when I saw them swing open a door at Jade Palace, Willie Gee's restaurant at the southwest corner of Bowery and Canal Street.

Jade Palace had settled a labor dispute earlier this year after some ugly picketing by angry waiters and a hunger strike. Willie still had it in for me because I wouldn't break up their legal protest. I walked across Bowery and watched from the other side of the street. I saw Willie in his distinctive prescription shades and black helmet of hair. He greeted the two men with an open-mouthed smile big enough for them to check his molars. Through the glass doors I could see Willie bringing them into the back of the restaurant, no doubt into the private room, and I lost sight of all of them.

I switched my radio back on. Immediately the dispatcher was calling me. I responded. Vandyne had been looking for me. I started walking south and said I'd meet him back under the bridge overpass.

They were putting the bodies into the back of an ambulance. English was sipping a cup of coffee that someone had gotten for him. He played with the tab of the plastic lid.

"That guy," I said, "went into Jade Palace with a buddy. I'm gonna follow up with Willie Gee tomorrow."

"That's good, Chow. Probably won't say shit, anyway, but why not make him sweat?"

Vandyne said, "Where are the people who reported the find?"

"Two tourists. Stopped Peepshow on his beat and brought him over to the bodies," said English. "Then they had a dinner appointment with friends."

"What kind of people find dead bodies and then go eat?" I asked.

"They're college professors. Peepshow got their business cards. They'll be coming to the Five later to make a formal statement. No one else here on the street saw anything, so this is how we're going to play it. You guys talk to the store owners in the area. They don't want to cooperate, tell them you might have to shut down the sidewalk area in front of their businesses for a while. That might make them talk. Maybe we can find out what the fuck happened here."

* * *

We went first to the fruit stand across the street. As soon as they saw us coming, the two men who had been unpacking crates jumped inside the store and locked the door.

I knocked on the glass and a man with a wrinkled neck that poked out of a dirty T-shirt shook his shaggy head. He said in English, "Close! Close!" I heard him through the vent above the door.

"Oh, closed, huh?" I challenged. I grabbed an empty plastic bag and started filling it with mangoes. I handed some bags to my partner. "C'mon, Vandyne! Fill 'er up!"

They watched us from inside the store and didn't make a move until we started giving away bags of fruit to passersby.

"Free! Free! Free!" I shouted.

"Hey!" yelled the shaggy-headed man. "What are you doing?"

"If you're closed, then all this must be trash!" I said. I rolled a pineapple down the street. Someone grabbed it and walked off.

The bolt slid out and the door, which had several bells and chimes tied to it, jangled open.

"I thought you people only stole an apple at a time!" the man yelled, grabbing our bags away.

"I thought you people kept regular hours."

"What do you assholes want from me?"

"We want to know what you saw down there."

"I didn't see anything! I heard sirens before I even knew what happened."

"Two men are dead. Their bodies are half a block from your store and you're not concerned at all?"

"I'm very concerned, okay? But I take care of myself. I concentrate on my store, my own business." He thumped his chest.

Not knowing what we were saying, Vandyne stepped back to the street and stared at the man.

"What's that black guy doing over there?" the store owner asked me.

"Oh, so now you notice things happening around your store?"

"I'm telling you, Detective, I didn't see anything and none of my workers saw anything."

"I guess you asked them already?"

"I don't have to ask! If somebody's looking around, they're not working. I'll fire them!"

Suddenly, I heard metal gates rolling down all over the block.

"Your workers are calling the other stores!" I said.

"I don't know!"

"How would you like me to shut down the sidewalk for our ongoing investigation of the area, pal? It might hurt your business a little bit if nobody can walk here."

"Don't you try to intimidate me, okay? I know who you are! You're the one who got that old man killed and harassed the toy-store owner until he had a heart attack!"

"Then you know I'm the wrong guy to mess with," I said, wondering if that could be construed as a threat in a court of law. "It was a stroke, not a heart attack, by the way."

"You're going to pay for all the damage you've done to this community!" He signaled for his workers to come out and pack up the fruit. "The gods always see that bad people get what they deserve—even a bad cop."

I smiled and handed him my card.

"I'm glad that we had this chance to chat," I said. "If you remember anything or want to talk for some reason, please give me a call at the precinct."

He growled and raised his hand over his head to throw my card to the ground, but he let go of it too early. We both watched it flutter slowly to the slimy sidewalk.

Vandyne and I went to an over-rice joint on Bayard near the Five for a quick dinner. We sat down and a waiter slammed a battered tin teapot on the wobbly table.

He sighed and brought over two thick teacups. I pushed the one that wasn't chipped to Vandyne. My hand shook as I poured some tea and topped off his cup. He tapped his fingers on the table in that fine traditional Chinese gesture.

I put my elbows up on the table and rubbed my eyes. I was tired, hungry, and still mad at that stupid store owner.

I had seen bodies, possibly tortured, in Vietnam, but that was in the context of a dirty war. What could possibly justify the deaths of these two young men here in America?

"Hey!" said Vandyne when I asked him about it. "What about all our black kids getting shot that nobody gives a damn about?"

"But black people do! The black community organizes and protests. Whether or not it gets picked up in the media is another thing. But Chinese people? Shit, they are just going to let this go. Nobody's going to talk about it. No witnesses are going to come forward. If those tourists didn't report finding the bodies, we would have had two bare skeletons before Chinese people said a word."

"If Chinese people don't care, then why do they live together and form Chinatowns not only in America but all over the world?"

"They're only together for the food. If you learn just one thing about Chinese people, Vandyne, it's this: They don't help their own in times of need. Oh yeah, if you've got money, they'll be glad to sell you something, probably at the best price you can find." I glanced at our smiling waiter who was slowly approaching us; he had no idea what I was saying. "But if you were in trouble or hurt, Chinese people wouldn't lift a fucking finger. They'd feel embarrassed for you, but that's it."

Our waiter, who had nothing to write with, came up and slumped over the back of a vacant chair at our table. He said, "Yeah?"

I turned to him and said, "Bring him chicken-fried rice and get me some sautéed bok choy over rice."

"You don't want any meat?" the waiter asked me, his breath reeking of cigarettes.

"I can't eat meat tonight," I said.

"Are you sick?" he asked. "Meat's good for you when you're sick."

"Not for what I've got."

"We have a lot of better dishes, like a fresh grouper," he said, turning to Vandyne. "So are you sure you just want chicken-fried rice?"

I told Vandyne to take it as a compliment when people talked to him in Chinese. Vandyne smiled and nodded.

The waiter coughed into one hand and scratched his back with the other as he walked away.

"I've taught you well, Vandyne."

"Oh yeah, smile and nod. Take whatever they give you."

"You got it down pat."

"What if the guy's telling me to go to hell?"

"Aw, he wouldn't do that." While you're with me, I thought. "Have you ever thought about trying to learn Cantonese?"

"Not seriously. It would be tough and, anyway, what would my ancestors think? What would *your* ancestors think, Chow?"

"Well, we're both speaking English right now. What would our ancestors think of that?"

"They would be extremely shocked, ashamed, and disappointed."

"To hell with their shame and disappointment! My ancestors don't pay the rent."

Our dishes swung in. Vandyne's tourist special came with a slightly twisted metal fork jammed in the side of the fried-rice pile. I got my chopsticks and probed the bok choy carefully. When you get greens sometimes tiny black bugs get caught between the leaves. It's always good to check before chomping.

Vandyne took a bite and then he put on a pained look.

"Hey, Chow, can you—"

"No!"

"But it needs some soy sauce for flavor!"

"They already cook it with soy sauce! If you add in more, you're giving yourself a ridiculous amount of sodium. You're going to end up with kidney stones or worse."

"I wasn't going to put that much more into it."

"Hey," I said. "You want to have dick problems?"

"Okay, okay, okay."

We both ate in about ten minutes. I signaled for the check, but the waiter waved me off. I left six bucks on the table to cover the meal with a generous tip. He cleared our table, shaking his head.

We came back to the Fifth Precinct on Elizabeth. Walking into the old brick house was like stepping back in time to 1881, because that was when it was built, and with no central air-conditioning or heating. The air conditioners stuck in our windows did little but drip water and raise a fucking racket.

Sitting at the desk immediately inside was the freckled face of Rip Mitchell. His first name was really Jim, but he used to have an extravagant mustache like Rip Taylor. He shaved it off, but he still liked being called Rip. The nickname had character and it wasn't insulting. Especially if you thought it stood for "rest in peace."

"How's it going, Rip?" asked Vandyne as we walked in.

"What's new, Rip?" I said.

"Vandyne. Chow," he said like he was taking attendance. He always said the least he could. He must have had a fat tongue from the lack of exercise.

I took a wide arc around Rip's desk to get as far as possible from the C.O.'s open office door and still make it to the stairwell. Damn, I thought, he's here late.

Our commanding officer, Sean Ahern, was short and thin, but he was as intimidating as a boulder rolling directly at you and picking up speed.

He had a small hairless spot in his right eyebrow, so we called him the Brow and, to his face, sir. You wouldn't want to piss him off. He had a bad temper and liked to stomp his feet hard and make you feel it in your chest.

Despite all that, the Brow had sparkling clear blue eyes that made him look incredibly innocent. He must have stolen them from some kid.

The Brow was out to get me because he had intended for me to spend my entire career as an NYPD prop at various Chinatown community events.

But I managed to break out and land investigative assignments. If I hadn't had the help of someone way up in the hierarchy, who was still anonymous to me, the Brow would have busted me down to guarding locked bicycles. My hockey skills during a benefit game against the fire department had impressed my guardian angel, and I wasn't sure if it was my scoring ability or my fighting prowess.

I thought I was in the clear, hiding behind Vandyne, when the Brow stomped his foot and yelled out, "Chow!"

I scuttled in and said, "Yes, sir?"

"Nothing," he spat out. "I just wanted to see how long it took for you to get here."

"Yes, sir."

"Get out!"

I saluted and left.

On the first flight of stairs, Vandyne let out a small whistle. "Goddamned Brow has got it bad for you," he said.

"He's got it bad and that ain't good."

"How do you know that song?"

"It's a song?" I said, surprised. "It was what a friend in Nam used to say all the time. 'We've got it bad and that ain't good.'"

Vandyne and I were on the second floor, which housed the detective squad and its small holding cell. Our precinct was a little unusual in that it had its own detective squad. I guess the powers that be figured there wasn't enough stuff crammed into our tiny building.

We walked into the squad room, sat down on the lopsided couch, and looked at English, who was at his desk, on the phone. He looked expectantly at us. I gave him a thumbs-down and he nodded.

Two tourists were sitting in battered chairs by Vandyne's end of the couch. The man was wearing khaki shorts, exposing two trunks of knotty varicose veins. He wore a dress shirt with rolled-up sleeves and a ratty collar. He had almost no hair and his face had been sunburned several times, making it harder to guess his age, which had to be north of fifty-five.

"Hi, I'm Herman Shepherd," he said to Vandyne, leaning in to shake hands. "Herman," he said again before reaching over to me.

Vandyne said, "Hi, I'm John." I nodded to Herman.

The woman shook my hand and said in perfect Mandarin, "I'm his wife, Irene." She was over forty but had worked hard at maintaining herself. Irene had a china-colored, heart-shaped face with dull green eyes and apparently had made herself up at the restaurant before coming in. A mid-length skirt showed some surprisingly great legs, especially in contrast to Herman's. I looked up quickly, but she had noticed and smiled.

"My name's Robert," I said to both of them. I think Irene was disappointed that I didn't speak Mandarin with her.

English got off the phone and came over. "Not much to expand upon," he said. "Herman and Irene are from upstate. They come into Chinatown every so often. Saw some group of people gathered—"

"*Chinese* people," interjected Irene.

English shrugged and continued. "So they went over to see what was going on. When the onlookers saw they were tourists, they dispersed."

"I didn't know what they were saying," said Irene. "I don't know Cantonese."

"It's tough to learn," I said.

"I've lived in Taiwan," Irene told me.

"I've never been there," I said.

"I was in Taiwan for a month," said Vandyne.

"Me, too," said Herman.

"What do you do?" Vandyne asked him.

"I teach geology at SUNY Buffalo. Sometimes I do exploration work for oil companies."

"I do translation work for the university's Asian studies journal," volunteered Irene. "I also lecture there, but I don't have tenure yet."

"Do you remember," I asked the Shepherds, "anybody who stood out at the crime scene?"

Herman frowned and looked at the floor. Irene said, "Well, I do remember this Chinese fellow in a red shirt, about average height. He gave us a rather menacing look. And I know that look. It's the resentment that they feel toward us." She looked at me. I glanced over at English, and he nodded at me. That was the guy who English had made out to be dirty and I had followed.

"That's about it," said English. "We'll be in touch if we ever need anything from you two."

"That's it?" asked Herman, rising to his feet. I half expected his veins to burst and bleed.

"We have to let them do their jobs, Herman," said Irene, a little too harshly.

They said good-bye and English escorted them out. When their footsteps in the stairwell had faded, I said to Vandyne, "Go ahead."

"Damn, that girl's got Yellow Fever. Bad, too."

"You know what, though? Yellow Fever's lethal."

English was walking back in. "Paperwork's lethal, too, guys. Let's get going."

"I'll do the bodies if you do the storm drains, Vandyne," I said.

"Now that's a deal, partner."

"Just make it neat, you two," said English. "I'm dealing with enough shittily typed reports from work on the FALN. If you can start sentences with capital letters, you're ahead of half of the meatballs who supposedly have more seniority."

Vandyne leaned into me. In a low voice he said, "I have that thing tomorrow. Remember, Chow?"

"I do," I said.

3

I GOT UP AS EARLY AS I COULD, ABOUT 0900, AND PAUL HAD ALready gone to his internship. That kid took an unpaid internship at a consulting firm that handled U.S.-Taiwan relations. I had helped to set him up at the job because my old girlfriend Barbara worked there.

Paul worked there mornings and came back to work in the toy store at night. That didn't sound like a fun summer for any kid. I shook my head. When I had met Paul he was in this downward spiral, beaten at home and spending too much time in the streets with his wannabe gangster buddies. He was so driven now it was hard to remember when he was loitering at Lonnie's bakery, taunting me.

I showered with sandalwood soap and Breck shampoo. Hey, it was on sale and you couldn't tell me that it was just for women, even though Lonnie had bought it and used it when she was over.

I threw on a blue short-sleeved buttoned shirt and black slacks. I passed over my regular heavy shoes and put on my black steel-toed boots because I was going into enemy territory. They gave a satisfying thump on each step when I went down to the building's front door.

I got a coffee from a bakery, but not Martha's because I didn't want to see Lonnie and maybe get softened up before I saw Willie Gee. I took a sip and grimaced. It tasted like it was yesterday's coffee reheated, but I still finished.

In the morning sun, Jade Palace stood out like a desert outpost to weary and hungry tourists too scared to go to crappy-looking restaurants. It was the biggest building on Bowery, and its shadow ominously fell across half the buildings on the block. For many tourists, including uptown Chinese, it was all the Chinatown they ever bothered to visit.

A truck was standing by the restaurant as two men with hand trucks wheeled crates of vegetables up a metal ramp and into the entrance.

When I reached the glass doors at the front, I swung open the one closest to me.

One of the deliverymen yelled out, "Hey, it's not open, yet!"

"I have a twenty-four-hour pass!" I yelled, flashing my shield. He ran away.

I walked into the main dining room. The lights were out and the tables looked ugly, without lazy Susans and new linen to cover up their chewed-up particleboard surfaces. I walked over to the private room at the side, but the door was locked. I heard an elevator bell go off. I turned and saw Willie Gee stroll into the dining room.

"Robert Chow!" he called out. "It's always a pleasure! I couldn't help but notice on our security cameras that you entered our premises outside of our business hours." He was wearing a gray polyester suit and a smile that could sell AMC Pacers.

I widened my stance and didn't shake his hand, which was aimed at my gut.

"Willie, I need to ask you about some customers you had last night."

"Of course, of course! Anything in the world that you want!" He pulled out two chairs from a nearby table. I moved my chair two feet away from his before sitting down.

"Last night around seven thirty P.M. two men came in and you seemed to know them. I think you brought them in to sit in the private room."

"Around seven thirty P.M. last evening, huh?" Willie surprised me by appearing to really think about the previous night. "What were they wearing?"

"One was about five-five, wore a red knit shirt. The other was taller, maybe five-eight or -nine, wearing a dark shirt."

"Both Chinese?"

"Yeah."

"Oh," said Willie, smiling and tapping his right temple. "I know exactly who you mean. These two gentlemen are Mr. Andy Ng and Mr. King Lam."

"Which one's the shorter one?"

"Mr. Ng."

"Do you know them well?"

"Mr. Ng comes in about once a week. Mr. Lam, less often."

"What line of work are they in?"

"They are both export-import businessmen, Robert. We do a lot of business with them. They entertain clients here. One time Mr. Ng bought out the entire dining room." Willie opened his face up in genuine surprise and raised his arms to his sides. "This whole room! Nobody's ever done that before!"

"What products does Ng import into the country?"

"I don't inquire the specifics of a man's business. That's rude, Robert! That's like asking every man who comes in if the woman he's with is his wife!"

"You seemed to be particularly glad to see him, like an old friend. Like someone you knew better than just a good customer."

Willie tilted his head at me.

"Are you kidding? Anybody who bought me out for the whole night would be my new brother! Even you, Robert!"

"What is the name of the company Ng works for?"

He inhaled deeply, then coughed. Willie hit his chest with an open palm. "Damn cigarettes," he choked. After he recovered more, Willie said, "Beautiful Hong Kong Limited."

He had another coughing fit and I slapped him hard on the back. He put up a hand asking me to wait, but I was already on my way out.

It wasn't unusual to have the word "beautiful" in the name of a business, because the United States is represented by a compound of the two characters "beautiful" and "country" in the written Chinese language, which is the same for the spoken languages Mandarin and Cantonese.

You know what the character for "beautiful" looks like—a lobster on its back with claws down, legs out, and tail up.

There were many companies in Chinatown that had "beautiful" in their name to show that they did business in the United States. Many of them had very ugly business practices, including not paying workers overtime, withholding paychecks, and firing pregnant women who couldn't stay on their feet.

I went down to Martha's Bakery to look in on Lonnie. The morning rush was over and she was wiping down the tables at the front. It broke my heart a little bit to see her doing this menial work, even though she was the assistant manager. I came in and patted her shoulder.

Victoria, the other woman who worked with Lonnie, was swishing a smelly mop around the floor by the counter. She winked at us. I waved to her.

Lonnie went behind the counter and gave me a small paper bag that contained two plain steamed rice buns. I still liked the hot-dog pastries, that Chinese-American creation that looks like a Viking helmet with both ends of the dog sticking out of the egg-glazed dough. Lonnie didn't let me have them very often. They were bad for me.

"I just came back from seeing Willie Gee," I told Lonnie as I checked the bag, unable to conceal my disappointment with what I saw inside. "I feel like I need a shower."

"You don't smell badly and you look all right. In fact, I'd say you look like a Breck Girl!" she said, smiling.

"Hey," I said, lowering my voice. "Keep it down, Lonnie!"

"It's funny, that's all. I'm trying to raise your spirits!"

"Anything interesting happen this morning?"

"Nothing, really. Just the usual. Well, everybody was talking about the two bodies that were found."

"Yeah, they're talking because there weren't any cops around."

"It was on the front page of all three newspapers!" That is, the KMT-biased one, the Communist-biased one, and the Hong Kong–biased one.

"Well, yeah, they can all agree on stronger sales."

Apart from having their own political slants, all three had sensationalist coverage of crime that bordered on ghoulish. About a month ago a man in L.A. had jumped from the roof of a building and the Communist-biased newspaper had run a photo spread showing the man plunging, frame by frame, to his death. I was disgusted at myself for buying a copy. Everybody in the detective squad flipped out when I showed it to them, but the midget had passed on taking a peek.

"Who do you think killed those guys?" I asked.

Lonnie gave me a hard look.

"Let's not talk about it," she said.

"Great idea. You're free tonight, right?"

"Yes."

"I'm going to send Paul to the midget's, then."

"Good idea."

I waved to Victoria, rubbed Lonnie's shoulder, and left.

"We have this year's Chinese Yellow Pages?" I asked English.

"We should. Check Lumpy's desk."

Lumpy was a guy who had retired early two years ago in a voluntary buyout during the city's fiscal crunch. His old desktop had become the detective bureau's unofficial library and condiment station. The drawers were crammed with packets of salt, pepper, ketchup, and mustard.

The Chinese Yellow Pages were published by the Hong Kong–biased newspaper. I flipped to the "importers" section and found three companies that could have fit the bill and set the book down on my desk, which was next to the drafty window.

I took a jar of Jif from Lumpy's bottom drawer. I wiped a plastic knife on my pants and then used it to spread peanut butter over one of the rice buns. I ate it quickly and washed it down with a cup of lukewarm water from our busted cooler.

I stretched out my hand and glanced at the rotary dial on my phone. There were marks all over the numbers on the dial from cops who had wanted to play Spirograph with their pens.

The phone for "Beautiful Hong Kong Peace" was disconnected.

There was no answer at "Beautiful Hong Kong Ltd."

A woman at "Beautiful Hongkong" answered the phone with a simple, "Hello?" I asked to speak to Mr. Ng and got what sounded like an aged man, surprised he had a phone call.

"Yes? This is Mr. Ng."

Finding a Mr. Ng wasn't so unusual. You throw a handful of popcorn in the air in the street and one or two will land on someone named Ng.

"Mr. Ng, is there another Mr. Ng who works there?"

"Well, no, there isn't. I don't actually work here myself, anymore. I closed this business years ago because the warehouse rent was just killing my margins."

"So 'Beautiful Hongkong' no longer exists?"

"No. Long gone. I keep telling them to delist my phone from the Yellow Pages, but you know, they never listen."

"Thank you anyway, Mr. Ng."

"Who are you?" he asked.

"My name is Robert Chow. I'm with the detective bureau of the Fifth Precinct."

"Well, maybe you can do something about my problem and get them to take me out of their book! I still get calls sometimes, strange calls."

"What kind of calls?"

"Asking in Mandarin for information about human tongues!"

"Human tongues?"

"Yeah! Scary people out there!"

"Well, I'll see what I can do, Mr. Ng. Have a good day."

I sat at my desk and thought about tongues, absently smearing another rice bun with peanut butter. I took a few bites and looked at the address for "Beautiful Hong Kong Ltd.": 220 Worth Street, sixth floor.

Worth Street is the unofficial southern border of Chinatown, cutting off Columbus Park, Mulberry Street, Mott Street, and Bowery at Chatham Square. It bordered the same block as Don's shabby apartment over on Park Street.

I got over to the building, but the name on the sixth-floor button was "Eight Stars Lion Dance Group." I rang the button and the door buzzed open. The stairwell was drafty, but it was still hot and humid in the building. I was sweating by the second floor. Luckily, like most Chinese buildings, there was no fourth floor, so I only had to climb to the equivalent of the fifth floor.

American buildings leave off the thirteenth floor. Why, I don't really know, except that thirteen is an unlucky number.

Chinese buildings don't have fourth floors because "four" sounds like "death" and it's bad luck to be associated with it.

This superstition applies double to "44" and triple to "444." A lot of Chinatown produce stands exploit this fear of four by pricing items four for a dollar, encouraging people to buy eight.

Here's a quick rule of thumb: American tea sets have four cups while Chinese sets have eight.

It helps that "eight" sounds like "prosperity," giving the number some charm. Chinese people pay extra for phone numbers and street addresses with eights.

Everybody says they're not superstitious, but it never hurts to have some insurance on the side.

The only door with light behind it was to the rear. I saw a woman sitting at the front desk through the door window, so I waved to her instead of pressing the buzzer. She put down her snack and buzzed the door. I walked into the air-conditioned room.

"Hello, is this Beautiful Hong Kong Limited?" I asked.

"Only in name," said the woman. Her hair was pulled back in a bun, a little unusual for a woman in her mid-twenties. Way too much makeup. She was wearing a dark green suit jacket over a flowery yellow blouse, all covered by flakes from her ham and egg pastry.

"Why just in name?" I asked, aware of some movement in one of the back rooms.

"This used to be the New York warehouse for the company, but it's been donated to a space for a nonprofit activity center for the youth of Chinatown."

"What sort of activities?"

"An affiliate of a Hong Kong–based lion dance group that practices here. We're also going to put in a table-tennis setup. It's not done yet."

"Do you know Mr. Ng?"

"Mr. Ng? You mean my brother? He's never here. I'm in charge."

"What's your name?"

"I'm Winnie," she said with emphasis, as if I should have known.

"My name's Robert Chow." I gave her my card. "This is purely an informational visit."

"You're with the detective squad! What's going on?"

"I just wanted to have a brief chat with Mr. Ng, that's all."

"I thought you might have been one of the contractors working on the floor here, but I guess you're not big enough, anyway. You're sort of built for desk work."

"Typing is tougher than it looks. Anyway, what's wrong with the floor?"

"Well, this used to be a warehouse space, so it's kind of rough all around."

I heard some more noise in the back. "You mind if I take a tiny peek back there?"

"Sure, go ahead."

I went down the hall and the carpeting ended almost right behind her desk. She stuck behind me. Soon I was walking on gray wooden planks. We went by some doorways, most without doors. At the end of the hall were two big metal doors. One was propped open with a cinder block.

We walked in. The floor was concrete. Eight gaudily adorned lion costumes were sprawled out in a row. Without people inside them, the glittery body sections were completely flat and the giant furry heads lay with their eyes and mouths open, tongues on the floor. The air-conditioning didn't reach back here and I fanned my face a little.

A man in a tank top and shorts was kneeling by a sparkling red lion with his back to us.

"Don't come in, Winnie!" he said. "These costumes are very delicate!"

"Brian," said Winnie. "We have a visitor."

The man put down a brush, wiped his forehead with the back of his wrist, and looked at me curiously. He was scarily muscular but had a friendly and very sweaty face.

"Hi. Welcome," Brian said.

"Hello. My name is Robert. How are you?" We shook hands briefly.

"He's with the police," said Winnie.

"What's wrong?" asked Brian.

"Nothing's wrong," I said with a fake laugh. "I just wanted to see what kind of business Mr. Ng operated. He's very well regarded in the community."

"Oh yeah? Well, maybe you can tell him to stop being so cheap!" spat Brian. "If he expects us to be a viable lion dance group, tell him to spend some money and get us new costumes, not these secondhand pieces of garbage that keep falling apart! Can't even put them on without the scales coming off!"

"Brian!" said Winnie.

"And while you're at it," he went on, "tell him to finish renovating this space! I feel like I've got my kids practicing in a junkyard. We're nothing but a tax write-off for a cheapskate!"

"It's not that bad here," I said.

"You don't see the rats right now! They come up right through the floor! The only thing Ng spent money on was the sound system." He pointed to two huge speakers that I had mistaken for Dumpsters. "But no matter how loud you turn them up, they don't make the studio look any better!"

"I thought lion dances were supposed to be done with live instruments?"

"Don't get me started on that! Oh, brother!"

"Mr. Chow," interrupted Winnie, "maybe you could come back some other time. I'll have my brother call you when I see him."

"Nice meeting you, Brian," I said.

"Hey, if you talk to Ng, remind him that I came from a respectable lion dance group to start this thing up!" he thundered. "I don't need to stay here—I'm good!"

I went back to the squad room and wrote down what I had learned in a notepad I kept in my top drawer for typing later on. You had to keep track of your day as it went by, because when it was time to type it was hard to tell what happened that day from the one before.

My phone rang. It was Vandyne.

"Tell me something good," I said.

"Can't do that because I'm not going to lie to you."

"Is everything okay? How did it go?"

"Well . . . ," he started. I could hear him shift the phone around and I thought I heard a door close.

"What's going on, Vandyne?"

"I just closed myself in the pantry here so I could talk more privately."

"So couples therapy didn't go so well?" I looked over at English, who was in the lounge watching TV. No one else was around.

"It went all right, partner. The doctor made me realize something. I mean, about what we both did in Nam, right?"

He was referring to the fact that each of us had justifiably killed a little boy.

"Yeah," I said.

"That's why I don't want to have a child. In my mind, I don't think I deserve to have a child because I shot one to death."

"But the kid you killed was shooting up your camp," I said. "It was kill or be killed!"

"I know, I know."

We listened to each other breathing for a little bit because I didn't know what else to say.

"You don't have to have kids," I said, hoping it would help. "It's not in the Pledge of Allegiance."

"Rose wants to have a kid before she's thirty."

"How many years you got until then?"

"Three. Well, more like two and a half."

"You know what, don't think about it for a year. Just let it all go for a year and then come back and see how you feel."

"But how the hell am I going to do that when she talks to her sister or when we see them and their boy and girl? She's even younger than Rose!"

"If you live your life wanting the good things other people have, you also have to consider all the bad things, too. I'm sure they're not as happy as you and Rose, Vandyne."

"Her husband's a doctor, a real condescending asshole. They live in a four-story brownstone in Manhattan with a nighttime view of the Hudson that looks like a postcard. They have a remote-controlled stereo system that the doctor showed off while we were having dinner. They also got a microwave oven and a walk-in refrigerator that holds their wine collection."

I got the feeling that Vandyne couldn't even bring himself to say the guy's name. I licked my lips involuntarily when he mentioned "wine."

"But you know what?" I said. "He doesn't have a gun, right?"

"He doesn't have a gun. He hates guns."

"But *you* have a gun!"

I finally heard him chuckle a little bit.

"I should be happy just because I have a gun?"

"Oh yeah!" I said, looking out the window at nothing. "Be happy you've got a gun! There's a lot of motherfuckers out there!"

4

AFTER I GOT OFF THE PHONE WITH VANDYNE, I PUT MY FEET UP ON the desk and did some more thinking about "human tongues." What the hell were those?

I picked up the phone and called the midget.

"Can you get away from the store for half an hour?" I asked.

"Yeah, why not?" he said. "Coffee, tea, food?"

"If you want."

"All right."

The toy store was just two right turns away from the station over on Mulberry Street. I shook my head as I walked in measured steps. So much of my life had revolved around this stupid toy store.

When I was a kid my best friend, Moy, who was the son of the owner, would let me play with everything and his dad would then take it in the back and reseal the boxes and put them back on the shelf.

When I came back from Nam, Moy's dad hired me for a pity job there.

When I was walking a beat, I was forced to throw Moy's dad out of

44

the post office on the Communist side of Chinatown where he had helped immigrants meet the requirement that all mail had to be addressed in English. Disgusted with what he perceived as police harassment, the old man put the toy store up for sale and then had a stroke. The midget then stepped in and bought the place.

I rounded the corner and saw the concrete step leading up to the store. I imagined a seven-year-old Moy sitting there, glaring at me.

When I came in, the midget hopped off of his stool and pushed his few customers out. "Hey, you have to leave right now! It's time to take store inventory."

"Do you really have to do this right now?" asked a young mother. "I was just about to pick out a present."

Without breaking his stride, the midget said, "I'm helping you out here. Just pretend that you've just walked around looking for twenty minutes, as you just have, and that you've now left the store. Then imagine the one thing you regret not buying and that's your present."

Soon he was standing on the sidewalk with the door shut and locked.

"Hey!" complained the mother. "Where are you going? I thought you were going to do store inventory!"

"Yeah, I do it all in my head," said the midget, pressing imaginary buttons in his left palm as we walked over to Mott.

"I'm sorry that you had to close up for a while," I said.

"It gives me a chance to stretch my legs a little. Anyway, if I can't tear myself away, then what's the point of being the boss?"

"You can fire anybody you want. That has to be a power trip."

"I don't want to deal with higher unemployment taxes. Anyway, only one person has left so far, and that was voluntary."

"It's too bad, what happened to that kid," I said, shaking my head. "He was working there during the day for, what, only a few weeks?"

"Oh yeah, poor Chris. Well, who knew he was going to get jumped by gang kids. Chris is only eleven, but I guess that's the right age to force a kid to join your gang."

"He might have left town. I haven't seen him around."

"Well, if you ever see him hanging out on a corner, go ahead and take his picture for your mug books. He was a bright kid but definitely headed downward." The midget looked at me. "You don't have the room to take in another kid, do you?"

"Jesus, I am not Mother Teresa! I can only save one kid at a time!"

"If kids only played more toys and games," he lamented, "they'd stay out of trouble."

"You ever get tired of running the store?" I asked him. "Don't you miss the fresh air and sunshine of Columbus Park when you used to play Chinese chess there?"

The park was south of Bayard and west of Mulberry, two and a half blocks away from the midget's store. For several years he was a fixture at the chess tables and became so famed for never losing a game, an American filmmaker came in and shot a documentary about him.

"Sure, of course I do! But you know, I have a fairly regular income now and I provide your roommate with a job. Also, it's a lot easier to take a leak now than before. Some of these restaurants along the park were getting downright unfriendly. Also, another upside is that I've been asked to join a merchants' association."

"Which one?"

"Golden Peace. The one that Willie Gee is now president of."

"Jesus, please don't join."

"Don't worry, I'm not. It's just another shakedown for an annual membership fee."

Before we got to the bend in Mott by Pell Street, we ducked down to a below-street-level teahouse run by a Taiwanese guy. I was psyched for this place because it was vegetarian only and they didn't put dried shrimp in their turnip cakes like most places do. I'm allergic to seafood.

An older waiter with bushy gray eyebrows came over and absently slid over an oddly clean ceramic teapot and two bright white teacups.

"Are these all new?" I asked.

"Yes, they are," the waiter said, looking away distractedly. "Enjoy them before they get dirty." He put his right hand in his pant pocket and jingled his keys.

"I'll have a turnip cake," said the midget.

"I'll have one, too," I said.

"Wow, two whole turnip cakes," said the waiter. "I wonder if you two will be able to finish them all."

When he was gone I asked the midget, "Did you piss that guy off before?"

"No way. Did you?"

"I might have," I said. "Or maybe he doesn't like midgets."

"Maybe he doesn't like cops."

The waiter came back with our turnip cakes.

"Hey," I said. "You know, you can catch more bees with honey than with vinegar."

"Why the hell would I want to catch bees?" he asked.

"Because they're really good workers," I said.

Nothing registered on his face as he walked away.

"Sometimes," said the midget, "I feel like I'm in a movie when I'm with you, Robert."

"Is it a comedy or a drama?"

"It's kind of both. I mean it's not a *good* movie by any measure." The midget cut up the turnip cake with his fork.

"Well, I'll take you to a good movie if you help me on this."

"What's up?"

"Why would someone ask for a 'human tongue'?"

"To eat?"

"No! Well, I don't think so. This guy gets phone calls from people asking in Mandarin about human tongues."

"Well, that's certainly a strange thing to ask for. And the person asking already has a tongue, I have to assume."

"Do you really not know what it means? I can't tell if you're joking now."

"Honestly, I don't know what it means. Maybe it's something kinky. Who is the guy getting the calls?"

"This guy who used to run an export-import business called Beautiful Hongkong. He may be getting misdirected calls intended for Beautiful Hong Kong Limited."

"The second company, what do they do?"

"They also used to do export-import, but their warehouse has been converted into a nonprofit recreation center with a lion dance group. They did it for tax reasons."

"Well, you know, about a decade ago those lion dance groups in Hong Kong were pseudogangs."

"You think this group here is a gang?"

"Naw, no way. These lion dance groups here are all tame corporate entertainment. They dance for hire. They don't attack each other with spearheads sticking out of the lions' mouths. Anymore."

"Is there a dance move called human tongue?"

"If there is, I sure don't want to see it."

We didn't stiff the waiter too badly. He had served us quickly enough.

I got back to the squad room and found Vandyne and English.

"Jesus," I said, looking around at the empty desks, "where the hell is everybody?"

"You tell me," said English. He glanced up at Vandyne and me. "You guys are still too new to have regular downtime hangouts. It's important in the summer to find a place with good air-conditioning."

"I didn't get any calls, did I?" I asked Vandyne.

"Expecting one?"

"Maybe. Hey, have you guys heard of the phrase 'human tongue'?"

Vandyne and English started laughing. It only proved that I had been right to go to the midget first. I crossed my arms and waited for the ribbing to stop. It could take a while.

"You mean this thing?" asked English, pressing a finger against his tongue.

"Well, it means something in Mandarin, some kind of slang. It may have something to do with the guy you fingered at the crime scene, English."

He shook off the funnies immediately and I explained.

"We don't have a case for probable cause to do a search at the lion dance studio," said English. "You didn't see anything out of the ordinary there, right?"

"Just a space that seems to be a fixer-upper."

"Maybe we can get someone from the buildings department to issue a bullshit citation and lean on them?" suggested Vandyne.

"Naw, let's give them some breathing room," said English. "See what happens. Maybe you two just sort of not obtrusively follow Ng and Lam around town. They'll slip up on their own."

I waited for Ng to call and then I called Winnie Ng a few times, but nobody answered. Maybe she was out getting her suit cleaned.

I walked over to the toy store, scratching a mosquito bite on my neck. I wasn't sure when it happened, but it was itchy as hell now.

"Is it okay for Paul to stay with you tonight?" I asked the midget.

"Of course. It's always okay."

"Thanks for telling me, Robert," said Paul.

"Hey, I had to clear it first. I couldn't just invite you over to his place. You have more fun there, anyway."

"The company's better," said Paul. "Smarter, too."

From my perch in the back, I made a man promise to buy a doll for his girl if she got straight As and then I saw two men in their forties walk in with much apprehension. One man had a few days of stubble. The other was neater and clean shaven.

I locked eyes with the stubbly man and nodded encouragingly.

"Detective Chow," he said in Mandarin as bad as mine. "Maybe you can help us." He was thin and slightly stooped. He had a lot of healed scars on his hands. His nose, mouth, and eyes were all straight single lines.

Up close the neater man had a big frightened face and his lips were stuck in a permanent pucker.

"What can I do for you guys?" I asked.

"I wanted to ask you," the unshaven man said, turning slightly to make sure no one else was near. "The bodies that were found. Was there a tattoo of the character 'open' on one of the men's necks?"

That was a detail we hadn't told the press yet. My heart sank for the man.

"Yes, there was."

The man's face folded in on itself and he trembled. The neater man nodded in silence.

"That was our friend's son. He was from our village in Fuzhou." These two men were Fukienese and obviously not well educated, though they probably knew how to corner a pig. No wonder they didn't know Cantonese and were bad at Mandarin.

"He was smuggled in with us, but once we got here they raised the fee and he refused to pay," the stubbly man said. "They took him and his friend away from the safe house!"

I knew what I had to ask them and what their answer would be. I felt a swirl of emotions go through me, and my heart hurt.

"I need the two of you to make a statement at the precinct."

"We can't!" said the stubbly man. "We're both here illegally!"

"How can we punish the bad guys if you don't help us?"

"We are too afraid! We've already worked too hard to pay off our smuggling debt to be deported!"

"What was his name?"

"We don't want to say!"

They made a move to leave.

"Wait," I said. "Does the phrase 'human tongue' mean anything to you?" I stuck out my tongue and pointed to it.

"'Human tongue'? No, not 'tongue.' 'Human snake.' We are the human snakes." He made a slithering motion with his right arm.

"'Human snakes'?" I asked.

"The people being smuggled are 'human snakes.' The smuggler is called the snakehead."

No wonder I was confused. "Tongue" and "snake" both sounded exactly the same in Mandarin—even the tone was the same.

"Who is the snakehead?" I asked.

"It's Brother Five. Now I've said too much already!" They quickly left.

"Hey!" I yelled, coming after them.

The midget stopped me at the door.

"They were probably followed here," he said, giving me a hard look. "Let them go or they'll get in trouble."

"You're right."

Some kid shook a toy that made a rattling sound and I jumped.

Back at the apartment with Lonnie, I told her about snakeheads and human snakes.

"That's so sad. Just so tragic," she said.

"Is it really better to be dead in America than alive in China?" I asked.

"They don't know they're going to die. You never think the worst can happen to you, right?"

"Didn't the Father of the Nation travel here with illegal papers? He had a fake Hawaiian birth certificate." I was referring of course to Sun Yat-sen, the man who brought down Manchu rule in China but tragically died before he was able to unite the Communist and KMT factions of the new republic.

"He was a Christian, too, Robert."

"Are you trying to get me to go to church on Sunday?"

"No!" she said. "But I'll have to go this Sunday. For confession."

We undressed quickly. We were good at it because we had only a few hours alone in the apartment at a time.

"I want you to bite me all over," she said.

I obliged.

"Hey! Not there," she said, pulling my head back. "Save that for last!"

We got up in the early afternoon and went to the Chatham Square Branch of the New York Public Library. It was just slightly into Communist territory, two blocks to the east of Bowery, but it was seen as neutral ground because of the number of non-Chinese who worked there and went there.

Lonnie had wanted to borrow an atlas to study countries around the world for one of her classes. The atlases at Borough of Manhattan Community College were for reference use only and couldn't be borrowed out.

The NYPL's latest atlases were also for reference only, but the librarian referred us to several boxes blocking the biography aisle. They were filled with library discards the library staff hadn't gotten around to dragging to the curb yet. I had found the first half of a 1970 atlas and Lonnie said it was recent enough. She was digging for the other half.

I contemplated a map that highlighted every country at war or having a civil war.

"Lonnie," I asked, "do you have any complaints about me? Would you change anything if you could?"

"Just your snoring."

"I snore?"

"Yeah! Don't you remember all those times when I elbowed you and you turned over and said you were sorry?"

"No. I don't remember at all." I put the half atlas on the floor and sat on it.

"I told Paul you snore."

"Why did you tell Paul?"

"Don't worry! He already knows you snore regularly!"

Lonnie pulled out an old magazine. "Hey, look at this! An issue of *National Geographic* from 1920!"

I looked at the cover, which was all words and no pictures.

"I wonder if they even had color film back then," I said.

I heard some shouting up at the front. A sheepish young Chinese man in clothes too big for him was standing up, holding a clear plastic bag of clothes over his crotch. His hair was a mess.

"I told you before!" yelled the old librarian, who looked like Mrs. Wilson from *Dennis the Menace*, only she had the temper of Mr. Wilson. "No sleeping in the library! You put your head down again I'll have a policeman here so fast it'll spin the chopsticks around your rice bowl!"

"I'm a policeman," I told her with restrained rage. "I can take care of this."

"See that you do," she snapped, and walked back to her desk to play with her crystal figurines.

"You don't speak English, do you?" I asked the man.

"I don't speak Cantonese," he said in Mandarin.

"Let's go outside," I said in Mandarin. "You've made the Americans too angry today. You can't sleep here. It's one of the rules." We walked out to the sidewalk.

"I can't help but fall asleep!" he said. "I don't mean to. I just want a place to sit during my break. I'm on my feet all day washing dishes." As if to prove it, he took his smelly dishwasher apron out of the plastic bag and put it on. He crumpled up the bag and shoved it into a back pocket.

"Where do you live?"

"I live in a safe house."

"You're illegal!"

He nodded and crossed his arms. "Want to take me to jail? I'll go. I'll go back to China, gladly."

"I'm not taking you to jail because I don't want to deal with the bureaucracy and the paperwork. Anyway, if you don't pay back your debt you're not going anywhere. The snakeheads will see to that."

"You know how long it's going to take?" he said. "I have to live in safe houses until it's paid off. But if I want to get a loan to pay off the smuggling debt, I'll be paying interest until I'm forty!"

"Where is your safe house?"

"It's hidden."

"How long have you been here?"

"Here? In New York? Only about a month. But before this I was in Boston for six months. I was in Philadelphia for almost a year before that. They say they keep moving us around so we don't get caught by authorities, but really I think it's because they don't want to give us enough time to come up with escape plans."

"Even if you did escape, they'd take it out on your family."

"If my family cared about me, they wouldn't have pushed so hard for me to come here. I'm not a human here. I'm a cow or a horse. I'm a work animal. They just let me have enough food and sleep to work another day." Then he paused. "You have a cigarette?"

"I don't smoke."

He turned to leave.

"Hey," I said, grabbing his shoulder. "Are you with Brother Five?"

He glared directly at me.

"I have to get back to the restaurant," he said, spinning away and out of my grasp. "See you, Generalissimo." He jogged to Bowery and crossed before the light said it was safe.

I had to smile at that dig at me. To a lot of the Fukienese I was, as an NYPD member, the equivalent of one of Generalissimo Chiang Kai-shek's foot soldiers. A KMT flunky. The enemy.

I went back into the library and found Lonnie waiting inside the doorway.

"I guess just the first half will have to do," she said. "At least it includes Asia and Africa."

"I'll try to find you a whole one at the Strand."

"Thank you. Hey, who was that guy you were talking to?"

"He's an illegal from Fujian."

"You were talking like you were old friends."

"Maybe a few centuries ago, our ancestors were fighting each other in battles to unite China."

"Now you're both in America."

"No. We're in completely different countries, Lonnie."

5

I WALKED INTO JADE PALACE, HEADING STRAIGHT FOR THE CLOSED doors of the private room. Two carts were strategically parked outside the doors. I pulled them away and yanked the doors open.

Mr. Tin, Don's father, had a white woman sitting in his lap. The dishes were pushed to the side as if to make enough room on the table for two people to roll around on.

"Irene, is it?" I asked the woman.

She leapt up gracefully and shook my hand.

"Oh, Robert, do come in. We're old friends, here, just goofing around."

"I'm not doing anything wrong," said Don's father. He shoved both hands in his pockets. When it became obvious that I wasn't going to beat a hasty retreat, he said, "Irene, how about you go do your eyelashes again?"

"Yes," she said. Irene left and closed the doors behind her.

Mr. Tin and I spoke in English. It just seemed appropriate because so many old boundaries between us had suddenly been redrawn.

"You're not going to say anything about this," Don's father snarled. "I'm a very influential man."

"I can see."

"I've made a lot of things nice for you. Not only because you were a childhood friend of my son's but because I think you're a good presence in Chinatown."

"What kinds of things have you made nice for me?"

"That toy store. The one that's run by the runt."

"What about it?"

"As a representative of the KMT and the executive chairman of the Greater China Association, I am one of the overseers of the community. You know the Greater China Association is where the various factions of Chinatown meet to resolve . . . business interests?"

"Yes, I know." Those interests included gambling dens and pross houses as well as more mundane points such as fixing prices on postcards and T-shirts.

"Well, that toy store is by Bayard Street. That's the historical border between two tongs. That toy store could have been subject to paying off two different protection rackets. But I made it clear to everybody from the moment that your friend took over—stay the fuck away from that store!"

"You should know that your message didn't get through all the way. You're not as powerful as you think. A kid who was working there got jumped by a gang. They beat the shit out of him."

Don's father nodded.

"The midget isn't as smart as he thinks. He slipped in right under his nose," he said.

"What are you talking about?"

"It's that old Trojan horse trick. That kid was part of the unruly, younger faction of a gang. He was keeping track of when the shop was slowest so that his buddies could come in and rip off the place. When I found out what he had planned, I had him fixed."

"That kid wasn't even twelve yet," I said.

"A kid that young can still pull a trigger, you know?" Mr. Tin said. "In fact, a kid that young is most anxious to."

"Do you know anything about those bodies we found under the bridge?"

"I have no idea. Honestly. What I can tell you is that nobody in the Greater China Association had anything to do with that! We ourselves are investigating through our own channels. It was probably a Communist-affiliated entity that is responsible."

He leaned forward and prepared to stand.

"Do you know anybody," I asked, "who is smuggling people in groups of twenty to thirty people at a time?"

"That many people!" he said, with full surprise. "No, that's crazy! How do you sneak in so many people all at once without getting caught and yet also in a safe manner?"

"You know what a 'snakehead' is?" I asked.

"No! I have no idea! Are you threatening me or something?"

He shot up to his feet.

"I don't mean anything," I said. "I was just wondering if you've heard of the term."

"The answer is, 'No'! Are you done, now, Robert?"

"About Don," I said.

He sat back down. "How are you doing with Don?" he asked.

"I'm having a hard time. A real hard time. I think he needs to go to the hospital. He needs to see a psychiatrist."

"No, no, Robert, he needs more time with you."

"I can't help him. I don't know what to do."

"You knew him when you both were young! You can speak Cantonese with him!"

"One dialect or another isn't going to help! We can take Don to a VA hospital. They'll pay for nearly everything. They'll put him on the proper medication, too."

"Robert. If word got out that my son has a mental problem, do you know what could happen?"

"No."

"People see mental problems as a family issue, understand? If they know that something is wrong with Don, they'll think that something is wrong with me, too. It would jeopardize my position in the community if it were known that my son needs to be on drugs to be normal."

Don's father closed his eyes and rubbed his eyebrows hard. I tried to remember the Don I knew, the one who had pressed, collared shirts when all the other boys wore undershirts that their fathers had outgrown.

Mr. Tin had bought that kid everything, but there was something genuine at Don's core that prevented him from becoming spoiled. Other kids were jealous, but Don had always shared everything that he could. That trait was definitely not genetic.

I couldn't deny, though, that this forceful man loved his son.

"I'll spend more time with him," I said.

"Considering everything I'm doing for you, you have to bring back my boy, and before the Double Ten holiday." October 10 was the KMT's national day to celebrate the 1911 uprising against the Manchu that was the beginning of the end of the foreign Qing dynasty. Once the Manchu, the Japanese, and World War II were out of the way, the battlefield was clear for the Communists and the KMT to have it out. The Communists' national day was October 1, to celebrate when they officially had swept the KMT off of the mainland in 1949.

The fact that the national days of these two bitter enemies are set at little more than a week apart is best appreciated by a people who see opposing forces entwined in everything.

"Mr. Tin, why do you need Don for the Double Ten holiday?"

"I'm set to visit Taiwan for a state celebration and I need my son with me. I won't be able to deflect questions about where Don is this year."

I got up and shook hands with him. I opened the door and found Irene chatting with one of the waiters, something about a garden in Taiwan. She saw me and smiled but said nothing.

After she was inside, two waiters came up and shut the room doors. Then they pushed together the serving carts in front until they bumped each other hard.

6

I MET BARBARA IN FRONT OF THE PRECINCT. SHE GAVE ME A BIG hug and I saw Rip flash me an okay with his right hand.

"Why didn't you call me when you first heard about Don?" she asked.

"I wanted to see what kind of shape he was in first. I didn't want to alarm you for no reason."

"Is he really that bad?"

"I'm not a doctor, but I think it's bad enough."

We walked south to Don's Park Street apartment. The streets were crowded with city workers and people on jury duty looking for lunch. It was tough to walk side by side, and I stepped into the street often to let people pass us.

It had been a few months since I had seen Barbara. It made me feel a little lighthearted and stupid, the guy I was before Nam, even though Barbara and her friends remembered me as a young gung ho American patriot. Cracker Jack, they used to call me, after the saluting sailor boy.

This is how stupid I was back then. I used to think that Barbara and I would be married and have kids by this time. After all, she was the first girl I had ever kissed. Just a few months ago, we did the toe tangle a few times before Barbara called it off and I got serious with Lonnie.

"As Don's ex-girlfriend," I said, "I figured maybe you could help him."

I had to keep in mind that Barbara's husband, a guy she had met at Harvard, was killed at Khe Sanh. I hoped the battle wouldn't come up in our talk with Don, and if it did I was going to ignore it.

"I wasn't really Don's girlfriend, Robert. We went on a few dates before his father put an end to it."

"What happened?"

"Don told me his father didn't want him to see me anymore because there was the daughter of a family friend they wanted him to meet. Probably an important business or political connection."

"Did you love him, Barbara?"

"Oh, come on!" She managed to look both amused and annoyed. "We don't really need to talk about this!"

"Sorry to bring it up," I said. "But I was hoping that when he saw you it might help to snap him out of it."

"People don't just 'snap out of' mental illness, Robert. They need medication and a therapist."

"He's taking something now that makes him sleepy. It seems to help."

"Is it Chinese medicine?"

"Yeah."

"Most of that stuff is superstition and nonsense."

"But it's our culture, Barbara."

"Our culture comes down to food and bullshit that's been handed down so long it doesn't smell anymore," she said. "How have you been?"

"Good," I said. "Busy."

"Can I ask what you're working on?"

"You know those two bodies found under the bridge overpass?"

"Of course I heard about it."

"What do you know about human smuggling, Barbara?"

"I know that it doesn't happen without some part of the government—in both the countries of origin and destination—turning a blind eye. Also, it wouldn't happen if there wasn't opportunity in the country of destination, and there pretty much always is."

"How do they know they'll be able to find work?"

"Because these people are always willing to take bottom-rung jobs and they'll work for less than kids in high school. They'll clean bathrooms, mop floors. . . ."

"And wait tables, wash dishes, and work in sweatshops."

"Why not? If you're an employer in Chinatown, you're already likely to be exploiting people in one way or another. As an employer you can increase your margins even more if you hire the most vulnerable employees—illegal immigrants."

I grumbled.

"Robert, this is nothing new."

"It seems like someone has been stepping up the smuggling."

"I hear Fukienese a lot more than I used to and there are places on East Broadway with food in the windows that I've never seen before."

We walked by a teahouse on the corner of Mott and Bayard.

"Remember there used to be a pharmacy here?" I asked.

Barbara glanced at the teahouse quickly and shuddered. "That place gave me the creeps!" she said.

"The old guy who ran that place, he was one of the original Toisan men left over from the bachelor-society days. He used to let me read comic books for hours."

Toisan was a desperately poor city in Canton Province that was in such a bad way that many of its young men left in the late 1800s to seek their fortunes around the world. All the Chinatowns in America were built up by Toisan men. Like my dad.

"The last time I was here," said Barbara, "it was to pick up some cotton balls. The guy gave me a condom and told me it was a balloon."

"He had a twisted sense of humor that maybe went too far."

"I think he was masturbating under the counter."

I took in a breath and held it. Maybe there was something behind the pharmacy's sudden closing.

We walked down Park Street's sharp decline and went around the corner to Don's building.

"This place looks like a dump," said Barbara.

I put my finger to my lips and pressed his apartment button.

The building door buzzed open and we walked in. There was even more trash piled up by the stairwell than before. What stood out to me were stacks of hacked-out layers of linoleum in blue and black diamond patterns.

"I think Don's been busy," I said as we went up to see him.

I knocked on his door.

"Robert?" he asked. I was relieved to hear that he sounded sleepy.

"Yeah, it's me. I've brought an old friend, Barbara," I said. I wanted him to know in advance. Surprises could only be bad.

"Barbara?" he asked.

"Hi, Don!" she said. "I heard you were back in town. I wanted to see you."

"Why?"

Barbara looked at me. I motioned for her to keep talking.

"Because we're friends."

Don didn't say anything.

"Look, Don," I said. "I thought I'd bring Barbara in so you guys could catch up. It's been a while since the three of us hung out together." The last time was right before the two of them broke off from me.

Don opened the door. I hadn't heard anything unlock and I was caught a little off-guard. His wild eyes were a little glazed over. He turned them slowly onto Barbara.

"You've seen me on the news, right?" he asked.

"I haven't been watching much TV lately," she said. "I've been really busy at work."

"Doing what?"

"Work stuff. A lot of reading and phone interviewing."

"I know you talked about me, Barbara," said Don, shaking his head slowly and sadly. "You told them everything, but I can't blame you. They tricked you with their lies."

Barbara flashed a wary look at me. I nodded.

Don stepped aside and I looked in at his apartment. Most Chinatown apartments had bumpy floors made of successive layers of linoleum floors rolled out on top of each other. Don's floors were hacked down to the bare wood, reminding me of Beautiful Hong Kong's offices.

"Why don't we all go to Columbus Park?" I suggested. It was across the street and I figured it would be far from walls, floors, furniture, and everything else that Don found oppressive.

"That's a good idea," Don said.

We went downstairs and crossed Mulberry Street. We found seats on a bench that looked like it had been chewed lightly by Godzilla. Barbara and I sat on either side of Don, who was sitting forward with his head down. He was sweating heavily but refused to take off his field jacket.

"Can I have some coffee?" he whispered. "I'd like three cups of coffee."

"I'll go," said Barbara. You'd better come back, I thought.

I watched two boys and a girl repeatedly trying to drink from a broken concrete water fountain. Old men played chess or chatted among themselves as the pet birds they had brought sat quietly in bamboo cages partially covered by sheets for shade.

"Remember running around this park, Don?" I asked.

"It could be a fake memory," said Don. "I think I'm really Vietnamese."

"You are definitely not Vietnamese. You were born here."

"I don't know where or when I was born."

"Just look at your birth certificate."

"It could be fake."

I suddenly thought about my father sneaking into the United States with falsified documentation.

"If you were born here, it's real," I said.

"Where is *here?*"

"Don, we're in Chinatown. New York. U.S.A."

He covered his ears and leaned back.

"It doesn't look the way it sounds," said Don.

Barbara came back with a bag of five coffees. She gave Don three of them and handed one to me. I peeled back the lid and took a quick sip.

Don drank one cup quickly. "It's too sweet," he said as he opened his second cup.

"I'm sorry," said Barbara. "Mine doesn't have any sugar. Do you want it?"

"No."

"Barbara was really worried about you," I said. "I told her you were having problems."

I looked at Don, who was on his third coffee, ignoring us. Barbara and I were just two more voices in his head talking about him.

To Barbara, I said, "Tell him a good memory you have of him."

She closed her eyes, drew her head back, and thought for half a minute. Then Barbara cleared her throat and bent down to try to look Don in the face.

"Don," she said, "do you remember getting on the Cyclone with me at Coney Island?"

"I remember," he whispered.

"You had fun that day, didn't you?"

He didn't say anything but nodded his head. After he had finished the last cup of coffee, Don said, "My head is a big radio and I can't control the dials. It keeps changing channels and the volume goes in and out."

"That sounds like schizophrenia," Barbara said to me. "I thought I had it in college."

"How do we take care of this?" I asked.

"We have to take him to a doctor."

"No doctor," I said. "His old man refuses to let me take him."

"Robert, he needs professional help!"

"Maybe. If I can't find something else first."

"Do you know how sick he is? He could hurt himself! Do you want that? Does his father want that?"

"Of course not! But how are we going to get him to a doctor without identification?"

"What?"

"He doesn't even have a wallet, Barbara!"

She paused and looked carefully at Don's face, making sure it was really him.

"You have to talk to his father," she concluded.

"That guy was an asshole to me when I was a kid," I said. "He likes me only a little bit more now."

"Well, he sure wasn't a fan of me, either," said Barbara.

Don got up and said he had to go to the bathroom. We followed him back to his apartment building and then watched him float upstairs like a lost kite.

7

FOR A WEEK I TRIED REACHING NG AT EIGHT STARS LION DANCE Group. When I was able to reach Winnie, I think she was getting the idea that I was really calling to talk to her.

Meanwhile Vandyne shadowed King Lam, but he worried that the guy knew he was being followed. I knew the first rule was to never try hiding from the person you're shadowing. But Lam knew where the underground passageways were, giving him a major advantage.

For example, Doyers Street, that little jug handle of a road where I got my hair cut, was originally the private drive of a large farmhouse. While the farmhouse was long gone, the subterranean grain storage areas remained intact, snaking along present-day Doyers Street and exiting on Bowery through the lobby of an office building.

The tunnels aren't a secret. In fact, there were even stores down there, little shanty shops selling everything from knockoff calculators and radios to foot massages.

Thing is, though, if you're not acclimated to the low light and forks and blind turns, you could easily get lost.

Vandyne tailed Lam down two flights into the tunnel when he lost Ng's pal and emerged only after buying a pair of slippers.

One day Ng suddenly came up to me outside my apartment when I was on the way in.

"How about we go for a walk, Robert?"

"Where to, Andy?" He smiled, seeing that he hadn't thrown me off-balance with the surprise visit.

"Let's just have a walk and talk."

"Are you going to have me shot, too?"

"What! Jesus fucking Christ, what's wrong with you? I just want to talk, brother to brother, you know?"

"Fine."

We walked west toward Chinatown.

"You don't have anything on me. You know why?"

"You're good at getting other people to do your dirty work."

"No. That's something my father's good at."

I turned to him. He was looking straight ahead.

"This is not going to be a surprise to you, Robert, but Beautiful Hong Kong isn't a completely legitimate business."

"You don't say."

"But under me, it will be. I'm transitioning the company from a legacy of triad businesses to a socially responsible and modern corporation. I've already created a space for our youth. They can learn to be proud of our culture, of who they are. An awful lot of our kids are at risk for delinquency now in Chinatown, but I don't have to tell you that."

"Yeah."

"I know you were born here, Robert. Are you proud to be an American?"

"Well, pride is a sin, so I'll just say that I'm very pleased."

"But you know what, brother, you're not really an American. You know what Malcolm X said? 'Sitting at the table doesn't make you a diner, unless you eat some of what's on that plate. Being born here in America doesn't make you an American.'"

"You've read Malcolm X?"

"Sure, I've read a lot! I went to the best prep school in Hong Kong. I went to Cornell University. I have an economics degree. But you know what I learned? What I know?"

"What?"

"I know that this country doesn't respect us, Robert. Western civilization in general despises us, in fact. They hate how inferior our culture is. How Chinese people are backward and worship blasphemous gods."

"Not everybody here hates us," I said. "In fact, you might say that we are our own worst enemies at times."

"I was at a wedding when I saw this white cop. I asked him about you and he readily gave me information about you. What if you had been working undercover? He would have given you up like that!" he said, snapping his fingers. "I didn't even have to come close to threatening him! Do you think he had even a little bit of respect for you?"

I didn't say anything, but I thought about Peepshow—it had to be him—squealing in pain as I bent his arm behind his back.

Ng went on. "You know what a brother would have said? He would have said nothing. You could have cut his hand off and he wouldn't have even said your name."

"And what kind of brother, exactly, would be torturing another brother like that?"

"I'm just giving you an example. I find torture repugnant, myself, but it happens. It's the reality."

"This is the reality, Ng," I said, pointing to a group of women walking by who were obviously coming back from a shift at a garment factory. They were carrying more fabric to cut and sew at home because they were paid by the piece.

"This is what I'm trying to get you to see, Robert! Look at what

America has reduced our people to! If they cared about Chinatown, we wouldn't be living in squalor, crammed into rooms, six people sharing a plastic basin to take a shower in, shitting in a toilet that doesn't have water! Our elderly should be taken care of and our young people should have more to do than just loiter in the street and shoot each other."

"I think you should be a social worker."

"I am a social worker! I'm fighting for change in Chinatown! Change that the Greater China Association doesn't want to see. Change we need! They only want to enforce the status quo and keep everything safe for the tourists."

"Are you a communist?"

He blinked.

"I am not a communist! Just because I want to improve our people's welfare doesn't mean I'm a communist! You ever meet a pinko with an economics degree?"

"Ng, while you were up at Cornell pushing your lunch tray through the fucking cafeteria, I was in the jungle fighting for my life. You're a rich mob boy with working-class fantasies of upsetting the order that your old man is a part of!"

"But we have so much more in common than not. We're the same age, mid-twenties! Two strong young brothers of the Chinese diaspora! If I had a man like you working with me, there would be no stopping us."

"What do you think of illegal immigrants?"

He shrugged. "I wouldn't know anything about it," said Ng.

"But you're not against it."

"I'm not. They want to come, let 'em come. Your old man snuck over, didn't he?"

"He became a naturalized citizen years before I was born!"

"Oh, yes, the Magnuson Act in 1943. Did you know that that was the first time the U.S. allowed any Asians to become naturalized citizens?"

"That was thirty-three years ago. That's old news in my book."

"Old news is history and if you don't know your history, you don't know where you're going." He broke off from me, but before he walked away he turned and said, "By the way, you can keep trying to keep tabs on me, but you're not going to find anything else. Why don't you keep an eye on your old pal at the Greater China Association? Check how clean he is!"

"He's a leader in the community! Okay, I'll grant you that he's not the nicest man in the world, but he is respected by many."

"In the courts and temples, maybe, but not in the rivers and the lakes."

"I know exactly what you're talking about."

He smiled. "See, we do have much in common!"

I walked into my barbershop in the elbow of Doyers Street. Since I was nearly there, I figured I would get my hair taken care of ahead of the holiday.

I walked in and the bell that was tied to the door let out a dull clang.

"Hey!" yelled Law, the barber who has been cutting my hair for as long as I wanted it cut.

The other barbers yelled "Hey!" at me and waved.

"You sit down!" Law said. "I'll be done with this guy soon. He doesn't have that much to work with." The seated customer looked up and wrinkled his nose at Law, who had no reaction.

While waiting in a chair I caught up on some of the papers' latest ruminations on the murders.

The Communist-biased paper had an editorial about how China-town residents needed to join together and demand improved social services and better policing.

The KMT-biased paper chastised those who had come over illegally instead of through proper channels. Rules must be respected and good Chinese people were always respectful.

The Hong Kong–biased newspaper asked readers to buy more

goods from Hong Kong. It would create more jobs in Hong Kong and people wouldn't have to go to the United States to find opportunity.

"Robert, put down those stupid papers," said Law. "Come over here and sit down. It's your turn."

He shook off a sheet, and although it still had some hair stuck to it and reeked of aftershave, he tied it around my neck. There was a cold and wet spot right under my chin. Why did I keep coming here?

"Law, what do you think about these illegal immigrants?" I asked. The shop used to have a radio, but it went bust. Nobody had had the heart to throw it out after all the years of service it gave, though. It stayed on the shelf, getting dustier.

"Listen," he said in a soft whisper that I'd never heard come out of him before. "It's okay to try to sneak in, all right? Many people have done it. But you know, if you're going to make the trip worth your while, you'd better be skilled in one of the three knives."

"Are you talking about kung fu?"

"No!" said Law. "I'm talking about cutting hair, cooking, or tailoring! Those are the three knives! If you're skilled in one of them, you can go anywhere in the world and make a decent living. If you don't have those skills, then you have to work shitty jobs for shitty pay for the rest of your miserable life. I have a feeling that the illegals don't have the skills."

"My dad didn't."

"No. He didn't."

Law didn't have to say it, but I knew he was thinking: That's why your dad had such a miserable life. Before he killed himself.

"Law, cut it short. I'm going to see my mom for the holiday. Make me look respectful."

Lonnie and I had been together a few months, but we agreed it was still too early for us to go to each other's parents' for holidays. You bring someone home to meet Chinese parents they'll pull crib parts out of the closet and set it up in the living room.

My mother had met Lonnie very briefly at an awards dinner a few months ago, but it was way too soon for me to meet Lonnie's stepmom and dad. I haven't yet figured out how I could shake the guy's hand instead of breaking his jaw for beating Paul regularly.

Lonnie's family didn't celebrate the Ghost Festival. As Christians, they shunned the holiday as a form of ancestor worship.

Both Chinese Buddhists and Taoists claimed to have originated the Ghost Festival, but my mother said it came from folk religions from before China was even united. Before getting on the subway, I stopped at the Golden Door market on Canal Street and loaded up on jars and cans of food. In the housewares aisle, away from the food for the living, I picked up Hell Bank Notes and incense.

One burns Hell Bank Notes to give loved ones money in the afterlife. Everyone goes to "hell" when they die, but if you have living relatives diligent enough to burn Hell Bank Notes on a regular basis, your account at the local Hell Bank branch should be nice and fat. Then you can buy your way out of the most excruciating torments of the afterlife and, if you have enough, buy mansions and hire servants.

Burning Hell Bank Notes was such an ancient religious practice that over the centuries it came to be seen as secular and as culturally Chinese as stir-frying. Some Chinese Christians and Buddhists objected to the practice, the latter because it was offensive to offer the dead material goods that had brought them suffering their entire lives.

Another thing that some Buddhists frowned upon was garlic, because it excited the senses. Eating it apparently could lead to a Buddhist monk or nun abandoning his or her celibacy vows.

I made sure to get a plastic take-out pack of water spinach sautéed with garlic, the old man's favorite. If my mom and I weren't reason enough for him to materialize, then the food might do it.

My mother lived in a brownstone past Bay Ridge in Brooklyn in a suburban Little Italy. Because she had learned English so well, she had gotten a job, years ago, sorting eighty-column cards in Midtown. It paid well and it was over the table. Now she was some sort of supervisor in the department—the only woman, she was proud to say.

"Robert! I was trying to call you!" she yelled out even before I had gotten inside. "I was going to ask you to bring some bitter melon!"

"Dad hated bitter melon," I said.

"It wasn't for him. It was for me! I was going to cook later this week. Guess I'll have to make do without."

She was trying to lay a guilt trip on me about the bitter melon and it put me in somewhat of a bad mood. I looked down at the bag I was carrying and felt the spinach sloshing around in the garlic sauce. I thought about the old woman who had cut in front of me at the take-out counter and yet gone on to complain how long the line was. I felt my grip tighten.

Then I took a deep breath. I didn't want this to be yet another night at my mother's that ended with me vowing inside never to come back. I looked up at my mother and smiled.

I had her strong nose bridge and expressive eyebrows, which she raised at me as she asked questions that she already knew the answer to. She was in her late forties and tried to come off as an Asian Jackie O. I'll admit—it was close.

My mother had already set up the dining room table for two people and three ghosts.

"Why three ghosts?" I asked her.

"I've been thinking that we should pay our respects to your father's parents. We haven't before and that's been my mistake."

"Aren't his parents still alive, Mom?"

"I mean your father's real parents in Toisan. They were the ones your father had been sending money to. They died during the Cultural Revolution."

"Yes, them. I know, I know. The parents in Hong Kong were the paper parents." Funny how the pretend grandparents were the only ones I'd ever met.

"Exactly, Robert. The ones on his fake documents. I talked to his biological parents only once on the phone before I left for here. We didn't want to jeopardize your father's position."

"As an illegal immigrant, you mean."

"Originally, yes, but by the time I came over, he was already a naturalized American citizen. He worked on a navy ship, so after the War Brides Act was passed he was able to bring me over."

I'd heard it all before, every year at this ceremony. Next would be the bit about how he had had to pay fifteen hundred dollars for the falsified documentation.

"Mom, I brought the spinach."

My mother took the bag and opened up the container.

"He came in under the family name 'Chin,'" she started. "He changed it back to 'Chow' for our marriage certificate. He had to pay two thousand dollars in 1928 for the fake paper. He was only fourteen years old."

"Wow, it's two thousand this year? Talk about inflation!"

"What are you talking about, Robert?"

"Last year you said it was fifteen hundred."

"With all the interest he ended up paying, it was probably more than two thousand."

I could already see the amount ballooning to twenty-five hundred bucks next year.

"An association in Hong Kong paid for it," my mother went on. "When he made it to San Francisco he was forced to join Wah Kung, a tong affiliated with the association, and he had to wash dishes in a tong-owned restaurant."

"Blah, blah, blah," I muttered.

Everybody knows about the tongs, associations formed by people who had the same family name, came from the same town, or had the same trade. They were founded to unite lonely Chinese men who had a common heritage and interests. But once some of these associations reached a critical mass, they went into organized crime, which was an inevitable step when like-minded people got together.

"It was a really big risk he took, Robert," said my mother. "You don't know how hard it was."

Impatiently I blurted out, "It was hard because he made so many mistakes in his life, Mom!"

"Don't you make mistakes, too? His only problem was that he was too trustworthy."

She went to the pantry to pull out her nicest large plate.

"Mom, his problem was that he never thought about us. If he had, he wouldn't have wasted all that money gambling and whoring."

My mother quietly put her head down and scooped the spinach onto the nice plate.

"That's not who your father was," she said. "He was a different man before."

I crossed my arms. "Who was he before?"

"He was a man who had his dreams of making it in this country. When those dreams fell apart, he tried to make it happen for you."

"Yes, he was such a nurturing soul," I said. I remembered one of our last conversations, when he said I should be a garbageman instead of a policeman, which was something that only a "fucking stupid idiot" wanted to be.

"Don't joke about your father. Sure, it's easy to laugh at him, the misfortune he had in his life."

"Mom, don't you get it? He brought it all upon himself. Wah Kung forced him to move to New York and keep working off his debt and then Dad borrowed even more money from them, right?"

"He only borrowed it to impress me with his new clothes and money. It was a different story in a few months. We had trouble making the debt payments and I was pregnant. As soon as I could, I went to work, too. We didn't have them all paid off until you were almost in high school."

"You can blame Pop for all the extra years it took."

"Well, you were no help, either, Robert! We knew you were running around in that gang and getting into fights!"

I shifted my weight and leaned against the wall. We had never talked about this before and now it was confrontation time—a decade after the fact.

"Mom," I started, "the gangs back then were a joke compared with now."

"I saw bloodstains on your clothes when I did the laundry. You think I didn't know? Your father told me not to bother you about it, because you had your own life to work out and you had your own way of doing it. All men do."

"Dad sure did have his way."

She slapped the oven door with her right hand and then leaned toward me, her face looking mean.

"He wasted a lot of money on you, Robert!"

"What are you talking about? He barely even gave me a glance!"

"Your father borrowed even more money to pay for extra photographs of you each year you were in school. He mailed out hundreds of pictures over the years to people he knew in China, Hong Kong, Taiwan, and the rest of the world. He wrote on every single one, 'This is my son'! It came out to thousands of dollars, Robert, but that's how proud he was of you, how much he loved you."

"He never said he was proud." Or that he loved me.

"You were the only thing he talked about in all his letters. How big, how handsome, and how smart you were. He never talked about his own hard work, the sacrifices and the suffering."

"Wait a second. How come I never saw any of these photographs he bought over the years?" I asked. I had always thought that my parents were too cheap to buy them.

"He kept only one photograph for each grade in his special box. But he burned them all when you told him!"

"Told him what?"

She burst into tears.

"He had such big dreams for you. He even told me once that he hoped you would rise up in the government and change the immigration laws so nobody would ever have to go through what he had to. Robert, when you said you wanted to become a policeman, it killed him! It really did!"

I had always seen my mother as the foundation of our family of three. My father cried many times, but not my mother. Never. Now I felt terrible seeing this strong woman choking up. I felt guilty as hell, and for the first time in my life I felt like I owed my father something.

"Mom, you knew I was never going to be a lawyer, Senator Chow, or anything like that. You knew I was a crappy student."

"Don't you understand, Robert? You were a genius to him! You knew Chinese, but you could speak English just like the people in the TV shows! He thought you could do anything!"

"He thought more of me than I did of myself. Anyway, is it really so bad that I became a cop?"

"He thought it was," she said, starting to dry her tears. "What was it all for if you weren't even going to college?"

"A cop is very important, Mom."

"But how does it honor your father's spirit? You probably won't make much more money in your life than he did!"

I bit my cheek from the inside and rubbed my mouth.

"That may be true," I said, "but here's something I can do—I can get these snakeheads."

"What?"

"Snakeheads, Mom. That's what the smugglers are called now."

"That's a good name for them."

"I can't go back in time and get the same guys who screwed Dad over, but I can help people stuck in the same situation now."

"Some things don't change, I guess. I read in the Chinese newspapers about those two bodies. In your father's time, if you couldn't keep up with payments, something could happen to you, too. Back then, when the American cops found a Chinese body, they would dig a ditch and roll it in. They just figured it was a criminal who got what he deserved. Your father knew men who were killed."

We set all the food on the table surface and lit the incense. A framed picture of my father at a young age leaned against a vase filled with stones.

"How old was Dad in this picture?"

"That's the picture from his fake passport. He's only fourteen or fifteen."

I stared at his young, smiling face. He was ten years younger than I was now. When I was that age, I was swinging a chain in the streets.

He looked innocent and utterly unprepared for his life's hard work. He couldn't have known how bad it was going to be. I thought about all the horrible things that were going to happen to that poor little boy in the picture, who looked like a perfect victim.

All that hope brimming in his eyes was mostly dead by the time I was born. I killed what was left.

I looked harder and I saw for the first time that I had his eyes.

Dad, I'm going to get these smugglers, I promised to his picture. Not for the father you were, but for the kid you used to be.

I lit up a hundred-dollar Hell Bank Note and watched it blacken and crumble in a metal bowl.

The veteran precinct detectives were out dealing with the FALN bombing and tried to stay out of the squad room as much as possible because the air conditioner was busted. The precinct detectives holed up in their hiding holes, the main one being Happy's on Baxter, above Columbus Park, where they hung out with Manhattan South detectives.

Happy's, which was one of the few big Italian restaurants left south of

Canal Street, wasn't the actual name, but it was easier to say. Everybody knew Happy's and everybody went there except for Vandyne and me.

Happy himself kept a semicircular booth in the front by the register that no one else was allowed to sit in but squad detectives, who were welcome anytime, even before or after closing. Three or four would come in at a time, wolf down steaks with a few shots of Johnnie Walker Black. If they had smaller appetites, Happy would probably give them the keys to the kitchen, but of course he knew better. A free meal or two per detective per day was enough.

I met Happy about a year ago when I was still on the bottle and stumbling through a footpost. Happy was trying to figure out how to hammer an old sign to the right of his entrance. Happy was doughy, in both shape and color, and about five-nine, 240, with a neutral expression on his face. He got his name because he had the most sarcastic sense of humor in the world. Or maybe he just hated everything, because his comments, which usually contextualized his own death, wouldn't register more than a flicker on his face.

"Do you like this?" he asked me after taking note of my NYPD uniform. "It's a family heirloom from Shanghai."

The sign was a reproduction of an old anti-Chinese cartoon that used to run in newspapers in the old West. A Chinaman with a long queue and ricepicker hat was standing and holding his head back with his mouth wide open. His right hand was holding a rat by the tail and dangling it just above his lips.

"Do you think people around here are gonna understand the parody?" asked Happy. "Or are they gonna wanna kill me?"

I smiled, but I opened up my right hand and laid it against my revolver. I entertained the thought of pulling the trigger, but the paperwork that would follow was a huge deterrent.

"They'll really wanna hang me for this one, huh?" asked Happy, his face smooth and frosty as beach glass.

"Let me see that up close," I said, grabbing the sign. It was light and made out of pine. I laid it down as a ramp from the street to the curb and stomped on it, snapping it in two. I picked up the smaller piece and handed it to Happy. "There you go. Less is more."

He kind of had it in for me after that. Fuck him. I didn't need to eat his ratty food. I had all of Chinatown for my ratty food.

Later I had heard that Happy had complained to the Brow about me, which didn't help my special relationship with my C.O. Well, fuck him, too. He was the one who was keeping me walking a beat and blocking my advancement to investigative assignments. The whole time I had blamed English Sanchez for not throwing me a bone.

I had unfairly hated English for a while and sometimes I felt bad about it. Lonnie told me that the Bible said that just thinking of sinning was the same as actually sinning, so thinking of killing someone was the same as doing the deed itself. Now I knew why so many cops had Blessed Virgin Mary cards shoved into the inside of their hats. Nobody had more murderous thoughts than an NYPD cop.

I came into the squad room and found that the heat and humidity were already comfortably settled in, shoes off and everything. I saw English and pointed at the dusty, dented air-conditioning unit perched above a blackened window.

"That thing ever going to get fixed?" I asked.

"Yeah, right after you finish that Apex Tech class," he said, never looking away from the newspaper on his desk. "They let you keep your tools when you graduate, you know."

We were alone in the room.

"Hey," I said. "I'm sorry I blamed you for not giving me investigative assignments."

"Forget it."

"I thought you had something personal against me."

"Never did."

"I thought you were a racist."

"I sort of am."

I chuckled a little. "Anyway," I said. "I'm not making a lot of headway on the two bodies."

"I didn't think you would."

"Because you don't think I'm up for it?" I growled. "You wanted to see me fall on my face?"

"That's not it." English flipped the newspaper closed and put his hands behind his head. "It's just that something like this gets forgotten. This FALN thing is going to get solved. People will go to jail for this one because white people were killed. Important ones. Two illegal Chinese guys dead? I don't need to tell you this: No one cares outside of Chinatown. Even inside Chinatown, most people probably feel like they got what they deserved."

"What about the smuggling, the illegal human trafficking?"

"It's all on the rise, but let the INS worry about that."

"So you gave me this assignment fully expecting me to not come up with anything."

"Yeah, I did." Now he was looking right at me. "But I was hoping you could surprise me. Pleasantly."

"This is a personal thing for me, you know?"

"That's not going to help you. Don't take the job to heart. It's not worth it. You don't need emotional scars when you retire."

"I already got 'em."

We each found other things to occupy ourselves with.

After a while, I asked English, "Do we know for sure that illegal immigration is up in Chinatown?"

"We see all the signs: There's a lot more trash, the streets are more crowded, and money-transfer businesses are booming. The illegals here, they always try to send as much money as possible back home."

"I can see all that. We should get the Immigration and Naturalization Service in on this and round up the illegals. It would be a humanitarian mission, stop the exploitation."

English sighed and shook his head.

"We tried that before. The Greater China Association threatened to file a racial discrimination lawsuit if we start raiding restaurants with the INS."

"We need the association's approval before we do anything?"

"They can make things easy or hard. Besides, let's say we raided a restaurant that was owned by a member of Greater China and found no illegals, which is a feasible outcome. Then what? Not only would the association come down on us, but also the ACLU, not to mention the fucking Manhattan D.A.!

"Anyway, Chow, the fact is that the Chinatown businesses benefit from the smuggling of aliens. They pay 'em less, work 'em longer, and if they treat 'em like shit, who the hell can they complain to? They sure as hell aren't going to try to organize a union or go on a hunger strike."

"I have reason to believe that these associations have a hand in the smuggling so that they get cheap labor for their restaurants and sweatshops."

"Is this from family experience?" English asked.

"Actually, from a certain family that's a friend of the family."

"I see," English said evenly, closing his eyes and rubbing his temples.

"You all right?" I asked.

"You know how much shit I'm getting over this FALN bombing?"

"What do you mean?"

"The new FALN spokesman has the same name as me! Manhattan District South guys kid around with me, but it ain't all kidding!"

"You're not Puerto Rican—you're American!"

"But my parents are from there! They've also got idiot friends who are pro–Puerto Rican independence who are not unsympathetic with the FALN!"

"If they live in New York City, they should have no say whatsoever over the fate of Puerto Rico."

"You tell them that. They're more loyal to Puerto Rico than anyone else."

"It must be an immigrant way of thinking. You feel loyal to the place that was so crappy you had to leave."

"I think they're nostalgic for the crap," said English.

"If this country keeps losing jobs, they won't have to be nostalgic."

8

I TOOK A SLOW WALK TO THE TOY STORE.

I could feel my father around me, which was a little strange because
the old man and I hadn't been close in years. When he came home,
tired and cranky, I used to wonder where the other guy went. The guy
who used to bring me candy, dried mango, or squid jerky. The guy who
discovered that I was allergic to seafood because of how violently ill I
became after eating squid jerky.

When he died, I couldn't feel anything for him. It was after I was
back from Nam, so that wasn't surprising. He had given me shit about
going to the police academy, so I just sort of regarded him as an annoying papa-san.

The mind is a funny thing. After I got on the wagon and fell in love
with a girl, I started seeing my father out in the streets. I didn't literally
see his ghost walking around, but I'd see his nose in profile on another
guy's face. Sometimes I'd be walking behind someone who had his
slouchy shuffle, his spotted ears, or the back of the head that looked like
an elderly porcupine with spikes gone soft and white.

One time a hand reached out to my shoulder and touched me exactly where he used to touch me from his chair after dinner to ask me to get him a beer from the fridge.

Of course it wasn't my father. It was an older guy who wanted to know if I was the guy whose picture used to be in all the Chinese newspapers. The man was almost completely bald and had two light brown spots on the top right of his head that looked like an imprint from a woman's high-heeled shoe.

He called me the Sheriff of Chinatown. I tried to get away from him as soon as possible, but he was one of those people who liked to say good-bye and then ask another question just when you're about to part. The guy ended up grabbing both of my hands twice before I was able to make the corner and get away. I checked that my wallet was still in my pocket, though, just in case he had been working me with a partner. I guess he was genuinely glad to meet me.

I get recognized less now.

My father died before he ever saw my face in the papers. I wonder if he would have been proud of me. Maybe he could have come to see that I made the right choice in becoming a cop. Then we could have been buddies. We could have gone to the father-son bowling tournament and chucked gutterballs.

I knew, though, that that never could have happened. The few years that my father was kind to me used up the last bits of humanity he had left. Dad couldn't even be nice to Mom by that point.

That smiling, hopeful teenager in the photo was long forgotten. Dad's spirit looking to pocket paper money and eat a meal during the Ghost Festival might not have recognized his picture. I can only hope his spirit was less bitter than the man. Working long hours at menial jobs to pay off his smuggling debt must have been like trying to save up for a new house with a paper route.

What it all came down to was that the smugglers made money from cheap labor to work in restaurants and factories owned by associations—maybe more money than they got from the people they brought over. The laborers made up a reliable workforce even after their debt was paid off and until the day they couldn't work anymore.

My dad was dead long before he fell off the roof. I really don't think he was holding out hope for me to make all his sacrifices worth it, like my mother said. If he was, then that was as foolish as taking that first step on the gangplank back in China to come here.

When I was drinking I used to be mad at everything that didn't come in a can or a bottle. I was focused now.

Stop the snakeheads.

Maybe, only now, years after my dad had passed, I was ready to do something for him and find some sort of resolution between us. Maybe my father's spirit had entered me and we were going to stop the snakeheads together.

Maybe I was just losing it.

Soon I was in front of the toy store. I went in and carefully scrutinized the two paintings behind the counter and felt my jaw tighten up.

The Guan Gong portrait was typically terrifying, with his bloodred complexion, war paint, and Green Dragon crescent moon blade weapon. His two-foot-long beard flowed into a point in his left hand. Guan was a real general during the Three Kingdoms period and is deified as a symbol of loyalty and righteousness throughout the Chinese community.

Yet Guan was also an outlaw, because before he rose to military greatness he had killed a corrupt official. Naturally the Chinese underworld felt a special bond with this aspect of Guan's life. They believed that Guan's story proved that criminal deeds are justified as long as you stay true to your brothers.

New members of associations and Hong Kong triads drank blood-infused drinks in front of his portrait, promising to be destroyed by knives and lightning if they betrayed their group.

The midget's other painting was a landscape of a series of lakes and rivers that looked like a Yes album cover.

"See something you like?" asked the midget.

"I see something I don't like," I said. "Why do you have Guan Gong hanging up there?"

"I like to remind people the consequences of shoplifting. Not only will you have to pay twice the sticker price, but this guy will kill you in the spirit world."

"You know a lot of gang members take oaths in front of Guan Gong?"

"Sure. We should take note of all the places that put up Guan's portrait for being potential gang hangouts. By the way, can you name even one restaurant that doesn't have a Guan Gong portrait or altar?"

"Can you explain the lakes and rivers portrait?"

"Explain?"

"Lakes and rivers. That's what members of the underworld refer to as the lives they live."

"Well, Robert, the phrase generally refers to a fantasy bohemian world, sort of like a Taoist *Lord of the Rings* or the Dungeons and Dragons crap that I sell. The gangsters misappropriate the term for their own purposes."

"But you know what people will think when they see that painting."

"They'll think, 'Gee, that little guy sure has great taste.'"

"All right, I'm going to just come out with it. Are you in an association? You are a highly visible guy in Chinatown. I just should have realized it before."

The midget slipped off his stool and came around the counter until he stood at my chest.

"First of all, I want to make it clear that the great majority of members of associations are just regular lonely men who want a place to socialize with like-minded people with the same family name or from the same village or province. They pay their membership fees and they get to come up and play mah-jongg and drink tea any time they want.

"It's the dozen or so people within any association who have ties to criminal activity. They use all the innocent members as a shield."

"Have you joined an association?"

"Yes, I recently have."

"Which one?"

"I don't want to tell you the name, Robert."

We spoke at a conversational volume as the kids around the store ignored us.

"I thought you said you weren't going to join Golden Peace!"

"I didn't. This is another group entirely."

"Is your association involved with illegal activities?"

"Some people may be, of course. I personally am not."

"Are they smuggling people into this country?"

"I don't know. They might be. I didn't specifically ask."

"Why did you want to join this association?"

"About a week ago a couple of guys came into the store and kindly asked me to join. The filmmaker doing the documentary on me thinks of himself as a bit of an artist. Naturally, he ran out of money. This group is one of the potential investors and would like to see one of their members in a high-profile role."

"Did they threaten you?"

"Well, I'm sure they would not have taken 'no' as an answer very lightly. Trust me. It was easier to join without protest."

"What are you getting out of this association?"

"We have some common interests." The midget shrugged. "Not everything, but many things."

"Is this one of the big associations?"

"No, definitely not. I would never have joined one of them. It's a little one."

I stared at him in silence.

"All right, Senator McCarthy," he asked, "do you want to see my membership card?"

"Yeah, I do. Are you sure this won't break any vows you took in front of Guan Gong?"

"Maybe, but the rest of the guys will get over it."

He opened his wallet and handed me a business card upside down. I flipped it over and read, "Little People of America, Inc."

"Oh, ha-ha!" I said.

The midget leaned against the counter and slapped his thigh.

"You know, Robert, I've got a bridge I want to sell you, too! I'll throw in a tunnel free of charge!"

"That's not funny. Stop laughing. C'mon, stop laughing! I'll see you later, all right?" I had to chuckle at myself. He had played me for a fool. It was easy to see why no one had beaten the midget at anything ever.

Vandyne and I sat in the Con Ed van parked in an alley off Henry Street. We had a big five-dollar bag of baked pork buns from a place on Canal. It was close to midnight and the streets were deserted. The area where the bodies were found was lit by lights hanging from the underpass above.

"I'm still thinking," said Vandyne, "that we maybe should have gone to Burger King instead. You know it was right next to the Con Ed facilities."

"I know. I was there, too. Remember? I guess these pork buns aren't doing it for you. You want to 'have it your way at Burger King now.'" I sang it out badly enough to make him cringe.

"Naw, I just think maybe I wanted some fries."

"I think barbecued shredded pork stands on its own. With the bun and chunks of fat, that is."

"How come these aren't light and fluffy like those other ones you got before?"

"Vandyne, these are baked ones. You're thinking of the steamed ones."

"I like them both, but these baked ones are sticky on the outside. They put a glaze on it that gets all over your fingers."

We both watched a guy shuffle to a phone booth, check the coin slot, and walk on.

"That glaze," I said, "makes them look better in the store. Shiny and new."

"Well, it doesn't make any sense to coat finger food with shit that gets all over your fucking fingers," he grumbled. "I don't suppose you grabbed some napkins."

"What do you need napkins for? Just lick your fingers when you're done."

"That's how Chinese people wash their hands, huh?"

"We like to stay neat, you know. Anyway, what do black people do when they eat finger food?"

"We bring some goddamned napkins and hand wipes, that's what! We ain't fools!"

"Well, right now we're both fools, sitting around and just waiting. But you know what? This is part of the job. One of the many sacrifices we have to make."

"If we can just stay motivated, we'll do fine, partner."

"I'm motivated, all right," I said. "Motivated like a motherfucker."

I reached down to my two insulated bottles, making sure to pick the one without the cracked lid, the empty bottle you always have to take on a stakeout. I drank a cup of coffee and screwed the lid back on.

"That coffee smelled good," said Vandyne.

"Lonnie mixed it up for me back at the bakery."

"Want to trade a cup?" he asked, holding up one of his two bottles. "It's Blue Mountain."

"Not yet, thanks. Say, where are you with that café idea you had?"

"Hell, this recession has to end before that really gets off the ground."

"I get it. Grounds. Coffee."

"Damn, how can you be this fast this late?"

A black sedan pulled in from Henry Street and slowed down. The driver then pulled a sloppy U-turn and scraped the car against the curb twice, front end and rear end. Vandyne and I both winced at the crunching sounds. As the driver's side rolled by we saw that the driver was Chinese.

"Damn! Chinese people are just the worst drivers in the world!" said Vandyne.

"We're good drivers. White people don't know how to lay out roads!"

"Hold up. Here comes another car."

A tan two-door came slowly up Market Street and stopped at Henry Street. The driver killed the lights. Someone got out of the passenger side and walked over to where the bodies had been found. It was a woman.

"What are you doing here!" I gasped.

"You know her?" asked Vandyne.

"Yeah, she's Ng's sister, Winnie. She works at the foundation he made by converting some old office and warehouse space."

She was dressed in a pants suit and walked stiffly, as if her platform shoes hurt. Every few steps, she lifted her right leg and picked at something at her heel.

We watched her walk up to the yellow tape and turn on a penlight.

"I'll take the woman," I said. "You stay here in case the driver tries to take off."

Vandyne nodded.

I jumped out and ran up to her.

"Police! Freeze and put your hands up!"

She screamed and dropped her penlight.

"I didn't do anything!" she yelled.

"You were looking for something. What was it?"

"Nothing! I was just curiosity-seeking!"

"You're interfering with a crime scene!" I said.

I heard the car start up. Vandyne hit the sirens and cut the car off. He leapt out with his gun drawn.

"Exit the vehicle with your hands up!" he yelled at the car.

"Get the fuck out with your hands up, asshole!" I yelled in Cantonese, in case the driver didn't speak English.

The door opened and Brian, the lion dance instructor, meekly held his hands up.

"Do not shoot, Officer!" he said in English.

"Looks like the gang's all here except for Ng," I said, turning to Winnie. "Where's your brother, Andy?"

"Jesus, please don't get him involved! He'll kill me!"

Vandyne was patting down Brian, who had his hands on the car roof, his legs spread. I grabbed Winnie's arm and walked her over to the car.

"This is a big misunderstanding!" Brian said. "We're just fooling around!"

"Fooling around a crime scene?" I said in a mocking voice. "That was really fucking stupid! You want to get your kicks, go to Coney Island! Winnie, put your hands on the hood and spread out your legs."

"This isn't fair, Robert," she wailed. "I didn't even do anything!"

"Well, you were going to! What was the penlight for?"

"I thought I was going to trip!" Then, looking over my uniform, she added, "You work for Con Ed now?"

"We're moonlighting," I said. "They don't pay cops enough."

Vandyne came over to me and said, "Maybe we should let them off with a warning. Driver's license is valid, they haven't been drinking, and all he had in his pockets were a couple of condoms."

"I say we drive the girl home and leave him hanging. Maybe she'll talk some more."

"You got a mean streak a mile wide," said Vandyne, smiling.

"And a mile deep," I added. "Brian and Winnie, we're going to let you guys off with a warning. Where do you live, Brian?"

"I live in Brooklyn," he said in English.

I looked at Vandyne, who nodded.

I said, "Now go straight home and we'll forget about all this. We're going to take Winnie home."

Brian gave a half-grin grimace and sank into his car seat. Winnie was completely silent as we walked her to the Con Ed van.

"I get it now," she said as she climbed into the backseat. "You guys are working undercover. You're just wearing Con Ed uniforms to fool people."

"To fool bad people," I said. "Like you and Brian."

"We're not bad people. But anyway, I'm glad you got me away from Brian. I didn't like the energy he was sending over. He's a distant relative, so that makes it even more disgusting. This is the first time he's asked me out and he makes me do this."

"Why did you go out with him?"

"He just wore me down. So I let him take me to dinner and a movie."

"Which movie?"

"*Midway*. God, that movie took forever to finish! That's the wrong movie to take a girl to."

Vandyne jumped into the driver's seat and started the engine.

In English I said, "Winnie, let's just talk like this to be polite to my partner."

"What is your name?" she asked Vandyne.

"My name's John. You're Winnie?"

"Yes. Hello, John." She reached up and shook his hand. "You're the first Negro I've ever met."

"Just say 'black,'" said Vandyne as he eased us away from the curb. "Once you go black, you never go back."

"You're not a Negro?"

"Listen, Winnie," I said. "When you call someone a Negro, it's like someone white calling you a Chink."

"White people do call me Chink. Is that bad?"

"When did this happen?"

"Well, you know I live with my brother in an apartment on Central Park South."

"I saw by your driver's license."

"Well, one day I was coming in and the doorman asked me if I lived there and the concierge said, 'That's one of the Chinks who live in 33 F.'"

"I'll kill that guy," I said involuntarily. "I'm sorry, that just came out of me. Did you grow up in Hong Kong, Winnie?"

"No, I was born in Singapore and lived there until I came here."

"I thought you spoke English with a little bit of an Australian accent."

"My English tutor was from New Zealand, actually."

"Vandyne, would there be repercussions if I walked her in and sapped the concierge?"

"Let it go," he said. "Sticks and stones, man. That jerk can throw around names, but he's Winnie's servant, basically. She pays his salary. She has power over him and he resents it."

"Winnie, did you live with your brother in Singapore?"

"Yes, with our mother, too. But he was born in Hong Kong. You know about our family situation, don't you, Robert?"

At this point, Vandyne made a small circle with his index finger, indicating that we were going to take the scenic route to give us more time to talk.

"I don't really know, Winnie. Tell me about your family situation."

"Well, Beautiful Hong Kong was started by our great-grandfather. He was an infamous triad member who was involved in a number of shady activities. Yet he also had a patriotic sense of duty to the Chinese. Nobody was more anti-Manchu than him! He gave a lot of money to Sun Yat-sen. We have a picture of him with Dr. Sun."

"Dr. Sun didn't mind being seen with triad figures?"

"Robert, you should know that the triads were founded by the Chinese originally to help bring down the Manchu regime. You know, 'Destroy the Qing, Restore the Ming!'"

"I know," I lied.

"God, Andy is obsessed with revolutionary slogans like that. Always has been. Anyway, so by the time Dr. Sun was organizing, the triads were already a couple hundred years old. They were key to financing the war on the Manchu. But then after the Manchu were finally brought down, the triads were suddenly at a crossroads. Many of them joined the new government of the young Republic of China. Others, they just went into full-time criminal operations."

"I guess your great-grandfather did the latter."

"No, my great-grandfather did the former. My grandfather did the latter and refined the triad into a worldwide association while making Beautiful Hong Kong sort of a front for many activities."

"I see."

"So my grandfather continued with the family enterprises, mainly in opium and prostitution. When my father came of age to take power, threats were made against his young son and wife, so he sent them to Singapore for safety. I was born shortly after."

"How clean is your association now?"

"It's still a little dirty, I'm sure. Just a little bit. But Andy is changing everything and getting rid of things that can't be, ah, reconfigured. He's making everything into a legitimate business. He's also very community minded. The lion dance group is just a start. He wants to start a program to send American-born Chinese like you to go back to Taiwan or Hong Kong to understand their history."

"Hey, I'm a Chinese American, not an ABC."

"What's the difference?"

"'American-Born Chinese' means that I was born in America, but I'm still really a Chinese national."

"You're not Chinese?"

"Chinese American!"

"Aw, shit," Vandyne moaned out loud.

"Vandyne, how would you like it if I called you Kenyan?"

"I might be, right?" he said. "What I mean is, I'm not sure if I am."

"Even if you are of Kenyan descent, you're still an American by birth."

We came rolling up to the address. "One-eight-eight Central Park South," I announced.

"You still want to get out and sap the concierge?" Vandyne asked me.

"I'm giving him one free pass because it would leave the lobby undermanned."

"This isn't the entrance," interrupted Winnie. "It's just a little farther down the block. This is the nigger door."

"What!" both Vandyne and I shouted.

"I came in through it before and the concierge told me to come in through the revolving door, not through the nigger door."

"I'll kill that guy!" thundered Vandyne.

"That's a bad word, Winnie!" I said. "Please don't ever use it again!"

"I'm sorry! I didn't know!"

"How come you know so much about Chinese history, but you don't know anything about American culture?"

"Because," she said slowly, "I'm Chinese."

A Triumph Spitfire suddenly swung in front of us and stopped at the main entrance to Winnie's building.

"That's Andy's car!" she said.

"Let's sit tight, everyone," I said. "You, too, Winnie."

"I will sit still," she said.

Two men got out. Andy and the man who Willie Gee told me was King Lam. Andy came around from the passenger's side and they did a two-arm embrace.

"Do you know that man, Winnie?" I asked.

"No, who is that?"

"A guy your brother seems to hang out with."

"Andy never tells me anything."

Lam jumped back into the car and eased toward Broadway.

"We've got to get on that one," said Vandyne.

"Jump out of the car, Winnie. We have to chase that guy. And don't tell Andy what we talked about tonight."

She jumped out.

"Don't worry, he never wants to hear anything from me. I'm a girl." She shut the door and we pulled away.

9

THE SPITFIRE WAS MOVING AS SLOWLY AS A CEMENT TRUCK.

"You think he knows we're following him?" asked Vandyne.

"That paranoid son of a bitch," I said. "We have a damn good cover."

"Con Ed—the only New York institution hated more than the NYPD. They provide shitty service and yet they're going for another electricity rate hike."

"I like how they didn't bother to clean off the graffiti before loaning us the van." Under the Con Ed logo on the back doors someone had spray-painted CAN SUCK IT.

"Why bother cleaning it off if they're just going to write something worse?" said Vandyne.

"Dammit! He's pulling over! What should we do?"

"We have to keep going. I'll do a lap around the block."

"That's good thinking, Vandyne!"

When we came full circle back to where we started, King Lam was leaning against the Spitfire, waving at us with both arms. Vandyne drove us up to him and I rolled down my window to talk.

"You two looking for the King Tut exhibit? It won't be here for two more years." He spoke English that had been weathered by some California sun.

I showed him my shield. "Now lemme see yours."

"I don't carry one on me, for obvious reasons. It's probably worse to have in my pocket than a gun."

"Are you bullshitting me?" I asked him.

He smiled and crossed his arms.

"Chow, he used the code words. He's for real," Vandyne admonished.

"Tell you what," the man said. "Let me get this car to the Manhattan South guys so they can comb through it. Then let's go get some drinks."

"Hey! He doesn't drink!" Vandyne shouted.

"I have a problem," I said.

"Let's go to a diner, then."

We followed the car to Manhattan South headquarters on East Twenty-first and picked up Eddie Ding, aka King Lam, when he got out. It was about one in the morning when we rolled into a diner on Third Avenue and Twenty-fourth Street. We all got cheeseburger specials.

"Why the fuck are you two guys trying to shadow people with a Con Ed van?" he said with several mashed fries in his mouth. "Can you even think of a bigger, more visible object?"

"A fire truck with the sirens on," I said.

"Like we said, Eddie," said Vandyne, "we didn't intend to be following anybody."

Eddie was brought in from the San Francisco PD by Manhattan South to lock down a tax-evasion investigation on Ng and Beautiful Hong Kong. They needed someone who was familiar with triad culture. Eddie had a master's degree in Chinese history and literature. His degree project was on Chinese criminology from the fall of the Ming dynasty to the present.

"How did you avoid the draft?" asked Vandyne.

"It never came for me because, you know, I had the academic deferment. I'm sorry I missed my chance to kill babies with you guys."

"You want a black eye for dessert, asshole?" I asked.

"Make that two," said Vandyne.

"You guys, come on! I'm just letting off steam. For crying out loud, that Andy Ng is putting me through a goddamned cultural decathlon. We played a drinking game about the 108 heroes of *Water Margin*. That was completely nerdy! I'm supposed to represent a Chinese triad based in Malaysia interested in buying certain criminal operations of Beautiful Hong Kong. I didn't know I had to be the guy's playmate, too."

"How are you going to nail him on taxes?" asked Vandyne.

"Soon I plan on entering the due-diligence phase in which Ng shows me the books on his operation. Well, when I have enough evidence collected on the cash flows of his little holding company, we take him down."

"Just like what they did to Al Capone," said Vandyne.

"Has he ever mentioned a single word about smuggling people over?" I asked.

"He hasn't said much about anything apart from *Water Margin* or *Romance of the Three Kingdoms*. It's like talking to a kid who has every single Superman comic and won't shut up about it."

I turned to Vandyne. "Those are the historical novels that Chinese gangsters worship," I said. "Like how the Mafia looks to the *Godfather* movies."

Eddie put his burger down. "Oh, but the worst is that sometimes he asks me about my personal life. At random times, the same questions. He's trying to see if he can trip me up. Do you know how hard it is to suppress the details of your real life and stick to what you've memorized for your fake life?"

"No," I said. "I don't." But my father did.

"I can feel he's still suspicious, but, shit, he lent me his car tonight because he said it was too expensive for me to keep renting mine."

"He's probably going to check how clean it is when you return it," said Vandyne. "If you do vacuum it out, he'll be really suspicious."

"I've got that covered," Eddie said. "See, I'll just say that 'as part of my thanks for loaning me the car, I went and had it cleaned for you and filled the gas tank, too!'"

"Smooth," I said.

"Can I ask you guys something?" Vandyne and I looked at Eddie expectantly. "How do you guys deal with living in this shithole? I mean, it was a close call a couple years ago, but New York might be heading back to bankruptcy. Then you'll all be fucked!"

Vandyne's jaw was locked shut.

I managed to work my mouth loose. "This city has a lot of heart," I said. "We've been through tough times before, but we'll get through it."

"You know what would really wreck this town," Eddie went on. "A blackout. You would have nonstop wholesale looting, murder, and rape. The entire city would be plunged into prehistoric times. With guns."

"You almost sound kind of gleeful, Eddie," I said.

"How about you stop trying to be a funny motherfucker?" Vandyne told him.

"Hey, I'm really sorry about that crack earlier about Nam," said Eddie. "I've heard about how a lot of guys were spat on at the airport when they got back here. That happen to you two?"

"Not me!" said Vandyne. "If any hippie spat on me, I would've scalped him."

"Not me, either," I said.

Eddie went on. "Two of the guys in my precinct, back home, they were in uniform and they had already been warned to wear street clothes, but they refused to. When these girls asked them if they had served in Nam, they started yelling at them, 'You white racist imperialists invaded our country and killed our women and children!!!' The hippies were crying and apologizing like crazy!"

"These guys in your precinct are Asian?" I asked.

"Yeah, one Chinese American, one Japanese American. But, you know, those girls had no idea."

"You have two other Asian guys in your precinct?" I asked.

"Oh, more than that. We don't have a whole lot of brothers in general. I think we're at two percent overall. Chow, you know, I heard you're the only one in Chinatown. Is that true?"

"It's true," said Vandyne.

"How much sense does that make?" said Eddie.

"Don't even get me started on this shit," I said.

"Well, you know, I heard all about it, already." Eddie wiped his mouth. "In fact, I met the guy who got you moved from bullshit photo-op assignments to the detective track."

A white woman in her late forties was on her way out of the diner when she caught sight of my and Vandyne's Con Ed uniforms. She simply assumed that all three of us were employees.

She walked over and yelled, "Break time again, fellas?"

Eddie turned to her coolly and said, "No, lady. We're still on the clock!"

Vandyne covered his face with both hands while I chewed on the insides of my cheeks trying to suppress a laugh.

She banged her fist on our table and stomped out.

"Eddie," I said, "you have a way of getting under people's skin!"

"I should," he said. "I went to a really good college."

Inspector Izzy Rosenbaum was not a tall man, but he projected strength like a column of stainless steel. His gray hair was in a crew cut from the fifties and his face was so crowded with muscles, it was tough for him to talk. It was just as well, because on the phone he barely strung three words together.

"You met Eddie," he said, shaking my hand in two brisk jerks.

"Yes, sir, he told me you were the one who helped me get out of the photo ops."

"Saw you play hockey," he said. His mouth was open in a way that was maybe a smile. "You're tough."

"I'm okay, sir."

"Scored two goals!"

"Yes, sir!"

"I know the Brow."

"You do?"

"Same academy class."

"Oh."

"Dirty little mick."

"You mean that with affection, right, sir?"

The captain stuck his jaw out and stretched his lips around it.

"Of course, back then my name was Israel Rosenbaum. Some guys had a problem with it. Most didn't. The Brow came up to me and said he felt sorry for me because my parents essentially named me 'Jewey Jew Jew.'"

"Oh, that's terrible."

"There was a fight."

"A bad one?"

"Good for me."

"What happened?"

He shrugged. "Stitches came out. They started calling him the Brow. Started calling me Lefty. We've never talked since."

"Wow."

"Heard his ugly voice in a bar few months back, complaining about how this Chow better not get hurt in the hockey game, because if he had to miss some community functions, the Chinks were going to hit the streets."

"That fucking asshole!" I said, shocking myself. I tried to suck the words back in. "Sorry, sir!"

"C'mon! Forget it!"

"Thank you."

"I saw the game. Saw you score. Saw you take a stand. Now you're detective track."

"I couldn't possibly thank you enough."

He swatted the thought away. "So you think you're ready for a test I got for you?"

"Sure!"

"It'll mainly test your memorization and ability to reach conclusions quickly."

"That's right up my alley," I said.

"But first, and I apologize for this, you have to meet my mentor here. He's a deputy chief, but he's kind of lost it. We keep him here at a desk. This is purely political, because technically I still report to him."

"I understand."

"He's not really qualified to do anything anymore and he rambles on, but try to be interested or at least look interested."

Izzy brought me down to the quiet end of a long hall and opened the door. An older man in a plainclothes suit sat at a desk that didn't even have a telephone.

"How are you, Lefty!" the man said.

"Good, good," said Izzy. "This is Robert Chow. Detective track, Five Precinct. Deputy Chief Barrett."

"Hello," I said, shaking Barrett's hand.

"I'll let you two get acquainted," said Izzy. "Remember to drop by my office when you're done, Chow."

"Okay," I said.

Izzy left.

"Well, first things first," said Barrett. "How do you like the job?"

"I like it fine," I said. "It's been better and more challenging lately."

"Where do you see yourself in ten years?"

"With a gold shield, I guess. I can assume that, right?"

"Yes, that's a safe assumption, but what about with a family? A baby boy and a baby girl?" He was smiling in a way that screamed, "I'm going crazy! Wanna come?"

"I don't know if I'm ready for that kind of talk."

"Look here, look here!" He pulled out his wallet and opened it. "This is my boy Michael when he was in first grade. That's college graduation. That's him now in front of his office park." Barrett went ahead and showed me pictures of his two girls, too.

All my experience in enduring various community functions had honed my skill at retreating within my consciousness to a tiny little safe space in the back of my head. There I could relive hockey highlights going back years; listen to Marvin Gaye, Stevie Wonder, and Neil Young; see Lonnie smiling in her uniform and then out of it. . . .

"Robert, are you here?"

"Of course I am. I mean, where else would I be?"

"Where else, indeed!" Was this Barrett dipping into the contraband?

"Deputy Chief Barrett, I'm currently on detective track now."

"Yes, I know."

"What would a man of your experience suggest in terms of advancing my career?"

"Travel!"

"I'm sorry, sir?"

"Travel! Go see the world! Do you know where I've been?"

"I don't know," I said. I thought of something and started looking around for Allen Funt.

"Guess! Be my guest at guessing!"

"Hong Kong? France? England?"

"Yes, no, and yes!" He also rattled off several more countries. "Do you know who I went with?"

"Your family?"

"My wife and kids!" Unbelievably, he stood up and reached for his wallet again. Boy, were me and Izzy going to have a few laughs about this. I looked at Barrett's kindly face and wondered what horrible thing happened to crack him up like this.

"Do you know where this is? You recognize that?"

"Is it the Panama Canal?"

"You're right!"

"The sign in the picture kind of gave it away."

"So it does! Oh, you have to go there! It's amazing!"

I nodded enthusiastically, hoping it would make him put his wallet away. He flipped through a dozen more pictures and blabbed about them. That man had more pictures in his wallet than I did in my photo albums.

"Well, it's time for my lunch, Robert. I've got to get going."

I felt my eyes light up and pure joy lifted me out of my seat.

"It's been a pleasure, Deputy Chief Barrett." We shook hands. I couldn't get out of that room fast enough.

I got back into Izzy's office and shook my head.

"Sir," I said, shaking my head, "you didn't prepare me for that!"

Izzy was all business, however. "You ready for the test now, Robert?" he asked coolly.

I nodded.

He took out a clipboard. "Names of the three children?"

"Deputy Chief Barrett's?" I asked.

"Yes."

"I don't remember," I said. My lips went rubbery and I could no longer feel them.

"What colleges did they go to?"

"I don't know."

Without standing, he reached and unfurled a map on the wall behind his desk.

"Come over here. Show me what countries he's been to." The map looked like any other I'd seen in classrooms, only there were no names on it whatsoever.

I walked over. I could feel sweat running down the insides of my thighs. I hoped it was sweat.

"Panama," I said, pointing.

"That's Nicaragua!"

I sat down again. There was a flashing white light inside my right pupil. Izzy pressed on, opening a binder to photographs of a dozen women in their fifties.

"Which is the wife?"

"I don't know." God, is college like this?

He flipped the page.

"Find three pictures he didn't have."

"I can't."

Izzy flipped the page again.

"Find the strangers who were in his pictures."

"I don't remember."

This was two to three times more excruciating than my session with Barrett although it lasted ten minutes, tops.

"I did terrible, right?" I asked.

"Average score is negative, because I deduct for wrong guesses. You got a zero. So you're above average."

"You're not gonna give me Panama?"

"I'll give half credit. Half a point out of a possible fifty."

"What did I need to pass?"

"There is no pass! You either get a fifty or you're shot dead!"

My mouth went dry. In some ways, the Brow was better than Izzy, because as much as the Brow pushed you around and verbally abused you, he never made you feel stupid. Well, certainly not to this degree.

"May I leave now, sir?"

He finally softened a bit. "Robert, you're always on the job. Pay attention to everything. Don't take anything for granted."

I met up with Lonnie for a quick dinner.

"What's wrong?" she asked. "You look sick!"

"That guy who helped me get on detective track just made me feel like the biggest idiot in the world!"

"What did he do?"

"He gave me this test and I failed it."

"Did you study for it?"

"It wasn't the kind of test you can study for. It was actually one of those life-lesson things."

"What did you learn?"

"That I have to always stay alert."

"All the time?"

"Yes. There could be bad guys out to kill me any second."

"What would you do if you saw a bad guy?"

"Well, you can't tell by sight if it's a bad guy or not. Maybe you can get a gut feeling, but you still have to watch him and see if he does something bad before you can move in."

"Would a bad guy do something like try to force you to hire somebody?" Lonnie looked a little timid.

"You were forced to hire somebody?" I asked. "I guess that's one way you can beat unemployment."

She sighed. "I didn't want to bother you and I know you have other things to deal with."

"Lonnie, what happened?"

"This guy came into the bakery with two women and tried to get me to give them jobs."

"Was he mean?"

"He wasn't mean, but he was forceful. When I told him we didn't have any openings, he said these two women didn't want to be prostitutes anymore and that I could help them out and give them both better lives."

"Why couldn't these women just ask for jobs themselves?"

"They didn't know Cantonese. The guy spoke to them in Fukienese and his Cantonese was pretty bad."

"What did the guy look like?"

"He was wearing jeans and a buttoned shirt. Not really anything that looked outstanding. His face would blend into a Chinatown crowd. But his teeth were kind of gray. You know how people from the mainland all have dark-colored teeth?

"I said I wasn't the boss, but I don't think he believed me. Then before they left, he actually tried to get me to give them free coffee and food! What nerve!"

"You told Shelly about this?" I asked, referring to Lonnie's boss.

"I called her right after. She said that this has happened a few times already at some of the other bakeries."

"Were those two women really prostitutes?"

"I could definitely believe it. They looked like they would do anything for money."

LONNIE WENT TO GO HIT THE BOOKS AND I TOOK A STROLL DOWN Mott to where it ended at Bowery, which was essentially the dividing line between the part of Chinatown loyal to the KMT and the much smaller community east of Bowery that was loyal to Communist China. Nearly all Fukienese lived in the latter.

The Communist-affiliated family and affinity associations were banded as Together Chinese Kinship and rivaled the KMT-affiliated Greater China Association.

Together Chinese funded two arts groups that featured mostly left-leaning Chinese Americans from all over the country who streamed into Chinatown after college to "find themselves" or "get back in touch with their roots." Greater China accused Together Chinese of spreading Communist propaganda through art, but Together Chinese said it was simply giving space for artistic expression, which by definition did not have political aims.

The two umbrella groups had had a major confrontation in early July when Chu Teh, the legendary Communist marshal, had died. Together Chinese flew a Communist China flag and blared out "The East Is Red" in tribute. Greater China demanded that they take down the flag and turn off the speakers. There was no response. Someone threw a lit gasoline-soaked rag in a wine bottle at the flag and nearly set fire to the entire building. Together Chinese took the burned flag down and turned off its speakers, but the song continued to play from several unknown points on the Communist side of Chinatown.

I walked up to Together Chinese's offices on East Broadway close to Catherine Street. The building was made of one-hundred-year-old brown crumbling brick. A blackened scar above the second floor marked where the fire had done its damage.

I pressed the buzzer and heard a door slam inside. I looked casually around and tapped my right foot. The men's bodies had been found only a couple blocks away. I got my right hand ready to grab my gun if I had to.

The door swung open and a thin girl in a tank top who looked about sixteen stepped out.

"Hello there," she said in English. "How can I help you?"

"Hi there," I said. "Are your parents home?"

"Very funny, big boy. I know I look really young."

I showed her my shield and said, "Can I talk to somebody regarding the Fukienese community?"

"You can come in. I'll find someone for you to talk to."

I stepped in and she shut the door behind me. The wood-paneled walls were bare with the exception of three portraits: Mao, Sun Yat-sen, and George Washington.

"You know, you guys couldn't have possibly existed even ten years ago," I said to the girl, who was still struggling with the locks.

"Times change, and attitudes change, you know," she said. "When we replaced Taiwan in the U.N., so many things opened up for us. Now that we have the momentum, we're threatening the status quo in Chinatown."

"What are you guys threatening to do?"

She shrugged. "Some people think the fact that we exist is a threat."

"Stephanie!" someone shouted in English from the second floor. "Who was that guy?"

"It's a policeman!" she shouted up. "He's inside now!"

Someone said something in Fukienese and I heard some scuffling and a door slam. Footsteps slowly came down the staircase. A man appeared on the landing. He wore blue twill shorts and a white short-sleeved buttoned shirt. I could see the outline of a sweaty V-necked T-shirt on his chest. He was about fifty, but he still parted his hair like a teen.

"Hello," he said in English. "How are you doing today, Officer?"

"Hi, my name's Robert. Do you have a place where we can talk?"

"Robert, I'm Mr. Song. I'm the chair of Together Chinese Kinship. Let's sit in here," he said, opening a side door to a small meeting room. We sat down at a nice worn-out walnut table that wouldn't be out of place at one of the upscale thrift stores in the city.

"Would you care for some tea?" he asked.

"No thank you, Mr. Song. I have to say, you seem to be working pretty late. It's almost seven o'clock."

"But that means eight in the morning in China. Sometimes we have affairs to talk about on the phone."

"You ever talk about illegal immigration?"

"Robert, are you implying that we have anything to do with smuggling people into America?"

I took notice of Stephanie, who took a seat at the far side of the table from Song and me.

"Mr. Song, I'm not trying to imply anything. The vast majority of illegal immigrants coming into Chinatown are Fukienese. Most Fukienese in Chinatown belong to groups under the umbrella of Together Chinese. Just tell me what you know about it."

"I personally don't know anything about the smuggling. But yes, I have also noticed the influx of Fukienese. I also concede that they likely are illegal entrants."

"Who are the snakeheads who are bringing them in?"

He breathed in deeply.

"Stephanie," he asked, "could you please boil a pot of tea for our guest?"

She got up, smiled at me, and left.

"She's a little new here, so she's still a little too curious," said Song. "Stephanie is a student at Yale, planning on going to law school."

"I could tell you didn't rescue her from a life of prostitution."

"She's my daughter, Robert."

I wiped the entire bottom half of my face with my hand.

"I'm really sorry, Mr. Song," I said. "It was an inappropriate joke. Is she getting relevant experience here?"

"You're Robert Chow, right?"

I nodded.

"Well, Mr. Chow, our biggest issue right now is finding Fukienese people legal representation to establish refugee status and apply for asylum. Most lose their nerve early on and disappear, but more people are coming in every day."

"How can I find these people?"

"They're kept in safe houses guarded by the snakeheads. Could be anywhere. They go back and forth from work to the safe house until their debt is paid off. It could take a year. Maybe two or three, even."

"You've met illegal Fukienese and you can't tell me where the safe houses are?"

"Chinese people are reluctant to reveal personal information even to people who could help them."

"Welcome to my world!"

"I'm not foolish enough to even ask. That would only arouse suspicion in the community. Together Chinese represents the people and we have to be able to earn their trust and keep it."

"Do you know anything about people asking bakeries to hire illegals?"

"I don't know anything about that, but I think we're reaching a saturation point in terms of employment. Look at our economy."

"Mr. Song, just be straight with me. Do you know who the snakeheads are?"

"I don't know, but I can say for sure that Together Chinese and all its affiliates have nothing to do with smuggling people over. For one thing, who owns the ships to bring all of them over? Nobody Fukienese, that's for sure. You should go look for who has the money! Who owns the transportation lines to bring them all the way here? Who has ties to the Taiwan government, because these smuggling ships fly the KMT flag? It's the Greater China Association, Robert!"

"You don't know for sure."

"Like hell I don't! A ship from Taiwan faces less customs scrutiny than any other from Asia!"

"That's not true."

"Well then, think about this! Who benefits from bringing in these particular illegal immigrants who are so disadvantaged, they're barely literate and can't speak or understand Mandarin or Cantonese? What's better than a workforce that's effectively deaf and dumb?

"It's those Greater China Association bastards and their cronies who are behind it all! After the workers at Jade Palace went on that embarrassing hunger strike, they've been looking for an effective replacement."

"That's a serious allegation, Mr. Song."

"I'm not alleging anything, Mr. Chow. And don't say I said all these things, because I'll deny it up and down. But you know it's true. It's the KMT continuing to systematically exploit the underclass Chinese instead of helping them!"

I stood up.

"I am not a Communist," I said. "I don't buy into socialist propaganda."

"In fact, you might say this sort of talk puts you to sleep, right?" Song stood up also. His smile gave me a creepy feeling.

"How did you know my name right off the bat, Mr. Song?"

"Do you remember a few months ago, you appeared for a restaurant opening on Division Street?"

"That was probably me."

"You were certainly there. In fact, I was one of the speakers that night. I looked over at you and you had fallen asleep on your upraised hand, elbow on the table. I didn't know that such a thing was possible."

"At the time I probably had a long day."

"I'm sure you did, Mr. Chow. A long day of long pulls at the bottle. A Mrs. Sun next to you remarked afterward on how you reeked of alcohol."

"I am an alcoholic. I've been sober almost four months now." My right palm hurt a little bit. I looked down and saw that my hand was in a tight fist, the fingernails digging in.

"Then we have something in common, Robert." Song put his hand on my shoulder. "I've been sober twelve years now. Some days are as hard as the first."

I shook his hand. "Twelve years," I said. "Congratulations. The next time I see you, it might be for a personal matter."

He nodded.

I opened the door and Stephanie jumped away. "You know, a pot that's never put on a flame never boils," I told her.

"Good-bye for now, Mr. Chow," she said, winking awkwardly.

I came home to see Paul watching the worst TV show in the world, M*A*S*H.

"Didn't we talk about this, Paul? They're trying to brainwash you and this whole country! They're trying to make you all forget about Vietnam!"

"Robert, it's a funny show! Maybe you ought to sit down and actually watch it sometime."

"Well, when I see them laughing and shit, I know that show isn't for me! If that was Nam, that entire fucking cast would have been dead, maimed, or insane by the end of the first season!"

I went over to the set and switched it to the Taiwan channel for the news.

"I don't want to watch this crap!" said Paul.

"You hate being Chinese that much, huh?"

"I'm Chinese and I live in Chinatown. I don't have to pretend to love everything that has someone Chinese on it."

I gave the show fifteen seconds. It was a feature on the cultivation of tung flowers.

"Okay, this is crap," I admitted. The Communist channel was just as bad, a blatant propaganda piece about the Taiwanese hero Koxinga, who had driven out the Dutch from Formosa. Only the show called him the *Chinese* hero Koxinga.

I shook my head. I used to flip between the two channels for hours, but I was less discriminating back then, because I was usually drunk.

"Let's just watch PBS," I said. "It's got to have something good for you."

A few seconds after I tuned it to channel 13, the *Nova* logo came up. "It's science, Paul. You like science."

The voice-over pondered loudly, "Why are sex drives strongest at certain times of day?"

"I'm not going to watch this show with you, Robert," said Paul.

"Maybe we should talk about, you know, human reproduction."

"Not in my worst nightmare do I want to talk with you about sex."

My phone rang.

"Thank you," Paul said to the ceiling.

I looked at the collapsible travel clock Paul used for his wake-up alarm—8:05.

"I'm coming," I said as I headed to the phone in the bedroom. When people have bad news, they're reluctant to call, so they set a time—usually on the hour or half hour. Those are times I never pick up the phone. But if the call is casual and spontaneous, it comes in at odd times. That's when I answer.

I picked up the phone and listened.

"Hello?" a man's voice asked.

"Yes?"

"Is Robert there?"

"Speaking."

"Robert, this is Don."

"Don! How are you doing?"

"I took my medicine. But I don't like the way it makes me feel."

"How do you feel now?"

"Like I'm on drugs!" Then Don laughed and I remembered the kid he used to be. "I'm sleepy, but my thoughts are more connected now!"

We decided to meet at an over-rice place off Bayard that was once one of the burger joints that the Darts gang hung out at.

"It's like all that history never existed," said Don. "The counter used to be there surrounded by all the stools. The jukebox was there. Even the floor and ceiling are different."

"I didn't come here much," I said. "Because, you know, I was in the Continentals."

"Didn't you have a good friend in the Darts, Robert?"

"Who?"

"His name was Moy."

"Ah, Moy. I don't know where he is now."

"His dad used to run the toy store."

"Yeah, I wonder where they went. We didn't stay in touch."

"Because he wasn't a Continental?"

"No, I have no idea where the former Continentals are now, either."

"You guys were just bullies, you know that? We were always a much smaller group, but you guys kept pushing the Darts around!"

"It was tough love. I'm sure you got some of that in Nam, too."

"Do you know what happened with that, Robert?" He smiled. "Did you know that I enlisted?"

"You weren't drafted?"

"No, I just signed up," said Don with a small, wistful laugh. "It was the first time I ever really defined myself. As Don Tin, an American. Not as Old Tin's son. My father just went fucking nuts. He had this whole college thing set up for me in Taiwan. I would still be there now, allegedly pursuing a Ph.D. from my penthouse condo."

"Don, you didn't have to prove anything."

"You don't know what it was like. He wouldn't let me be friends with Cantonese people, including you, Robert."

"I thought he had something personal against me."

"That might be true. Anyway, he kept telling me that we were really Shanghai Chinese, not these lowly, uneducated Cantonese who do manual labor. We were just living here in Chinatown temporarily, rebuilding our support base. After the KMT defeated the Communists our family was going to take back our mansion on the Bund."

"Yeah, that's gonna happen."

"He hates speaking Cantonese."

"He's not that good at it."

"My Cantonese is pretty good, though, right?"

"It should be. You were born here in America."

He smiled. It was a nice thing to see. "Thank you, Robert."

"Don, your dad pulled something in Nam, right?"

"What do you mean?"

"I mean, he had connections that got you discharged after you enlisted, right?"

"He didn't. What happened was that during basic training I started hearing voices talking about me. I would look around, but there wouldn't be anyone there. The weirdest thing was that the voices would be next to me in the cafeteria, but I would know they were coming from outside the building. I'd go outside to try to follow the voices, but they kept moving."

"What did these voices say?"

"They would make fun of me, saying I wasn't strong enough, my cock was too small, or I was just ugly. The voices would also say horrible things about people right next to me and it made me feel embarrassed.

"I went to see a doctor about it, but he thought I was just trying to get out of the war, you know? Jesus, I wanted to go so badly! It was the first thing I really wanted to do on my own. I wanted to fight for democracy in Vietnam and win my own independence, as well.

"Can you believe that they originally were going to make me a combat photographer because they didn't want me to have a gun? They said it would be for my own safety, otherwise I might be mistaken for a Vietnamese."

"Imagine that," I said.

"I managed to cover up my problem with the voices for a while. One day our infantry unit was being brought to the front in a helicopter. We got shot down. I was treated as if I had a concussion, but they finally figured out that I was schizophrenic because I had no physical head injury. And because of that, my father got me back.

"I didn't want to come back, Robert. I would have rather died in Nam than come back here and live under his thumb."

"He really cares about you, Don. He asked me to look in on you."

"He asked you last, Robert. After he'd exhausted the patience of all our family and friends."

"Don, you told me you thought there were men behind the walls in your apartment."

"Yeah, I know. It sounds crazy." He clasped his hands together. "In my mind, I know it's completely irrational. But the constant voices, they overpower everything—reason, memory, thought. In the end, it's these fucking voices that have managed to separate me from my dad, so it's not an entirely bad thing."

"Don, you don't take your medicine regularly, do you?"

"I take it kind of at random."

"Even if you hate it, you have to take your medicine or else you won't get better."

"But don't you know, Robert, these pills don't make the voices go away. They just make them a little softer. I can still hear them now."

Suddenly he stared at me in the eyes and his face took on a haunted look.

"Shut up," he said softly to the voices. Then to me he said, "Do you want to come with me to get more medicine? The store's closing soon."

"Let's go," I told him.

Outside Heavenly King Herbs a huge sign took up the entire space of the storefront window. Only one phrase at the top was in English: REIN- VIGORATION TABLETS, $20 FOR 10 DOSES. The rest of the sign was filled with increasingly outrageous claims in Chinese characters for what the tablets could do: "Cures headaches. Prevents blood-vessel inflammation. Stops sleepwalking. Regulates magnetic polarity. Heals arthritis. Burns fat. Fights cancer. Reverses aging process."

"Don," I said, "how long have you been taking these bullshit tablets?"

"About two years," he said. "But of course not regularly, so maybe I'm not giving them a fair chance."

"There's a fair chance that this medicine is bullshit," I said, pointing at the sign.

We went inside and Mr. Lee, the proprietor, greeted Don like royalty. "Mr. Tin, it is so delightful to see you!" he said. Mr. Lee was in his late fifties and dressed in a loose-fitting white linen shirt with cloth buttons. He had a white streak in his otherwise black hair that made it look like Pepé Le Pew's tail. All along the back wall were closed drawers of dried herbs filed away like library cards. An ancient balance scale sat on the front counter, next to a mortar and pestle.

Don nodded and kept his head down, his eyes on the scale, which was slightly tipped even though both pans were empty.

"Mr. Lee, how are you?" I asked.

He did a double take. "Are you Policeman Chow?" he asked.

"Yes, that's right."

"Oh my God, you look great!" said Mr. Lee. "Congratulations on being sober!"

"Thank you."

He looked closer at my face and smiled. "You have a girlfriend now, right?"

"How can you tell?"

"I can see that you shave regularly!" He laughed. "I can see the little scars from razor nicks!" Then he asked Don, "Fifty more doses?"

"Yes," said Don.

Mr. Lee dropped into a crouch and disappeared under the counter. I heard him open a drawer and rummage around.

"Mr. Lee?" I asked.

"Yes?" he said from the floor.

"What are these tablets really doing for Don?"

Mr. Lee stood up again and said, "Well, they're helping him to manage his disorder."

"So you admit they're not really effective! Those are some pretty wild claims you have in the window."

Mr. Lee put five small boxes on the counter. "Well, maybe those claims are fanciful, but they are part of an old poem, Robert. It's merely a decoration for the window. Besides, the tablets really are doing something. They're keeping him somewhat sedated so that he doesn't try to kill himself."

"So great. Now he's sleepwalking through life. How are you going to cure him, though?"

"I can't. He needs to go to a doctor."

"Meanwhile you're making all this money off Don's dad. You're as crooked as this crappy balance scale."

"I've told him again and again that his son needs anti-psychotic medicine prescribed by an American doctor. You know what he did? He sent Don to an acupuncturist. His joints are working fine now. By the way, the balance is strictly ornamental. I use an electronic scale that's less aesthetically pleasing."

"The anti-psychotic medicine, will it really help him?"

Mr. Lee leaned forward and put his elbows on the counter.

"It will help him manage, just like my tablets. I'm not exactly sure what Don has, seems like manic depression or schizophrenia. But you should know, Robert—there is no cure. Don will be on medication for the rest of his life."

"There's nothing you have that can bring him back?"

"Chinese medicines treat the body. Herbs can lick a sore throat, tennis elbow, or even nerve damage. But we've always had a stigma about mental and emotional diseases, to the point where we didn't bother to try to come up with natural cures."

"Historically, how were the mentally ill cured?"

"When they killed themselves or were killed."

He pushed the tablets to Don, who put a hand over them and nodded.

11

SOME STUPID GANG KID SHOT ANOTHER ONE INSIDE THE PAGODA Theater on Elizabeth Street. The theater typically had a live Chinese opera show onstage before the film. They started shooting right when two scholars were singing about what qualities made a virtuous man.

When the shots rang out, everybody either hit the floor or ran out into the street. By some miracle, only one gang kid had been shot, a bullet through the chest. They had such bad aim usually only bystanders were hit.

After the gang kids had run off and the ambulance had taken the victim away, everyone filed back into the theater and settled back into their seats. There had been a delay in getting the movie up and the audience was getting ready to riot or, worse, demand their money back. Giving out full refunds was a nightmare to Chinese businessmen, worse than having paying patrons shot on the premises.

When Vandyne had arrived on the scene, the movie had just started and the owner behind the box office window refused to stop it. If he did, he told Vandyne, the audience would kick in his door and drag him and the cash register out. He assured Vandyne that all the eyewitnesses were still inside and that it was best to talk to people after the show.

"So what'd you do?" I asked Vandyne. We were leaning against our desks in the squad room, eating Chinese beef jerky out of a plastic bag.

"He asked me if I wanted to sit down inside and I said, 'All right.' Then he wanted to charge me for going in! Of course I wouldn't pay, so then the guy pulled up a chair for me and I sat by the exit doors." Vandyne screwed his face up and said through his teeth, "I've been chewing this thing like five minutes. It's like a baseball mitt. And it tastes like chewing gum and red pepper flakes!"

"Part of the pleasure of the hot-fruit flavor is in the chewing," I said. "Would you rather have curry beef? There's also chicken jerky. Maybe that's more your speed?"

"No, man, I've been chewing on it so long, something's gotta give soon."

"So, back to the theater. The movie ends, everyone comes out and just avoids you."

"Well, I've learned that it's easier to talk to the younger Chinese because the older ones . . ."

"I'll say it. They're scared of black people."

"I see that sometimes. Anyway, nobody young or old would talk to me. So that was a bust. I went to the hospital to talk to the shooting victim and they told me to come back in a few days. So this morning, I went in and saw the young man." Vandyne suddenly smiled. "Okay, there it goes! This piece of meat is breaking up!"

"So what did the kid say?"

"Wouldn't tell me anything. In front of his mom and dad, he put on this act like he was at the movies with his friends while they were at work. Those friends of his that were sitting around that room, well, let me put it to you this way—we've got all of them in our mug books. So after the parents left I said, 'Don't you want to get those guys back?' Probably the wrong thing to say, but he just smiled and said, 'I'll take care of it.' I think we can count on at least one more shooting this sum-mer."

"Depends on when he's getting out."

"Bullet missed his lungs, went out through the side. He'll be out in less than a week."

"Why do these kids think they live in such a hopeless world?"

"It's capitalism," said Vandyne. "They're programmed by TV. They see these people flaunting their cash roll, jewelry, and cars."

"Those goddamned kids are going to study and work hard to get what they want."

"How hard did you study and work, partner?"

"Not that hard and I never got what I wanted. So let my example be a lesson to them."

"You talk like your life is over. You still have thirty, forty years to achieve something."

"Right now, man, the only things I'm focused on are snakeheads. They're basically slavers, you know that? They hold people in prisons they call safe houses while forcing them to work off their debt. Nobody would cry if a snakehead got his neck broke while 'resisting arrest.'"

"Chow," said Vandyne. "Let's get real. They should suffer through our justice system and have their names splashed all over the media."

"What if they got off?"

"Then we didn't have a good enough case against them. If we don't have a presumption of innocence and we just went out shooting people we thought were bad guys, then it's going to be like Nam. Just going into villages and wiping them all out." Then he walked over to a gar-bage can at English's empty desk and spat out the beef jerky.

Vandyne left to get to work on the hopeless task of trying to talk to potential witnesses around the Pagoda.

"How come I can't get a line out?" I asked English. I was trying to track down remaining members of the San Francisco association that my father had belonged to.

"Is this phone call work-related?" he asked.

We didn't look at each other as we continued to talk.

"Yeah."

"Is it long distance?"

"Yeah, but I'm not trying to call China. It's continental U.S. We can't call out of state anymore?"

"Well, we're having a little dispute with the phone company right now. This call can't wait until you get home?"

I shook my head. "I need to call California during business hours."

"Well, just unplug your phone and use the jack under Lumpy's desk. He had a pal at the phone company who set up the line back in the fifties for permanent free service."

"What did Lumpy have to do in exchange?"

"You don't want to know. Hell, I don't want to know. Could have been anything. Shit, it was the fifties. If Frank Serpico thought cops in the sixties were bad, they were Girl Scouts compared with the bulls in the fifties."

I brought my phone over to Lumpy's desk and found the jack on the floor. English and I continued to not look at each other.

"What kind of cop was Lumpy?" I asked.

"Jesus, I've heard stories. You know, a long time ago Lumpy was a real crack detective. He was a one-man army, busting up drug and prostitution rackets all over the Lower East Side. He had the right pocket in his pants tailored to be extra large. That way, he could stick a notepad in there and write down license-plate numbers and other details without taking his hand out of his pocket."

"Damn, that's amazing."

"But it all fell apart one day when he was about to collar a pretty notorious pimp. When he grabbed the guy and turned him around, he was looking right into his own father's face."

"Did he bring his father in?"

"No. The story goes that he let him off, destroyed all his notes about the case, and bounced around different precincts. Finally ended up festering here in the detective squad. Spent his last years slumped over his desk calling up Dial-a-Joke in cities across the country. He could have made the inspector rank, but instead he ended up being a lousy precinct detective."

"Being a precinct detective isn't lousy."

"It's the lowest form of a detective, Chow. Don't get caught up in the yuk-yuks of *Barney Miller*. When you get your gold shield, don't waste too much time. Get yourself on the Anti-Crime Unit or something else. Just get the fuck outta here."

"I promise," I said. I picked up the receiver and heard a dial tone. I spun the numbers slowly into the rotary dial.

An old man answered with a warbling, "Hello?"

"Hello, who am I speaking with?" I asked in Cantonese.

I heard a sudden inhale. "Oh, I never hear plain speech anymore! So many Fukienese in my neighborhood now!"

I'm sure the man was exaggerating, as change-averse older Chinese are prone to do. When Cantonese people overhear some Fukienese, the reaction is, "There goes the neighborhood!"

"Hello, Uncle. I'm the son of Ah Chow, also known as Ah Chin. Are you Mr. Lau?"

"Yes, yes, I am. Of course I knew your father. You sound like you're calling from far away. I can hear my voice echo like we're talking across a great divide!"

That was a profound observation. This man speaks like a poet, I thought. I only read poetry by accident, but, still, I liked his voice.

"My name is Robert Chow. I'm calling from New York City."

"Ah, Old Chow said he would send a son someday to visit me. I did hear he passed away a few years ago. I was so sorry to hear it. He was such a dear man and a hard worker. He did all he could for our association, even trying to set up the New York branch, but I guess it was destiny for everything to fall apart."

"Yes, yes," I said. It figured. The father I knew could barely keep himself together.

"You know by now that he came over as a paper son of someone in the association and that he had to pay that debt back. It took many years."

"Yes, yes," I said. If he hadn't paid up they would have hunted him down and knifed him like he needed breathing holes in his back.

"Your father said he had many bad memories. The things he saw and the things he had to do. Say, I've been keeping a box of your father's belongings from his early days in the country. It was too much for him to take across the country."

"Mr. Lau, what do you have?"

"Some papers, some books, and I think a diary."

"A diary?"

"I've never read it, out of respect. Your father kept telling me to get rid of everything, but he was just worried that it was too much trouble. It really wasn't, I assure you. I've kept everything locked in a briefcase, just waiting. I knew you'd show up someday!"

What in the world did my father write about? I thought about his picture, that young man looking back at me, ready for the rest of his life, ready to pick up all the gold nuggets that were rumored to be strewn around the streets in America. He couldn't have known that he'd be spending decades paying back the association for sneaking him into the country.

He didn't know that he was being set up for heartache, disappointment, and bitterness.

"How did you know my father, Mr. Lau?"

"You're not going to believe this, but we came over on the same boat. It was a long ride and we were friends for life. I didn't see him after he left for New York, but we wrote to each other at least once a month all the way to the end.

"When we got here the U.S. immigration officials had us locked up on Angel Island for a month or two, bringing us out for questioning a few times, to see if they could catch us in a lie. But we were both young, we had great memories, and we kept our stories straight. Boy, I tell you, they did not want us to come into this country!"

I glanced back at English, who was drinking coffee, staring at a wall.

"I know what you mean."

"Well, when are you coming?"

"I'm sorry, what do you mean 'coming'?"

"Don't you want to pick up your father's stuff?"

"I was actually hoping that you could mail it."

"I can't mail it. I think it's too heavy."

"Could you take it to a UPS office or something?"

"I don't know how to do such things," he said, laughing.

Chinese people laugh a lot, though rarely to express that they find something funny. Laughing is more like something to do when you're done with your sentence and want to expend the leftover air in your lungs in an inoffensive manner.

Lau went on. "I'm an old man. I don't know how to box and ship things. It's too complicated. Please forgive me."

I begged him to try. But when I had to tell him my address three times, I abandoned all hope. Lau had a great memory, but his brain was full. Nothing else could be added.

"I will try to do this, Robert. I will do my very best."

I felt the defeat already plainly in his voice. "Thank you very much, Uncle."

After I hung up, English came over and sat on the edge of Lumpy's desk.

"Who was that?"

"An old friend of my father's."

"What'd you talk about?"

"Well, hell, I'll tell you. My dad came over to this country illegally. I am the son of an illegal immigrant."

"I kind of already assumed you were."

"What do you mean, you assumed?"

"C'mon. Chinese guy your age? How the hell did your dad get over here before the Chinese Exclusion Acts were repealed?"

"He could've been the son of a railroad worker."

"There were almost no Chinese women then. They weren't allowed to immigrate. Plus all the anti-Chinese riots basically scared almost all the Chinese back to China, as bad as life was under the Manchus. Chinese didn't really build lasting communities here until all the associations and tongs took control and offered a measure of protection, along with various illegal activities."

"How the hell do you know all this history?"

"It's my business to know. This is the community I'm supposed to protect and serve, right?"

"Yeah, but how did you find out about all that?"

"I picked up a bunch of pamphlets from one of the Communist-backed art-group meetings here in Chinatown. You just have to read between the lines of all the propaganda to get to the truth."

"A little bit of knowledge is a dangerous thing," I said. "Now just picking up those Communist pamphlets shows you have a connection with radical groups like the FALN."

"Don't start that shit with me. I don't even know Spanish."

"But you look like you do and people judge you by your looks. Believe me, I know."

I plugged my phone back into the jack by my desk and it began to ring immediately.

"You should have left it unplugged," said English.

I picked up the phone. "Detective," I said.

"This Chow?"

"Yeah. This Eddie? Are you calling from a pay phone?"

"Yeah. I'm by the Kelly Restaurant on Pell. Do you know it?"

"Sure I do. What about it?"

"Can you get down here? There's too much for me to explain."

Pell was only a few blocks from the Five. I was there in less than five minutes.

The Kelly Restaurant was a smallish joint. It didn't have particularly outstanding food. The barbecued meats were all right, but they didn't do the little extras, like handing you a calendar with the New Year or handing you a clean napkin.

Eddie was pacing the floor. It was ahead of the dinner rush and the chef was sitting at a table in the back, smoking with a waiter. The owner, Mr. Wong, was standing in front of the cash register, his arms folded in front of him.

I came in and both Eddie and Mr. Wong ran over to me, yelling.

"Hey, come on!" I said. "I can't understand either of you!"

"Make him file a complaint, Chow!" yelled Eddie.

"What happened?"

"Nothing happened!" yelled Mr. Wong. "Officer Chow, who is this guy? What's wrong with him?"

I made Eddie sit down at a table in the corner with me and speak English.

"For Christ's sake, man, you gotta keep a lower profile," I said. "Make a fuss like this and someone's gonna make you!"

"Let me tell you what happened first! This group of eight kids came in here and ate like animals. When the check came, one guy just signed it with a gang name and they all left without paying. Mr. Wong was whining and complaining about it to the chef and waiter that they were coming more and more frequently to eat here. I told him to file a complaint with the police and he refused. So I called you to convince him to."

"Eddie, you're getting off-course by pursuing this. You have to let this go for now."

"What the fuck? 'Let this go'? If Mr. Wong does nothing, this is a slap in the face to the brave people who do file complaints against the gangs!"

"Right now, we don't have the manpower or the time to pursue an entrenched kind of criminal behavior. I'm focused on finding those snakeheads. You're after a guy for tax evasion. Stay on target."

"Like these criminals only focus in one area, Chow. You know they have a fucking hand in everything!"

"Let's just take on one hand at a time! Otherwise we're arm wrestling with an octopus!"

"When you take on one arm at a time the other ones are doing all kinds of shit behind your back! Bullshit like this only goes on because people are willing to take it! If all these store owners banded together and stopped paying protection money and stopped giving away meals, the octopus would die!"

"Eddie, I don't know enough about octopuses to keep going in this direction, but again, to get back to my original thing, you have to let Mr. Wong handle it his way. He can go to his association and make a complaint. Then someone from his association lodges that complaint with the association that has loose ties with the gang. Then they reach some sort of compromise. Chinese people just don't come out and make a direct and public statement. Even if it would help people. You know this, Eddie."

"That's great, Chow. Just have them all police themselves. That was exactly how your old man got fucked over in America. He'd be real proud of you now."

"Don't talk about my dad, Eddie. You don't know how the hell he felt about anything."

"Sorry about that, dude. I was just trying to get you personally invested."

"What did you call me?"

"Dude?"

"Are you making another dig at me?"

"Naw! It's just like saying 'man.'"

We got up.

"Mr. Wong," I said, tipping my cap.

"You take that man away, Officer Chow! He's nothing but a trouble-maker!"

When Eddie and I hit the street we went off in opposite directions, and quickly.

I hadn't heard of Cunningham Park before, but when I found out the minority officers' picnic was going to be held there, I knew I had to go. I had to make up for my shameful appearance at last year's picnic when I pulled a lot of the usual gags, including dancing on the table and the daring breakfast-in-reverse crawl. Worst of all was that I didn't remember any of it.

Lonnie and I took the F train out to Union Turnpike and then caught a bus to the park. I was amused that Lonnie carried subway and bus tokens on a twine loop strung through the "Y" cutouts in the centers of the tokens.

"That's very Chinese, carrying strings of coins."

"It keeps them separated from change in my purse."

"You know what? We should have hoarded them. I knew they weren't going to change the token!"

When the New York City Transit Authority was getting ready to raise the fare to fifty cents in 1975 from thirty-five cents, they lied and said a new token was being minted and warned the public not to bother stocking up on the soon-to-be-worthless tokens. The NYCTA even made a few fake redesigned tokens that were shown on the news.

But it was all bullshit and soon we were paying fifteen cents more for the same old tokens. It was the kind of scam that made people in Chinatown praise their ancestors for having the wisdom to create a community where everything one needed was within walking distance.

"This park is far!" said Lonnie. "It must be really nice!"

"I just hope it's worth the trip. There better be a serious barbecue." We were sitting near the back and I noticed people were looking over their shoulders at us. You never know how the Cantonese language will go over outside of Chinatown. At least we weren't speaking Fukienese.

The picnic went fine. Lonnie and I settled into a table with Vandyne and his wife, Rose. A young Indian guy named Gupta joined us. He hadn't been around at last year's picnic, because he was willing to sit at the same table with me.

"I'm a double disgrace to my family," Gupta said. "I eat meat and I'm a cop." He was making short work of a triple-decker cheeseburger that was dripping bubbly red grease onto his plate.

"Being a cop is an honorable and honest profession," said Vandyne. "It's got decent pay, benefits, and you can't beat the pension that lets you retire after twenty years."

"It sure as hell beats humping it through a jungle," I said.

"You guys were in Nam!" Gupta exclaimed. "What was it like?"

"It was good and bad," said Vandyne.

"It was all bad in the end," I said.

"Can I ask you guys something? What did it feel like to kill?"

Rose turned away from Gupta, but Lonnie put on a fake at-work smile.

"Let me say this," said Vandyne. "When you kill someone, you don't feel anything immediately. Right there it was a kill-or-be-killed situation. But that act is with you the rest of your life. You think, 'That guy I killed can never enjoy a picnic like this. He can't sit here with a beautiful woman. He can't stuff a cheeseburger into his mouth.' Now I can appreciate all of those things on one level because I'm alive, but on another level I am thoroughly disgusted with everything."

Vandyne got up, turned his back, and walked stiffly to the horrific park restroom.

Gupta stood up awkwardly.

"Why do people always ask the same fucking question!" I yelled at him. "Next time you're on the footpost, why don't you pop someone and find out what it feels like to kill!"

Gupta excused himself to Rose and Lonnie and scampered away. I suddenly realized that I had been standing with my finger pointed at Gupta's forehead. I sat down and tried to open a fun pack–sized 3 Musketeers bar. I was having a hard time because my fingers were greasy.

"Robert," said Rose. "I wanted to tell you something."

"Sure, Rose. What is it?"

"Well, do you know that we're in couples therapy?"

"I do."

"Damn it, he really does talk to you more than to me."

"He's my old partner. We would take a bullet for each other."

"John doesn't talk to me as much as he used to. Even in therapy it's like pulling teeth. Have you noticed it at all?"

"Honestly, he seems the same." I thought about that phone call I got from Vandyne when he was shut up in the pantry. Maybe that was a little weird.

"For July Fourth we went to see one of his old friends in Philadelphia."

"I knew about that, too."

"Of course. Well, anyway, some kids had set off some fireworks a little early and it caught John off-guard."

"What happened?"

"He ran into the bathroom and jumped into the tub and stayed down."

"That's probably the best place to be in the house when you're under fire."

"I'm trying to be serious, Robert! You're making a joke out of everything!"

"I'm serious, too, Rose! That was just a part of his training that kicked in. If he wasn't in that tub, in his mind, he would have had an arm or a leg blown off."

"But he's not in Nam anymore!"

"He is, Rose. We both still have one foot there."

"But you didn't have—" She caught herself. "You've managed to stop drinking, though."

"Rose, you know that I killed a little boy in Nam, right?"

"John told me that a few years ago."

"I've seen that little boy again."

"Not for a while now, though," added Lonnie.

"Yeah, but he could show up again," I said.

"How do you manage to keep going on, Robert?" asked Rose.

"I stay focused on reaching my near-term goals. Right now I'm trying to find snakeheads—people who smuggle over illegal Chinese and hold them under abusive conditions until they work off their debts.

"These snakeheads are the same type of people who made my father's life so miserable. They made him the lousy father that he was."

Lonnie and Rose nodded in agreement. Could they really say any differently? I wondered if Vandyne was going to be okay.

I finally got the puny 3 Musketeers out of the wrapper and pushed it into my mouth. I didn't even really like 3 Musketeers, but after all the effort I put into it I wasn't going to let anybody else have it.

THE NEXT DAY, LATE IN THE AFTERNOON, FOUND LONNIE AND ME standing off Bowery, two blocks away from meeting my mother for an early dinner.

"How do I look, Lonnie?" I asked.

She came over and pulled my collar one way. "You look fine," she said. Lonnie was looking me over, her face marked with concern, eyebrows coming dangerously close to the bridge of her nose.

"What's wrong?"

"It's just that, this shirt's a little old."

"Old?"

"It's not even red anymore."

"You can tell it's red. She's seen it before and anyway, it's not like I have time to go back and change. Anyway, I think you're too dressed up. This is not a formal thing."

Lonnie had on a white blouse with a knee-length black skirt.

"I'm so embarrassed," she said. "I don't have panty hose."

"My mother isn't going to be checking out your legs."

"Women always inspect each other. I'm just glad I had some makeup with me at your place."

My mother had decided to make a mad dash through Chinatown for groceries on the weekend and called my apartment from a pay phone, asking to meet up for a meal.

I was naked when I had answered the phone and I felt weird talking to my mother.

"Tell your friend to come out, too!" my mother had said.

"I'll see if she'll come," I had replied, looking at Lonnie, who was in bed, pulling the pillow over her head.

My mother was always at least ten minutes early to any appointment. I think she liked to catch the other party slightly off-guard and before they had a chance to settle in. Sun Tzu would have been proud.

She'd be strategically seated at the table, sipping tea when you came in. Because there was one bad chair, you'd have to sit on either side of her. She'd quietly judge you awkwardly pulling out a chair for your girl-friend and then stumbling over to your own chair.

"Mom," I said, "you remember Lonnie, right?"

"It's a pleasure, Mrs. Chow," Lonnie said.

"Lonnie, you're so young and beautiful!"

"Thank you."

"Is Robert nice to you?"

"Of course he is!"

"Does he get you presents?"

"Sometimes."

"It's okay that he's a policeman, right? He's not going to get you a new house and a new car, you know."

"Mom," I said. "Lonnie is a smart woman. She doesn't judge a man by how much money he makes."

"My son was never really that good in school," continued my mother.

"Part of that is my fault. I wasn't around enough to force him to study harder. If I had, then maybe he'd have a better job and get you better things to wear."

Lonnie's left hand shot to the bracelet on her right wrist. "Robert didn't give me this," she said. "It's something I've had for a long time. It's a present from an old friend who moved away."

"Oh," said my mother.

I knew exactly what she was thinking: Was that old friend a boy or a girl? And of course it mattered. If it was a boy, it may mean that he could come back someday and steal Lonnie away from me. If it was a girl, then maybe the bracelet meant that they had done drugs together.

"I need to wash my hands," Lonnie said.

When she was far away enough, my mother tapped my hand and said, "Was the bracelet from a boy or girl?"

"I don't know."

"What do you mean you don't know? You didn't even ask her? You're a policeman. You should be asking questions!"

"Shouldn't we get menus and order?"

"I've already ordered for us. So are you two going to get married?"

"It's too early to talk about this! Don't bring it up!"

"You don't know yet? You don't think she's the one? You have to make a decision someday, and the sooner the better!"

"It is way too early to talk about marriage. Let's just enjoy our meal together."

"Your father and me, our relatives basically agreed we would marry unless we strongly objected. We hadn't even met at that point. We just had pictures."

"We don't do it that way in America, Mom."

"Don't do what?" asked Lonnie, who was now back.

"We don't drink hot soup to stay cool," I said.

"Lonnie, you're going to really like the food here," said my mother.

"It's not common like a lot of Chinatown places. They have a good chef here and they don't use illegal immigrants."

"How do you know they don't?" I asked.

"I can tell. They're all professional here."

"This is a nice restaurant," Lonnie said.

"It isn't cash-only, too," my mother added. "See, they take Master Charge, BankAmericard, and American Express. This restaurant is well certified! Those financial companies wouldn't let just anybody represent them!"

The food was all right. I don't think I can appreciate fancy dishes the way my mother can. Simplicity may sometimes be a sin in Chinese culture, but chopped barbecued pork and vegetables and garlic never did a man wrong.

I made sure to keep all the teacups filled. I think Lonnie was a little nervous, because she was drinking a lot. She had to excuse herself again, throwing me back to the lions.

"How come she didn't wear panty hose?" my mother asked.

"I'm not sure. Let's check with her when she comes back to the table."

"Don't be stupid, Robert, okay? It's one thing if you can't help it, but I know you're doing it on purpose."

"Mom, are you really against going to restaurants that employ illegals?"

"Of course! You think I want to continue to patronize low-class places like that?"

"But those places gave Dad his first break."

"Robert, they exploited your father until he went off to the war and got citizenship. Boy, they changed their tune after that!"

"People who are illegal now, they have almost no way of getting citizenship."

"They shouldn't have come over, then."

"They're here now and they're suffering."

"Robert, how many times do I have to tell you? Don't try to help them. Help yourself. Get a promotion, get more money, get married, and move out of Chinatown. I can tell you one thing—nobody helped your father and me."

"I have a better idea, Mom. I'm going to stop the snakeheads." I dropped my voice and leaned into her. "I'm going to put them in jail or kill them."

"Robert!" my mother shout-whispered. "Don't say that!"

"I think Dad would have wanted to see them executed after all the suffering they caused him. He wouldn't want to see more people go through what he did. Dad was one of the luckier ones, but it's hard to see how much worse his life could have been."

"Life can always be worse, Robert! Jesus, did you know that he was going to name you 'Humphrey'? Your father loved Humphrey Bogart because he was the closest thing to a Chinese actor in the movies. Dark hair, too thin for his clothes. I insisted that you be named 'Robert' after Robert Mitchum. Now that was a man's name—a good name!"

I sat back in my chair and crossed my arms. I had only seen two of Mitchum's movies and both had knocked me horizontal on the couch.

"Your father," she said evenly, "would have wanted you to forget all about it and do the best for yourself. Maybe you should even think about going to college."

"I've got two dead bodies, Mom. You want me to forget about them and take a stroll around the quad? You want me to forget Dad's struggles, too?"

"No, don't forget him. But remember that he would have wanted you to keep moving forward."

"Ignoring history isn't very Chinese. I want to put these guys away for Dad."

"What are you talking about? All those criminals who did him wrong are long dead, Robert!"

"Their work still goes on, though. They're here in spirit and so is Dad. Or did he not show up that night for his food offering? That would be just like him to be out carousing instead of coming home, right?"

That wound her up a little bit.

"You don't know whom you're dealing with and you don't know what you're going to find!" she warned. "You think it's so easy to tell who's bad and who's good? Let the INS deal with the snakeheads! It's not a police matter! You're just going to end up causing trouble, Robert!"

"I can handle trouble, Mom. You and I both know Dad was no saint."

"You have a choice. You can be with this nice girl and have a bright future. Or you can slide back into the past and get trapped there, because the only thing you're going to find is that it's too late to save your father."

Lonnie came back from the restroom. They cleared our dishes and brought over a plate of cut-up oranges.

"You two eat," insisted my mother. "I'm going to cook later. I don't want to get the orange smell under my fingernails."

"What are you cooking?" asked Lonnie.

"Some special dishes. I had to come in to get fresh vegetables. I ran out of some sauces, too."

"Are you having friends over?" asked Lonnie.

"Just one friend," said my mother, smiling and looking down. "From work."

I jumped in and said, "A girl or a boy?"

The next day at the toy store I told the midget what my mother had said about going forward and forgetting the past.

"Chinese people live in the past," he said. "They live in their ancestral villages and eat the same food their great-great-grandparents ate. Hell, they even use the same pots and pans!"

"Right! It's in our culture."

"But that's also why we're in the state we're in. Any time there was a great invention, something that could level out society and spread the wealth, it was never broadly implemented. We invented paper, but more books have been lost than we have in print. We invented the compass, but we never explored the entire world. We invented gunpowder, but we couldn't defend ourselves against Europe, Russia, the U.S., and Japan."

"What happened to China?"

"I don't know."

"What do you mean, you don't know?"

"I should say, actually, that I don't know for sure because there were a whole bunch of things at work here. For one thing, there's the old Chinese smugness that everything foreign was inferior, so there was no sense to going out and having icebreaker events with barbarians. That stifled growth and the culture became more inbred and weaker.

"Another thing is that Chinese society is cellular. The national identity is much weaker than family and village bonds. The Cultural Revolution was supposed to break those regional bonds for the sake of a stronger and more unified country, but it only sowed chaos.

"Also, there is no such thing as advancement in Chinese society. If you're a peasant, you'll always be a peasant. You could go to Harvard and be a multimillionaire, but you'd be seen as a rich and educated peasant. Nobody was going to hand you the keys to the kingdom. Great minds and great ideas died in the rice paddies because of lack of recognition. That's why when Chinatown people make it, they move out to the suburbs instead of staying and helping to build community groups to help other families. The elitist pro-business umbrella groups—both KMT and Communist—wouldn't allow it."

"But you're here. You obviously don't need to be in Chinatown. Why aren't you selling toys in Gramercy?"

"There's no good Chinese food there."

"Good point."

"But anyway, this whole thing about being stuck in the past or moving on, I think your mother's right, Robert."

"About what?"

"I don't think you should go after the snakeheads, honestly."

"So I stand by and just let them make people suffer?"

"Honestly, most people in Chinatown have horrible jobs and tough lives. It's not really that much worse for the illegals. Also, if you go after them, you might not catch any of them and they'll only go further underground and become even more ruthless."

"I have to get them. I just have to catch one and make an example out of him."

"Let's say you do get one snakehead. It will be taken out of your hands, anyway. INS will take over the case and someone else who is better connected than you will get most of the credit."

"Then that's one I stopped, though."

The midget stretched his arms and then folded them across the counter. "If you really want to advance as a detective, hang out more with that guy at Manhattan South who likes you. Try to get transferred to something more prestigious than squad detective, like the Street Crime Unit. Think of how many collars you could get! After all, you're a member of the *New York* Police Department, not the *Chinatown* Police Department."

"If I do that," I said, "then who's going to stop the snakeheads?"

"Nobody. But if you don't go, you might get stuck in Chinatown the rest of your life."

"Like you."

The midget smiled. "Not quite like me. I'm popular."

13

I RAN INTO PEEPSHOW IN THE STAIRWELL OF THE FIVE. I GAVE HIM a quick nod and was preparing to head down to the toy store, but he put out a hand and touched my shoulder lightly.

"I'm so sorry, Chow!" he said.

"About what?"

"Well, you know I've been working some Chinese weddings when I'm out of the bag?" Chinese weddings always involved a lot of cash and jewelry gifts. They would often hire an off-duty cop to guard the door in case some punks got the idea of coming in and robbing everybody.

"Yeah, I know."

"I was at this wedding several days ago at Jade Palace. It was set apart from the rest of the dining room by one of those folding wall things. I had just gotten set with a whole plate of Chinese food and a Coke, but there were no forks. I had to go into the kitchen and get one from the kitchen staff."

"I don't understand why you're apologizing to me."

"Because when I came back out there was a guy sitting in my seat. Not just any guy, either. That guy Ng that you've been following!"

"Yeah."

"I went over to him and before I could say a word, he stood up and showed me a picture of you!"

"A picture of me!"

"Yeah, it was a Polaroid! A little blurry, but it was definitely you. Ng asked me if you were a cop!"

"And what did you say?"

"You have to understand, Chow. His English was so good! He caught me completely off-guard!"

"You told him!"

"Jeepers creepers! He asked me point-blank! I'm so sorry."

"It's okay, Geller. He already had my card."

"So it's all right, then, huh?" Peepshow looked at me with sad piglet eyes. My heart went out to him a little bit. How many times had this poor bastard gotten his ass kicked in school or at home? He had earned his nickname because his street clothes had a rip in the ass that no one ever told him about.

"Yeah, it's all right," I told Peepshow. "I wasn't undercover and I've already talked to his sister and then to him in person."

"Oh, man!" he said, breathing garlic into my face. "I am so relieved! It's a load off my shoulders."

"But Geller, I hope you've learned to shut the fuck up in the future. Unless you want me to hand you over to Internal Affairs for moonlighting at weddings that may include criminal elements."

"I will remember!" he said. "I will, I will, I will!"

Lonnie had gotten a top grade on a feature story she had written about the history of Chinese Americans and how their many contributions to this country had gone overlooked in the Bicentennial celebrations.

I had heard enough about the railroads, but the part about Chinese fighting on both sides of the Civil War was new to me. I wanted to show it to Vandyne, but I wasn't sure I'd want him to know about Chinese fighting on the side of slavery.

The professor liked it so much he said he'd check to see if the *Staten Island Register* might want to publish it.

To celebrate, I took Lonnie out for dinner, but before a full meal she wanted to stop earlier at the Taiwan place on Mott for some turnip cakes.

"Are you sure you really want to go there?" I asked. "The last time I ate there, the waiter was a total jerk to me!"

"Maybe he was having a bad day," said Lonnie. "You have to give people a second chance sometimes. People at the bakery aren't always in a good mood, but I have to think our buns and cakes make them happier. Anyway, it's your favorite place to get turnip cake!"

"If he's mean again I'll stick a turnip up his ass," I muttered.

Lonnie smirked as we went down to the below-street entrance.

Once inside, I was surprised to see that the place was busier than ever. It was only half full with about a dozen people, but that was about a dozen more than I expected ahead of the dinner rush.

We sat down and a new waiter quickly brought over a teapot. He was in his mid-thirties and had a worried look.

I said we were ready to order and he nodded. When I asked for two turnip cakes, he looked a little confused. I pointed it out on the menu and he held up two fingers.

"Yes, two," I said.

He said, "Thank you," and left.

"Jesus," I whispered to Lonnie. "That guy's Fukienese!"

"What's wrong with that?"

"He's probably an illegal alien!"

"That's a discriminatory remark, Robert!"

"I haven't seen him before."

"That doesn't mean anything!"

Our waiter came back with the cakes.

"Hey, how's it going, man?" I asked him in Cantonese as he set the plates down.

"Um," he said. He clearly had no idea what I was saying. He gestured to the owner, the heavyset Mr. Chen.

"Is there a problem here?" asked Mr. Chen, who needed to learn how to do a better comb-over. His horn-rimmed eyeglass frames made him look like a giant balding owl.

"No, no problem," I told the owl. "Say, what happened to your old waiter? The sourpuss?"

"Oh, that guy!" Mr. Chen stuck his chest out. "I gave that bastard the boot! Stuck-up Shanghainese guy. Always said he was going to finish school. Always said he was a scholar, not a waiter! He can go live on the sidewalk with his books now!"

"Where did you get the new guy from?"

"An employment agency got in touch with me. He's Fukienese."

"A-ha!"

"Huh?"

"You hired a Fukienese guy!"

"I hired two Fukienese guys! They work for much less. Also, the Fukienese dialect is almost the same as Taiwanese, so I feel like I have my kinfolk with me here. But I had to lower my menu prices by five percent to bring back those customers who were turned off by that Shanghai dickhead."

"Hey, watch it," I said. "We've got a lady present!"

"I've heard you say worse, Robert," said Lonnie.

"Not tonight, though. Mr. Chen, are these guys legal?"

"Of course they're legal! They came in through an employment agency."

"Which one?"

"I have a card." He fished in his pocket a little bit. "Here. Look."

It read: "Beautiful Hong Kong Ltd., 220 Worth Street, sixth floor."

* * *

"How is the Pagoda-shooting thing going?" I asked Vandyne. We were sitting in a New York Telephone van at Worth Street and Columbus Park, keeping an eye on Ng's office.

"About as far as Totie Fields got on her diet," said Vandyne.

"Aw, man, that's not funny! You know she lost a leg?"

"C'mon, Chow! She'd be the first one laughing. In my opinion, she's the best working white comedian right now."

"Well, anyway, about the shooting, Vandyne—Chinese people just don't want to get involved. You have to pretty much threaten them. If you're uncomfortable with that, let me know if you want me to lend a heavy hand."

"Yeah, I might be calling on you." He shook his head. "Someone gets shot in a crowded movie theater, couple hundred people pour out onto the street, watch the punks run away, and yet no witnesses."

"Did I tell you about that editorial in the Hong Kong–biased newspaper?"

Vandyne said, "No," but I knew he was just letting me tell the story again. We were close enough so that we allowed each other to tell and retell the same stories, sometimes with key details changing to make the teller look better and better.

"It said that these gang shootings only happen because the kids know that the police allow them to happen!"

"The silent majority allows crime to happen by refusing to press charges or testify," said Vandyne, shaking his head. "Say, partner, I think I will take you up on your offer. Could you talk to the kid in the hospital?"

"Is this punk still playing tough?"

"He's playing quiet. Won't tell me shit except that he's going to square everything out himself."

"I'll see if I can set him straight."

"Yeah, but don't beat him up! You understand?"

"I never get out of hand. Anymore."

"You've managed to save one gangster wannabe. Maybe you can save another."

"I'm still waiting for that one to pay off, but he's on the right track," I said. "So far."

After a little while, I said, "You know, I feel bad about something I did the other day."

"What?"

"That guy Eddie was trying to force a restaurant owner to file a complaint against some gang kids who ate a meal and left without paying. I told him to drop it."

"Why?"

"See, the guy wasn't going to do it anyway and Eddie was running the risk of blowing his cover because he was attracting so much attention."

"Then when does it start, Chow? When are people finally going to get fed up and file complaints, identify criminals in a lineup, and then testify in court?"

"I don't think it happens. Just the nature of Chinatown is that it's built on a cycle of exploitation. You just keep your head down and try to get through it. Once you're able to save enough money, you move the hell out. You're not thinking about improving the neighborhood if you don't have long-term plans to stay there. Then someone worse off moves in and takes your place."

"You mean new people like those illegal Fukienese immigrants."

"Exactly, partner. And the store and restaurant owners don't want to file complaints because they don't want bricks or bullets flying through their windows."

Vandyne rolled his neck until some bones cracked.

"This talk is depressing, man," he said, feeling the dashboard over. "This stupid car is outfitted with an eight-track player but no cigarette lighter?"

"I'll go get you some matches if it will keep you awake and alert," I said.

"And in a good mood."

I thought about what Rose had mentioned at the picnic.

"You got it, man," I said.

I slipped out of the van quietly, not even closing the door, and walked west along Worth Street, away from Beautiful Hong Kong. At the intersection with Centre Street I found a small twenty-four-hour grocery run by Italian Americans. I poured a cup of coffee at the self-help station and brought it up to the counter and asked for a book of matches.

The man looked back at me with the same cold calculation as a hunting lioness on *Wild Kingdom*. He was wearing a filthy apron and hadn't shaved in a week or longer.

"I'm supposeta give ya free matches with your coffee?" he asked.

"You want a nickel for them?" I asked.

"I hate chu people! Ya disgust me!"

I realized pretty quickly it wasn't a race thing. Instead I was meeting a big fan of New York Telephone. I was dimly aware of my right hand trying to wipe off the logo from my chest.

"Every time one of youse come in here, ya want the free napkins, free spoons, and free matches! When are ya gonna get rid of the buzzing in my shitty phone that ya charge me for every month?"

"You need to call our maintenance department and set up an appointment."

"I did! Three times! No-shows, all of them! I'm keeping track! I have a paper trail!"

I took out my wallet and threw a dollar bill on the counter.

"There," I said. "You can keep the change. Please, can I have a book of matches?"

"You take this, pal," he said, tossing a pack that had half the matches ripped out. "Don't worry about it being used. Those matches work, unlike my phone!"

Damn, switching our cover from one hated utility to another only made me realize that maybe it wasn't so bad being a cop. Or maybe people treated police better because we had guns.

I slipped back into the van and handed the matches over to Vandyne.

"What the hell is this?" he asked. "You find this in the street or something?"

"That's the best people will do for a guy from New York Telephone."

"I'm ready to strangle those guys, myself. Every other phone call gets crossed with another line. I've called the maintenance department to set up appointments, but the guys never show up! But I have to keep paying because I need a phone line! It's blackmail!"

"It's blackmail of a black male."

"You know, I would laugh if I weren't so pissed off at them." He lit up and inhaled deeply.

"Anything happen when I was gone?"

"Well, a delivery truck pulled up at the funeral home around the corner."

I looked at the truck that was backed up to the loading dock. "The only time you can deliver coffins is in the dead of night."

"Damn, that's a good one!" said Vandyne, finally cracking a smile.

Up above, probably at Beautiful Hong Kong's office, speakers blared out some lion dance songs.

"Man, what is that racket?" asked Vandyne.

"It's for the lion dances."

"They need to play that now?"

"Maybe they have a show tomorrow. Lion dances are used at all sorts of celebrations through the entire year."

"Why do they only use percussion instruments? That makes it particularly annoying to listen to."

"You have to make loud sounds to scare away the ghosts, and what could be louder than drums, cymbals, and gongs?"

"How about neighbors yelling at them to shut the fuck up?"

"That's no good. If you complain about the noise, these dancers will come out and kick your ass."

"Dancers. Real tough. Like the Jets and the Sharks."

"These guys *are* tough, though. Lion dancing is related to kung fu, you know."

I saw a light go on in one of the apartments above the funeral home.

"Vandyne, do you remember me telling you about this old friend of mine who cracked up in Vietnam?"

"Something like that. What about him?"

"I think that's his light that just went on."

"He lives above that funeral home?"

"Yeah, and he's fighting some ghosts of his own, too. He takes Chinese medicine because he's paranoid and hears voices. He thinks men are coming to take him away."

"What's his name?"

"Don."

"Up until this point you avoided saying his name because you were trying to disassociate yourself from him. You were trying to depersonalize your relationship with Don."

"Did you learn that from your couples therapy?"

"Oh yeah. I've also been learning just a little bit about a thing called delayed-stress syndrome."

"What's that?"

"It's when you are so traumatized you kind of ignore it, but then it sneaks up on you and you freak out and don't even realize it."

"Rose told me about you jumping in the tub in Philly."

"See, and when that happened, I thought it was completely normal for me to do that. And I was right back in Nam when those fireworks went off. There was no doubt in my mind that I hadn't come back to the World yet and that I was under fire.

"Maybe you didn't notice it, but in the last newsletter from the VA there was a small thing about delayed-stress syndrome. Did you happen to see it?"

"Everything from the VA I throw straight into the garbage."

"Are you insane, Chow?"

"Listen, man! Every time I used to open one of those letters, I'd read something that would send me into a drinking rage! I don't want to revisit any of that!"

I looked into the lighted window, waiting to see if Don would walk by.

"When was the last time you had a flashback, Chow?"

"About a month ago, I think. I jumped out of bed and crawled under it. I just slept there because I felt safer."

"What set you off?"

"I don't know. Maybe I heard something. Maybe I *thought* I heard something."

"At the VA hospital they have some rap sessions that may be of some use to you."

"What's a rap session?"

"You all get in a circle and just talk about what comes to mind."

"That sounds more like a Tupperware party! You mean you don't get to go anonymously and talk one-on-one with a therapist? The men there all see each other?"

"It's a safe space. Nobody's out to rat on the other person and you can say anything you need to."

I shifted in my seat. "You know, I already talk to you, Vandyne."

"Of course you do."

"What could I say to a bunch of guys I don't even know? They're all going to think I'm crazy."

"We all think we're a little crazy. In fact, most statements begin with, 'You're going to think I'm nuts, but . . .'"

"Vandyne?"

"Yeah?"

"Have you been going to these rap sessions?"

"I went to one."

"Are you going back?"

"I don't know."

"What does it cost out of pocket?" I asked.

"Actually, they pay you."

"They pay for this?"

"They pay you ten dollars for each complete session you do. If you get up and walk out early, you don't get your money."

"Is there somebody writing down everything you're saying?"

"No, but there are doctors observing you. They have a federal grant to study the syndrome. If they get enough subjects, they might be able to upgrade it into a full-fledged disorder."

"Why doesn't the government just give that grant money directly to the vets? They don't trust us, so they give the money to people to watch us like we're animals in a zoo?"

"Honestly, if they gave us the money, a lot of it would go straight up in a lot of vets' arms," he said. "Now these doctors are trained to help people like us."

"Did it really help you, though? I mean, honestly."

"Let me tell you something. Originally I had called the number and committed to attending a rap session. At the time it sounded far off enough, but it seemed that all of a sudden that day rolled around and I didn't want to go. But I'm glad I did. Just talking about it made me feel better. I told them all about how I shot up a tree and there was a little boy hiding inside who had been shooting up our camp."

"What did everybody else say?"

"They could relate because there were all kinds of booby traps around. A flap in the ground would open up and a gun would start shooting at you."

"If I start hearing stories like that again, Vandyne, I don't know how

I could stop myself from getting a drink," I said, and looked directly in his eyes. "I swear to God, I don't know how I could take it. I could drink a beer right fucking now." Or cry.

"There is a risk of, uh, open containers during the meetings," Vandyne said.

We stopped talking for a while.

After about fifteen minutes the lion dance music shut off. A few minutes later the light went out in Don's apartment.

"Should we wait until someone comes out of Beautiful Hong Kong?" I asked Vandyne.

"Yeah, let's just hang here a bit." He lit up another cigarette. "Damn, there are only two matches left."

"When you run out, it'll be your turn to make a run to the store. Tell him you're giving him a credit on his phone bill to make up for the poor service."

After about another ten minutes a group of people came out of the building. I recognized some of the kids from the unofficial and illegal mug books of Polaroids we kept at the Five. I knew some were peripheral gang members or former members. I didn't see any hard-core members, ones who would be packing a gun.

"Interesting mix of people," said Vandyne. "Some former rivals mixed in there."

"I think Paul knows some of those guys."

"They still come around for him?"

"Naw, living with me has made him kryptonite to the gangs. On the other hand, nobody wants to be friends with him anymore."

"Man, that's sad. But the righteous path is a lonely path. A lot of people like to drag you down with them." Vandyne had grown up locked alone in the apartment in Philadelphia, practicing the guitar. His mother would force him to learn a new 45 every week.

"I'd rather have Paul grow up lonely than grow up dead."

"Have you ever met Paul and Lonnie's parents?"

"I've seen their dad before, but I couldn't go up to him and introduce myself. That guy's useless. Lonnie's stepmother is Paul's birth mother."

"All right," said Vandyne.

Some girls came out onto the street, which was a little unusual because traditionally only men and boys were allowed to do the lion dances, including playing the musical instruments. I recognized one of the girls. It was Stephanie from Together Chinese Kinship.

It looked like the group might go hang out, but it split up with a few heading east to the Communist side of Chinatown and the rest heading up Mott Street, probably to a restaurant open late.

Ng's lion dance group was doing some amazing work in bringing different people in Chinatown together. He was doing a lot of good, especially for the young people. I couldn't imagine any association being that inclusive.

Brian the instructor came down last and alone, holding a duffel bag. He lit a cigarette and stretched his back. Brian switched his bag to his left arm, went down Worth, and turned north on Bowery.

Without a word, Vandyne started up our van and followed. We didn't have to go far. After a few blocks Brian hopped up the steps to Jade Palace and went in.

"What should we do?" I asked Vandyne.

"Wait until he comes out and see who he's with. Could take a while."

"Aren't we just wasting time? Couldn't we just walk up and take a peep?"

"Don't worry about wasting time," said Vandyne, maneuvering the van into the southbound lane of Bowery about ten yards away from Jade Palace's doors. He killed the engine and lit another cigarette.

We got some action right away. An old woman with a disturbingly wide nose knocked on Vandyne's open window.

"Yes?"

"Hey, you! You fix!" She pointed at the public phone we were parked next to. The phone booths in Chinatown all had metal pagoda-shaped cutouts on the top. Using them was like sticking your head into a small altar.

"No. Later fix," said Vandyne. "I promise." I used a hand to block my face so she couldn't see that I was Chinese.

"Hey, you! Soul brotha! You fix!"

"Aw, shit," said Vandyne. Under his breath he muttered, "You're not going to help me, are you, partner?"

"It would just prolong it. If I start speaking Chinese we'll never hear the end of it until the phone is fixed and sparkling clean."

"We have to do something. She's attracting way too much attention here."

"Ask her if she saw the shooting at the Pagoda. That'll get rid of her."

Suddenly she slapped the hood of the van hard. We both jumped. I would have hated to be one of her kids. She disappeared up the street behind us.

"You know what?" I said. "People really are meaner these days. Maybe Eddie's right about New York City being on the verge of collapse. We're going to eat each other up alive before 1980. I just want to get all the snakeheads before I go. Then I could die in peace."

"Chow," Vandyne said slowly, "you weren't thinking of taking the law into your own hands?"

"What do you mean?"

"You're talking about dying in peace. Sounds like you're ready to take a few snakeheads with you."

"I could do it, but I don't think I will."

"Well, don't do it! If you shoot them, you're playing right into the criminals' hands. You're going to make it easier for other criminals to continue to operate because of the backlash against the police. As defective and slow as it is, you have to allow the judicial system to work."

"What if we arrest these guys and they get off?"

"Then we try to catch them again."

"And then what if they get off another time?"

"That would never happen. Once these criminals get caught—even if they're not convicted—they are convicted in the public's mind. They pass on responsibilities to someone else."

"That's the same game the restaurants and garment factories play. If they get caught in labor violations, they close down and reopen 'under new management,' although it's the same group of owners. And they don't rehire the troublemakers who blew the whistle on them."

Just then Brian came out of the restaurant and lit up a cigarette. Eddie came out behind him and said something. They chuckled a little.

Suddenly there were two loud popping sounds—obviously small handguns—from the next block over, where some of the lion dance crew had gone.

We heard girls screaming and boys yelling.

I felt something crash into us from the back. It was the parked car behind us that Vandyne had just backed into.

14

VANDYNE LURCHED THE VAN OUT AND WE SPED DOWN BOWERY and went up the wrong way on Mott. We saw some kids running in different directions.

We stopped on the sidewalk. I jumped out and grabbed a running boy.

"What's going on?" I asked him.

"I don't know. We were just standing in the street. I heard a gun and I just started running." He was about fourteen and wasn't a known gang member. Just to be sure I frisked him.

"What are you doing?" he protested.

"I'm just making sure you aren't hit," I lied. "Where did the shots come from?"

"I'm not sure."

"Chow!" said Vandyne. He pointed up the street at a cook in an apron standing and smoking.

We walked up to him. The cook had come out of Jade Palace's back doors after hearing the shots. He had seen a black car speed away to the south, didn't get the plates.

We had just missed the car when we turned up Mott.

"Hey!" yelled Willie Gee, who suddenly popped out of a back door. "What are you doing, talking to these two cops!"

"I'm helping them," said the cook.

"I don't pay you to stand around and talk!" Then to us, and in English, Willie said, "Leave him alone! He doesn't know anything! He's a very simple man from the Chinese countryside!"

"What are you doing out here, Willie?" I asked.

"I saw that one of my kitchen staff was missing, so I went looking for him."

"You didn't hear gunshots?" asked Vandyne.

"Gunshots? No! I heard nothing! You guys heard a truck backfiring and it gave you one of those crazy Vietnam flashbacks!"

I pointed at the cook.

"I need to take your personal information," I said.

Willie stomped his foot.

"If you talk to this cop," he said, "you're going to be investigated as a suspect even if you're just a witness. You will put your job and your family at risk. One slipup and they're going to deport you!"

"That's not true!" I said.

"Are you going to pay him?" asked Willie. "What does he get out of it? Do you even guarantee him protection?"

The cook dropped his cigarette and twisted his foot on it. "Willie's right," he said to the ground. "I get nothing out of it and plus I bear all the risk."

"I saw how smart you were the day I hired you!" Willie said, beaming.

"Think about the fear people have to live in," I said. "Shootings every week now, and it's just going to get worse."

"I think I was just hearing things," said the cook.

Vandyne didn't understand what we were saying, but he knew what was happening.

"Willie," he said. "How would you like it if you were extorted or robbed on a regular basis and nobody helped you?"

"My association has its own preventative crime measures. You two only take action when there's already a victim and it's already too late."

"What sort of 'measures' do you take?" Vandyne asked.

"For one thing, we make sure to provide training and employment for our people. Most crime in the community stems from shiftlessness."

"Do you happen to provide employment to illegal Fukienese immigrants?" I asked.

Willie turned to the cook. "You see this?" he said. "They are already trying to frame me for a crime and I was just standing here talking."

The cook nodded and went inside.

"You're hindering an investigation," I warned Willie in English.

"Investigation into what? Nothing happened!"

"You made sure nothing happened!" Vandyne accused.

"You know what?" said Willie. "You two have no credibility in this community! An alcoholic and a black! What a team you guys make! Hunh!" With that he stormed back into the restaurant and locked the door.

"I can't believe he called you an alcoholic," I said to Vandyne. He made a tight smile and shook his head.

We met with Eddie a few hours later at a twenty-four-hour Greek diner on the Upper East Side by a firehouse.

"What was going on with Brian?" Vandyne asked him.

"Beautiful Hong Kong apparently is trying to put together a lion dance group of kids from all over Chinatown, regardless of political beliefs or past affiliations with gangs," said Eddie. "Ng wants to have his lion dancing in both the October 1 and the October 10 parades. It's rubbing a lot of associations the wrong way and they're not afraid to make it known."

"Where did those gunshots come from tonight?" I asked.

"Beats me," he said. "It could have been anybody shooting at anybody. Seriously. We do have a shoot-a-kid-per-week quota to make in Chinatown, don't we?"

"Don't fucking joke about kids getting shot!" I said.

"What, are we supposed to cry instead? I don't know about you guys, but the way I see it, most of those kids who get shot are hoods themselves. You only get pressured to solve the shootings where the tourists get wounded. Vandyne, you were looking into that kid who got shot at the Pagoda, right?"

"Don't act like it's over," Vandyne said.

"That was one gang kid shooting another, right?"

"Allegedly."

"And the shooting happened in a crowded theater and yet there were no witnesses, right?"

"Yeah."

"You know what I say? Screw it. Let that kid get out of the hospital and go kill the guy who shot him. Save the taxpayers some money."

"And let him get away with murder?" I asked.

"Naw. Someone from the other gang will shoot him and finish the job, this time."

"We would have half the town trying to kill the other half in no time," said Vandyne. "Then the whole country would all start shooting each other."

"Let's get it on!" said Eddie. "I'm ready!"

We all laughed. I didn't know about Eddie, but Vandyne and I really were ready for a full-scale war at any second. Neither of us could eat a meal without our guns at our sides, even at home.

"But anyway, about Brian . . . ," I started.

"Yeah, so, Ng has Brian training these kids in lion dancing. It's associated with martial arts because traditionally a kung fu master can't charge his students for lessons. The lion dances for hired entertainment were a way to make money."

"I thought the lion dances were basically extortion schemes from the associations," I said.

"Well, they're that, too," Eddie said.

"Why should Beautiful Hong Kong have lion dancers?" Vandyne asked. "They're not a kung fu club."

"Ng, that wonderful humanitarian, wanted to bring all Chinese people together, and the lion dancing is something that he thought combined the culture with physical activity, which is important. Kids are like dogs. They have excess energy and go fucking crazy if they don't have a chance to burn it off. But here's the thing: I'm thinking Brian has different ideas."

"Such as what?" I asked.

"For one thing, he's old-world. Brian was one of the premiere lion dancers in Hong Kong. Back in his day, they tied knife blades to their shoes so they could cut up the costumes of their rivals. He was teaching for a long time and had his own dancing group for a while, but after a business disagreement with his landlord he's here."

"Let me guess. He doesn't see eye-to-eye with Ng about letting in just anybody, right?" I asked. "He wants it segregated with just Hong Kong kids, right?"

"Naw, I think he actually wants everyone willing to come in and do the work that is necessary to get it done."

"Then where do you come in?" Vandyne asked.

"Me?" asked Eddie with a wide smile. "Oh, I'm the guy who's supposed to get the kids guns so they can be an organized gang under Brian!"

"Does Ng know anything about this?" I asked.

"I'm pretty sure he doesn't. Brian has a warped sense of reality. He thinks that with Ng tied up with business all day, the kids could be his personal muscle."

"Maybe we should take that fucker down," I said.

"Aw, just leave him alone!" said Eddie. "He's a talker, not a walker. He'll never do anything. Even if I got him a gun, he'd be too chicken-shit to point it at anybody. Leave him alone. I got bigger fish to fry."

"You're watching Brian all the time, right?" asked Vandyne.

"Yeah, I am. Believe me, if he actually has the balls to make a play for anything, it's going to be for Ng's sister, Winnie."

"You know, we picked up both Brian and Winnie one night," Vandyne said.

"Yeah, Brian told me. He said that once he had his gang going, you two were going to show him respect."

We all laughed at how stupid an idea that was.

"What kind of things was his dream gang going to get into?" I asked.

"Oh, the usual boring kind of stuff, competing with other gangs for work from the associations. Lookouts for the pross houses. Guarding the gambling dens and escorting the winners home—without robbing them."

Eddie added that last part because one of Chinatown's gangs had become known for mugging the people they were supposed to protect. The association who had hired them got a rival gang to take over their turf.

"What are you going to do?" I asked Eddie.

"Delay for a while, I guess. Seriously, when those gunshots rang out tonight, Brian was running like it was a fifty-yard dash. When we bust Beautiful Hong Kong, that coward's going to be swimming across the Hudson to Jersey before we have the door kicked in. I'm actually pretty close to wrapping up the tax-evasion case on Ng."

"How's that going?" asked Vandyne.

"It's sloppy, but I think we can get a case together that will stick. I was lousy at economics back in school, but that's actually working out to my advantage. Ng was getting so fed up with trying to teach me different accounting methods that he introduced me to his finance guy. He showed me the ropes on how to cook the books. I can't wait to put this guy away and get this thing over with."

"What are you going to do when you're done?" asked Vandyne. "You're not going to stay out here, are you?"

"No way, man. The humidity sucks and I don't want to see what winter's like. I'm going to the beach and inspect some bikini lines!"

"How hard is it to transition from a crime empire to a legitimate enterprise?" I asked the midget. "Won't a part of it always be dirty?"

We were sitting in the toy store. I was helping to sweep up because Paul was working late at the consulting firm.

"All businesses to some degree operate in a gray area," the midget said, not looking up. He was flipping through the day's receipts and marking off entries in a book. "Part of being a capitalist society is that you have to give freer rein to the businesses because they will create jobs for the people and pay taxes to the government. The more money the companies make, the more jobs they can create and the workers pay more taxes. So you have to cut them some slack. You give them tax breaks on building new headquarters and facilities in your state and you let them come clean about dirty money without penalty."

"Then it's like an amnesty program. If you said, 'Hey, I was going to launder all this money I made from drug deals, but I want to pay taxes on it instead,' then the government would be fine with that?"

"Sure they would! If Al Capone had simply paid taxes on all that bootlegging, he never would have been convicted of any crimes."

"So when I was fighting Communism, I was basically protecting a system that favors big business over the little guy."

The midget looked down at himself and then at me. "Who says the little guy can't open his own business?" he asked.

Paul came in, drinking the last from a can of Coke.

"Working sucks," he said.

"You know what sucks more than working?" I asked. "Not working."

"So then you're not going to retire after twenty years and start drawing your pension because it would suck to not work, right?" Paul asked me.

"If I'm not dead after twenty years, it will be a sign from God that I should retire. I never argue with God."

"You never go to church with Lonnie!"

"I have a strong personal relationship with God, but it's on an informal basis," I said.

"Well, speaking of personal relationships," said Paul with a wink, "I talked a little bit with Barbara today."

I smiled. "How is she doing?" I asked.

"She's busy—very busy. Anyway, I told her about Lonnie's article about the history of the Chinese in America and she got very interested in it. She has a friend who works at a newswire service and she thinks maybe Lonnie can get a job there."

"That would be great!" I said. I had a vision of Lonnie bagging up coffee and taro buns for sweaty Cantonese jerks during the morning rush. She was getting a college degree—something I hadn't done yet. Lonnie deserved a better job.

"Barbara wants to meet Lonnie first before getting in touch with her friend. She was talking about dinner with the two of you."

"Is she seeing anybody?" I asked.

"She's too busy to date, she says."

It was going to be an awkward meal, but I was willing to do it if it meant a potential job for Lonnie in this crappy economy. She had been sending her résumé around trying to get her foot in the doors of some newsrooms, but papers and magazines were laying people off.

The three Chinese-language newspapers were doing well but only because they were subsidized by the KMT, Communists, and the Hong Kong government.

Lonnie said it was all just propaganda and that she would rather keep the bakery job than work at any of them because it was honest work.

In reality, she made her job honest work. When I saw her drop a pastry on the floor one day she amazed me by throwing it away instead of restocking it. If her boss had seen her, it would have been a firing offense.

15

BARBARA HAD INSISTED ON TREATING US TO A DINNER AT A
swanky midtown Sichuan restaurant. The consulting group had an account there and she could finagle it as a business expense, she had said.

Lonnie dressed in a formal blouse and skirt. I had put on my best
collared shirt, the one I took out of the cleaners' paper wrap only for my
birthday. It made me look as clean-cut as I can get, and I was glad I wore it.

Barbara was already seated but stood up when she saw us. She was
wearing a slinky black dress that had a dangerously low neckline and
seemed form-fitting. It was too sexy to wear for a work function or for
any other event that didn't end in a bedroom.

I had to stop thinking like this immediately.

I squeezed Lonnie's hand.

Barbara waved.

We sat down and I introduced Barbara to Lonnie.

"Your brother is so smart. He is an absolute genius," Barbara gushed.
"He's the fastest in the office on the calculator. Does intelligence run in
the family?"

"He is much brighter than me," said Lonnie. "He always has been."

I noticed how Barbara's makeup reshaped her face from the last time I had seen her. I don't think she even had lipstick on when we were with Don in the park. Her cheekbones seemed to stretch her skin out to the point that it exposed light blue veins underneath, contrasting with her chocolate-chip brown eyes.

"Robert, have you lost weight?" Barbara asked.

"It's mostly the way this shirt is cut," I said. "But I've also lost some pounds since I've stopped drinking."

"Is this a permanent sort of change?" she asked, glancing at Lonnie.

"Barbara, I'm an alcoholic."

"I guess we're not going to be having cocktails, then. Damn, and I kind of needed one today!"

"You never really need a drink."

"The food is the main thing, anyway," Lonnie said.

Barbara had already ordered before we arrived, to save time.

I was pretty partial to this chicken-and-chili-pepper dish until some sauce slid against the back of my throat and it felt like someone had stuck a lit Zippo in my right nostril. I tried to play it cool and swished water around, but that just made the heat spread over the entire roof of my mouth.

There wasn't any rice to shove in my mouth and absorb the hot oil with. The fancy Chinese places served meat only with some vegetables to show how upscale they were. Eating rice was for the lower classes to make themselves feel full.

I continued to simmer lightly in my private, single-seating hell as I let Lonnie and Barbara have a conversation.

"How is your Mandarin, Lonnie?"

"It's okay. I'm able to understand it pretty well, but when I speak, the tones are a little hard."

"You have to be fluent for this job, which is really a paid contract position. There aren't health benefits or paid vacation time, but you're not getting that now, are you?"

"I get some holidays and American holidays off, now that I've been there almost two years," said Lonnie.

"Let me tell you more about the job. You're going to be assisting an old friend of mine at the United Nations. Have you heard of Presswire?"

"No, I haven't."

"It's a wire service that competes with Associated Press and UPI. They're small but feisty. Basically, you'll be checking the daily schedule of media events and attending some of the events. You have to be careful, though. You might read about, say, a panel on improving health care in Southeast Asia. Sounds interesting, right? But when you show up, you find a bunch of people blowing hot air. You're going to find out pretty quickly that what sounds good on paper usually doesn't live up to the description in real life. Oh, could I see a copy of your résumé?"

"Yes, I have it right here." Lonnie opened up a binder and pulled her résumé from a plastic flap inside the cover.

Barbara scanned it quickly. "So you're going to be done with your associate's degree at the end of the summer?"

"Yes. I've worked really hard at it."

"Do you know what you're going to do after that? Before Presswire can hire you for a full-time position, you need to have a bachelor's degree."

"I've already been accepted as a transfer to NYU. I'm going to start in the spring semester."

"NYU! Now that's a good school!"

"Of course, it's not as good as Harvard!"

"Well, I think it's just fine. You know, eventually you'll be replacing my friend at Presswire. He's going to be burnt out in a few years. He's the same age as Robert and I—we're all much older than you! You're just a baby!"

"I'm not that much younger."

"Your skin is so light and smooth! I wish I could have it!"

"You have many wonderful features, Barbara. I'm the jealous one!"

"I thought of something else, Lonnie. Once in a while you'll have to do radio broadcast spots. How well can you speak English?"

"I can speak English fine," Lonnie said in English.

"I hear a little bit of an accent," said Barbara. "It might be charming, though."

The waiter had been ignoring my distress signals, which were now just short of jumping on the table and tap-dancing.

"Barbara," I broke in, "what are the chances of getting a bowl of rice? I have a hot spot that's just not going away."

"Robert, why didn't you say something?" she asked. Barbara turned her head and the waiter was immediately by her side. "One bowl of rice, please. Lonnie, you want one?"

"No, thank you," Lonnie said.

After I had the fire out I ate a little bit more but found most of my appetite gone. I excused myself to go wash the dried sweat from my face. I went down the red-carpeted stairs. Before I reached the restroom a private banquet room door opened and Ng stepped out. We looked at each other as he eased the door closed behind him, cutting off a wave of laughter.

"Andy, what are you doing here, so far from Chinatown?" I asked.

"I might ask you the same thing, Robert."

"I'm just here eating. Do you own this place?"

"No," he said, smiling. "This is neutral territory. We're simply ironing out a bad misunderstanding between groups."

"Does this have anything to do with a shooting after your lion dance group met?"

He laughed. "What shooting? There was nothing! What I'm doing tonight is just bringing together new friends."

"I understand you've been running an employment agency from Beautiful Hong Kong's office."

"Not seriously. It's all rather informal. When I know of people looking for work, I try to find them jobs. For each man employed that means one less person to cause trouble."

"You're getting jobs for Fukienese."

"What's wrong with that? All Chinese have to help each other!"

"Are they illegal, Andy?"

"They have the right paperwork, Robert, and anyway it's none of your business. Your problem is that you're too American for your own good. You're steeped in that fine tradition of xenophobia."

"Does 'xenophobia' mean 'fear of foreigners'?"

"Yes."

"Well then, I'm not, Brother Five!"

"What did you call me?" asked Ng with a frown that had a hint of amusement.

"Brother Five. That's what they call you, right? One of the surname characters for 'Ng' means 'five.'"

"That's true," said Ng, nodding. "It's also true that that is my family name. But nobody ever calls me that."

"Are you sure?"

"Hey, Robert, I don't have anything personal against you. I know you're just trying to do your job. But your judgment is clouded and the Chinese people aren't foremost in your mind. I am sure, though, that someday we will both be able to celebrate our brotherhood."

"If I find that you're involved with anything illegal, we're going to be celebrating ten years in jail for you. While you're in the process of cleaning up Beautiful Hong Kong, Andy, I really hope it isn't making you dirty."

We walked away from each other, Andy to the pay phone and me to the restroom.

While I was washing my face someone came out of the bathroom stall and stood at the sink next to me. When I was done wiping my face I saw that the guy next to me was a gang member. To anybody else he looked like a young college student.

"Didn't I take your Polaroid in the park?" I asked him.

He jumped about two feet in the air.

"Jesus, what are you doing here?" he asked.

"Never mind why I'm here. Are you in the group that's meeting in the private banquet room down here?"

"Yeah, I was invited to the dinner. Do I need a passport to leave Chinatown, or something?"

"No, you don't. But I still want to know what you're doing here."

"It's an off-site meeting for the young people of Chinatown that Andy Ng put together. He wanted to show us the story of Chinese people in the global historical context."

"What did he show you?" I was surprised to see genuine interest light up in the kid's face.

"He had a slide show of the highlights of the Tang and Ming dynasties. He showed the sea routes that Chinese took almost a decade before Columbus. We went everywhere! All the way to Africa and probably even to the west coast of the United States!"

"What kind of talk is that?" I asked.

"They found stone anchors off the coast of San Francisco that were exactly the kind the Chinese used during the Ming."

I left the restroom, walked down the hall, and threw open the private banquet room door.

I had expected to find a room full of Chinese guys, cigarettes dangling from their lips, hunched over cards.

Instead it looked like I had walked into a classroom. Everyone had a book open and was following along with Ng, who was standing by a chalkboard that featured a time-line comparison between Europe and China. Incredibly, rival gang members were sitting side by side, mixed in with each other.

Most of these boys had dropped out of school—some even before high school—and despite having attention spans shorter than the time it took to chew a Tootsie Roll, here they were quietly learning. They may have still been animals, but now they were fit for a petting zoo.

"Sorry," I said. "I thought this was the lost and found!"

"Officer Robert Chow!" said Ng, who stepped off to the side. "You are no stranger to the fellows in this room!" The guy I ran into in the restroom shuffled in past me and took his seat. "I hope I'm not judging you unfairly, but you are a perfect example of a Chinese who may have lost touch with his roots."

"I know who I am!" I retorted.

"You're all right with me, Robert." Ng walked over to me and put an arm on my shoulder. "This man is my brother," he told the boys. "Whenever you see him in the street, give him the proper respect that an elder deserves. Anybody who even speaks badly about Officer Chow will have to answer to me! Okay?"

The kids nodded. I was caught off-guard. So much so that before I left I shook Ng's hand and waved good-bye to the class.

I came back to the table and found Barbara and Lonnie tussling over the check.

"Robert, are you all right?" asked Barbara. "You were gone quite a while!"

"I ran into someone I knew."

"You look a little shaken," said Lonnie.

I took the opportunity to grab the check. "Barbara, I've got this," I said.

"Don't be silly!" she said. "My firm does so much business here they'll probably just waive the check!"

"We don't need any more favors from you, Barbara. But you have to get Lonnie this job."

"It's signed, sealed, and delivered," she said. "I have a lot of ins with Presswire."

"Isn't this great, Lonnie?" I asked.

She smiled a little too wide. "It is wonderful. Thank you so much for your help, Barbara."

When we got to my apartment, Lonnie let me have it.

"I can't believe that woman!" she said. "She still obviously has feelings for you, and she's willing to dress up like a high-class call girl to get you to look at her!"

I was sitting on the couch, but Lonnie remained standing.

"She's an old friend, Lonnie. We grew up together."

"You were more than just friends!"

"We had to see her to get you this job. Otherwise, I would never hang out with her anymore."

"While you were gone she had the nerve to say that since she had gotten Paul a job and now me, she should get new jobs for my parents!"

"I'm sure she was just kidding."

"The way she talked about Chinatown made it sound like a backward third-world country!"

"See, Lonnie, the Chinatown Barbara and I grew up in was so different from the way it is now. All the kids spoke English and we had a malt shop to hang out in. It all changed like a decade ago. All these Hong Kong kids came in and took over and Chinatown became a foreign country to us, you know, because we're Americans."

"Did you ever wish you had a real American girlfriend like Barbara?" Lonnie asked, finally dropping next to me on the couch.

"You are an American, Lonnie."

"I mean born here."

"It doesn't matter to me. Look at us. All the other Americans think we come from Hong Kong, anyway."

"But I am from Hong Kong!"

"And you're the best thing from Hong Kong, ever!"

"Robert, how did things change when those kids came over?"

"Oh, man. They were friendly at first with the American-borns, but then they learned to resent us for not being Chinese enough. Guys like me had to deal with racist jerks in high school and then Hong Kong jerks at home. Back then high school was only about thirty percent Chinese—not like now where we're the majority."

"So the American-borns fought with the Hong Kong Chinese?"

"There wasn't any organized fighting and the gangs back then had a mix of the two kinds of Chinese. It was a lot of stupid boy stuff, hitting each other with rolls of steel washers and doorknobs."

"How do you hit someone with a doorknob?"

"You put a bunch of them in a sack and swing it around."

She shook her head. "I can't believe you became a cop."

"I can't believe I'm still alive."

"That's only because you guys didn't have guns. You weren't shooting each other."

"Speaking of our troubled youth, Lonnie, whatever happened to those kids who used to hang out with Paul at your bakery?"

"I'm not sure. You know Paul was their leader. After you put him to work, they didn't hang out there anymore."

"I think I saw some of them tonight."

"At the restaurant?"

"Yeah, I saw a whole bunch of delinquents in a private room eating together. I thought I saw some of Paul's old friends."

"Sometimes when gangs have disputes, they go outside of Chinatown to work things out peacefully."

"This was different, though. They were listening to a lecture about Chinese history."

"That doesn't sound right, Robert."

"I know."

She shucked off her high-heeled shoes.

"Robert, could you please run the hot water in the tub? I'm going to soak my feet in there."

I kissed her forehead and got up.

"Why do women wear shoes that hurt?" I asked.

"Because men like the way we walk in them."

I walked to the bathroom, wiggling my ass to make her laugh. I kneeled down by the tub and plugged the drain. I turned on the hot water, admiring how clean Paul had kept the tiles.

I thought about how close he had come to becoming the next China-town casualty and now the kid was a responsible young man, much more than I was when I was his age.

Did those gang kids who were in the banquet room have the same potential? Maybe all they needed was a sense of responsibility and some-one tough who cared about them. The parents were working twelve-hour shifts in sweatshops and restaurants and were pretty short on patience and sleep when they crawled home. The illegals coming in and working longer for less money made everything even worse for everybody.

I wondered what was happening on the other side of the world, in Fujian. How long did it take human snakes to scrape together the de-posit for the snakehead to smuggle them to America? How long did it take for them to realize they were paying to dig their own graves?

As I leaned on the side of the tub, I realized that it was shaped like an open casket and I felt uneasy. I stood up quickly and looked down at the rippling reflection of my face resting at the head of the coffin.

16

"CHOW, HOW ARE YOU FEELING?"

Vandyne sounded so genuinely worried I looked into his eyes carefully. He really was shaken. I thought I saw flecks of green in his brown pupils. Maybe I wasn't really awake yet.

It was about six in the morning. We were sitting at a large round table in a Taiwanese restaurant in the alley that ran mid-block between Elizabeth and Bowery. The table sat up to eight, but we were alone.

"I'm doing good, man," I said. "Is everything all right with you?"

He shook his head and reached for the sugar for his fried-dough stick. I got mine with the oily baked bread sheath the Taiwanese like to shove the stick into, making a bread-bread sandwich. With a bowl of warm soy milk sweetened with some sugar, it was a great way to greet the dawn.

I had a big bite of the doubled dough in my mouth when Vandyne leaned in and whispered, "I had a dream that you died, Chow."

It made it that much harder for me to swallow and gasp, "Jesus fucking Christ, don't tell me something like that, man! Don't you know how superstitious Chinese people are?" I spooned warm soy milk quickly into my mouth to clear off the oil film on my tongue.

"I'm sorry. Let's just forget it."

"The horse is already out of the barn. Tell me what happened in your dream."

"You sure you want to know?"

"Yeah. You've already cursed me. Might as well tell me everything."

"You were walking along a column of soldiers. I couldn't see their faces. Then some guy broke out and ran at you. He stabbed you in the chest with a knife."

"What did he look like?"

"He had black hair."

"I'll be on the lookout for him."

"They were all Asian, Chow. I think it was Nam."

"Are you absolutely sure that it wasn't a flashback you were having? Maybe you were remembering something you had suppressed down there."

Vandyne shook his head. "It was a premonition," he said, dragging one end of the stick through a small sandbar of sugar on his plate. "You can heed it or not."

"Even if I wanted to heed it, what would I do? Avoid groups of Asians? Stay in bed all day? I don't think Paul's going to change my bedpan."

"Just keep it in mind," said Vandyne, looking out a window to the alley. "Last time I had one of these was when I met Rose. I saw us walking down an aisle."

"And the next thing you know, you're walking through aisles in Macy's."

"No, that was after the wedding, when we went shopping for bedsheets."

"That must've been fun."

"I had another premonition in my life that also came true. I saw my guitar string break when I played the first note to the solo in 'Brown-Eyed Handsome Man.' I wasn't surprised at all when it happened, either, because I knew it was a premonition when I saw it, and the string snapping off felt exactly the same."

"Didn't you just make the string break? You *knew* it was going to happen, so you subconsciously plucked the string too hard."

"It was destined to happen. I wouldn't have done it on purpose or by accident."

"How do you know?"

"I was too good a guitar player to simply snap a string."

"I've got some great eight-sided Taoist mirrors to sell to you. They'll deflect all the bad luck heading your way to somebody else."

"I already have one," Vandyne grumbled.

"I'll take it as a warning. I'll watch out, I promise." I dipped a stick into my bowl of soy milk and swished it around. I watched a slick of grease vibrate on the surface and poured more sugar on top of it.

"That is kind of like dipping a donut into coffee, Chinese-style," said Vandyne, who had passed on getting a bowl of soy milk.

"Why did you get a cup of decaf?" I asked.

"I've been getting irritable. Rose says it's the caffeine. I think it's the therapy."

"I think you're getting cranky in your old age."

"I'm married. I have a right to be cranky."

"I'm in a relationship and I'm still smiling."

"Marriage is a whole new level. You have to do a lot of unpleasant but politically good things."

"I wouldn't mind doing anything for Lonnie."

"Then go over and have dinner and see a Broadway show with her parents." I frowned and he laughed. "Don't get all cranky now, Chow! You love the girl, you gotta love her family."

"I already live with her brother. That's as much of her family as I'll take for now."

I looked at the empty chairs around us.

"Where do you think she'll want to sit?" I asked.

"I think she'll want to sit right next to you. You are her type, after all."

"I don't want to get involved with someone old enough to be giving me grades and checking my grammar."

"You can learn a lot from older women, partner. They're very worldly and usually pretty well-off. Young buck like you could probably get a lot of nice presents from Irene. New suit, shoes, silk underwear—"

"Let's stop there! Sounds like you've thought about trying to find a setup like that."

"I think it was a movie I saw a while ago."

"How did it end?"

"If I remember correctly, the husband walked in and shot both of them."

Irene came in wearing a Chinese shirt with cloth buttons and dark slacks. Eyes turned to her angular white face that sailed over to our table like a comet in time-lapse photography.

"Irene," I said, interrupting her bow with a handshake.

"Thanks for coming," said Vandyne.

"Thank you both for accommodating my schedule!" she said, taking a seat one down from me. She set her bulging purse down on the chair between us. "I've got a tape recorder in there."

"For recording us?" I asked.

"No, no. I'm interviewing a contemporary poet later. He works down here."

"Irene, you've said you had some things to tell my partner and me about Mr. Tin."

"We do have a close association, you know that," she said, glancing at me. "There are times we've been together when Mr. Tin had some problems to deal with. Sometimes people come up to him and start speaking Mandarin immediately because they don't think I can understand."

"That's their mistake," I said.

"I'll say. It's a new racial prejudice," she said, appealing to Vandyne with one hand on her chest and the other outstretched to him. He responded by crossing his arms.

"Is there something in particular that happened? Do you know if Mr. Tin is involved with illegal smuggling?"

"I haven't heard anything like that, but he's been helping to hire people that I believe to be illegals to work at various restaurants. One time when I was coming back from the restroom I heard two men talking about Brother Five and 'piggies.'"

"Piggies?" I asked. "Is he smuggling livestock?"

"'Piggies' is another term for the people who are being smuggled. It's similar to 'human snakes.' Of course, these are people who are probably handled in a worse manner than livestock."

"We've heard of the character 'Brother Five' before," said Vandyne.

"That's coded language, also. It may be a name with five strokes in the character. Like 'Tin.'"

"Sorry, Irene. 'Tin' has six strokes," I said.

"No, Robert, it has five," she said.

"It's a field," I said, with some force. "It's a four-sided box with a cross in it. Four sides and the two lines inside add up to six."

I looked at Vandyne and we nodded to each other.

"Robert," started Irene, with a sheepish smile on her face. "You're wrong. The top of the box and the right side are a single stroke. So it's a total of five strokes. You've forgotten that character strokes are counted by using a brush on paper. I mean if it were clay tablets we were dealing with—"

"You're right, Irene," I said, cutting her off. "I was completely wrong."

Goddammit! I had been so sure that Ng was the lead candidate for Brother Five. Mr. Tin was actually just as plausible.

I took out a Polaroid of Ng and showed it to Irene.

"Have you seen this man?" I asked.

She looked it over carefully. "No, I haven't."

"Are you sure?" asked Vandyne.

"I'm positive I haven't seen him. He has a very Cantonese face, though."

"What do you mean, 'Cantonese face'?" I shot.

"I mean the facial structure typical for southern China. Like yours, Robert. A bit elongated to a pointy chin. Similar to a fox. Northern Chinese have stronger, more squarelike heads and are physically bigger overall. Some say more attractive."

I took in a deep breath.

"Irene," Vandyne said quickly, "let's lay off the physiology a bit. I can appreciate that you know a lot about the Chinese people and culture, but don't treat my man like he's a museum piece and you're reading the sign next to him."

"I didn't mean to cause offense. I'm just very excited about Chinese culture!"

"I'm sure you didn't mean to cause offense," I said. "In any case, the man in this picture is Andy Ng. I had reason to believe that he is Brother Five. His Cantonese name 'Ng'—you know it as 'Wu'—happens to mean 'five.' He also eats in the private room of Jade Palace."

"I don't remember meeting anyone by that name," said Irene. "Point well taken about 'five,' though."

"The fact, which you've pointed out, that 'Tin' has five strokes puts him in play, in my mind. Have you ever seen Tin personally involved with 'piggies'?" I asked.

"I haven't, honestly. You know, I'm not blinded by affection for Mr. Tin, either. You might say that I'm sort of working for the other team."

"The Communists?" asked Vandyne.

"No, I mean the Taiwanese opposition, the native Taiwanese, that is. They have an ax to grind against the KMT and their followers who fled to Taiwan from the mainland after losing the civil war. The KMT outright stole private and public lands and distributed them among their cronies as spoils. They still impose martial law on Taiwan as if it were still actively at war with the Communists."

"How did you get involved with the native Taiwanese?" I asked.

"I've been studying Chinese poetry for many years, and when I moved on to contemporary Chinese poetry I found the native Taiwanese poets the most intriguing. By their ability to pinpoint a society's direction, poets are by nature at the head of cultural movements. The ones that I'm most personally involved with are overtly anti-KMT.

"There was a massacre perpetrated on the native Taiwanese people by the KMT not long after they arrived from the mainland, and the poems from that time are just so agonizing! It's as if Picasso's *Guernica* were rendered in Chinese characters.

"Of course, they've only been published in underground, unsanctioned journals. I hope to get them published in English at some point to let Americans know about the atrocities committed by the dictatorship that they support."

"In the meantime," I asked, "why are you with Tin?"

"Oh, I just pick up on mundane sorts of things that help my friends. You know, the latest legislation issues—what highways are going to be developed, what land areas are going to be commercially zoned. With that information in hand, they can develop countermeasures."

"Are you meeting one of those anti-KMT poets today?" I asked.

"No, someone different. This is more of a professional rather than personal meeting, related to the university's Asian studies journal. This poet is a native Cantonese speaker, and as a young college student in Hong Kong he anonymously composed poems about cats that were widely anthologized. I found him by placing an ad in one of the Chinese newspapers."

"What's his name?" I asked.

"I've promised not to reveal it." She looked at me and added, "I'm quite discreet."

I felt a slap at the back of my head. I turned and saw nobody. I looked the other way and saw the midget shaking hands with Vandyne. He hopped into a seat next to Irene and said in Mandarin, "You guys all finished up here?"

"Of course it's you," I said in English to include Vandyne. "You're a famous poet, too?"

"Well, not 'famous,'" conceded Irene. "Let's say 'well-known.'"

"Why did you write poems about cats?" I asked the midget in Cantonese, making "cats" sound like they were the dumbest things in the world.

He blinked. "Why are you alive?" he asked.

"I don't know."

"There you go."

The midget put a paper bag on the table.

"Hey!" yelled the cashier in the front. "No outside food allowed in here!"

"It's not outside food! It's from inside Chinatown! Anyway, bring me two coffees!"

"The fried dough and soy milk here are very good," I told the midget.

"That stuff is gross," he said, taking an egg tart out of his bag.

"I didn't know you wrote poetry," Vandyne said.

The midget said in English, "I write a long time ago. So what. Some people like."

A waiter came by and put two paper cups of coffee in front of the midget and frowned when he saw the egg tart. The midget raised an eyebrow to him and the waiter scurried off.

The midget took a sip of coffee and halfheartedly began to pry the egg tart from the aluminum cup. In Mandarin, he muttered, "It is way too early to be talking about poetry."

"You said this was the best time for you," Irene replied in Mandarin.

"I was trying to scare you off, lady!"

Vandyne and I said good-bye.

"I need to talk to you later," I told the midget. He nodded and blew across the top of one of his coffees.

Vandyne and I were both tired but also too awake to nap up in the precinct's lunchroom, so we walked a big lethargic loop around Chinatown. We came upon Willie Gee, who was out in front of Jade Palace inspecting an onion in front of a deliveryman.

"How long has this been in storage?" Willie asked.

"A day at most," grumbled the man.

"It feels a little wet," said Willie.

"Your fingers are wet."

"Are you trying to cheat me? Trying to fool me into buying old onions?"

The man sighed. "Okay, ten percent off." He kicked off his hand truck and pushed it up a ramp into Jade Palace.

"That's a deal, then," Willie called after him. "Don't try to cheat me again!" He took a few steps back when he saw Vandyne and me but recovered quickly. "I'm glad you two are up so early!" he said with an ugly smile. "I feel safer already!"

"Can it, Willie," I said, "or we'll round up all the illegals you've got working in your kitchen."

"Everybody's paperwork checked out fine," he seethed.

"Sure would look ugly to have the INS running into your restaurant, wouldn't it?" asked Vandyne. We kept on walking.

"Just try it! I dare you!" Willie called after us. "I'll be waiting! Right here! With my lawyer!"

"That guy . . . ," started Vandyne.

"As long as people just care about eating cheap in Chinatown, guys like Willie are going to be in business," I said.

We came up to Canal and turned left.

"We're pretty much walking your old footpost," Vandyne said.

"Boy, I don't miss it. I was walking in the same circle every day."

"There's something to be said for having a good, steady routine."

"How do you ever learn and grow from constant repetition?"

"Routine isn't really repetitive, though. Even if you walked the same beat at the same time every day, it would still be different."

"Maybe, but you'd never notice the difference."

The morning rush hour traffic on Canal was so loud we had to shout toward each other's ears. To the east Canal became the Manhattan Bridge and to the west it became the Holland Tunnel. Essentially, Canal connected New Jersey with Long Island and was one of the busiest roads in America, which explained why parts of it were always under construction.

We walked west along Canal and then we turned south on Mott Street. Vandyne and I went by the Greater China Association's imposing façade of three stone balconies and iron doors. Up on the roof the KMT flag fluttered in the morning sun in tandem with the American flag.

"How can you fly both flags?" asked Vandyne. "You can only be true to one country at a time, right?"

"If you're practical, you salute them both just in case."

"In case what?"

"In case you have to run from one country to the other."

"Are you happy in America, Chow?"

"I love America so much that I would kill for her. Is there anywhere else you would live?"

"I thought Vietnam was beautiful except I didn't like the birds."

"Which birds?"

"The ones that kept dropping napalm and defoliant." We both laughed. "Seriously, I've been reading about Angola, Rhodesia, and South Africa. The military junta in Nigeria. If we can take a stand for democracy and freedom in Vietnam, why can't we invade Africa and try to make things right?"

"C'mon, the white people are too scared to go to Africa! The rootin' tootin' rednecks won't be able to fly their Confederate flags."

"Speaking of which, I have to say that while I am no fan of Ford, there is no way I'm voting for Carter!"

"Why not? Don't you think the grin will win?"

"Maybe he'll win, but I'll be damned if I vote for a man whose brother brags that he's a redneck."

"You can't judge a man by the actions of his brother. Otherwise we'd be putting entire families behind bars."

"Well, maybe we should. Might get this country straightened out. Don't forget that motherfucker was talking about 'racial purity' before."

"Hey, he apologized for it! He said he misspoke!"

Vandyne grunted and swiped at nothing in the air.

As we came to the turn in Mott by Bayard Street there was a loud crash.

"What the hell was that!" yelled Vandyne.

Suddenly music filled the air with drums, cymbals, and other percussion.

"That's more lion dance music," I said.

"Why the hell are they playing this at seven in the morning?"

"Let's go see."

We went to the end of Mott and I rang on Eight Stars Lion Dance's button. The door buzzed and we trudged up the stairs. The music was becoming unbearably loud.

"It's a good thing Chinese people never complain about noise!" Vandyne yelled up at me.

"Good for whom?"

I pounded on the door, and a big, burly Cantonese guy answered the door.

"What?" he asked.

"How about you turn that music down!" I said.

"How come?"

Vandyne came up on the landing and yelled, "Hey, turn that music down!"

The big guy said, "Okay," and shut the door behind him. After a few seconds, the music dropped by about a tenth in volume.

I pounded on the door some more. "Hey," I said after Burly came back, "it's still too loud!"

"Are you guys cops?"

"Yeah, we're cops."

"This is private property. You can't come in!"

"Where's Winnie?"

"Winnie ain't here, now."

"Where's Ng?"

"He ain't here, either."

"Who are you?"

"I'm a contractor. I'm renovating this place and since I have a permit to work, that's exactly what I'm going to do." He slammed the door and locked it. The music surged to a volume that was louder than it was originally.

"Like a crabby teenager, huh?" said Vandyne.

"He says he's renovating the place," I said.

We went back down the stairs to the sidewalk and walked west on Worth Street and then north on Mulberry Street. A box truck was blocking the sidewalk by the funeral home. We walked around it and found Don sitting on the curb in his field jacket, his head in his hands.

"Don! Are you all right?"

"We got an EDP here?" asked Vandyne. Emotionally Disturbed Person.

"No, I know this guy! He was the one who was in Nam!"

I put my hand on Don and he felt stiff like a mannequin.

"Hey, are you all right?" Vandyne asked him.

At Vandyne's voice, Don looked up. "I'm in trouble," he said, giving a sad smile. "My dad is sending men through the walls to take me away."

Vandyne looked at me and I shook my head.

"Don, let's take you home," I said.

He rose to his feet. "Can I have some coffee?" he asked.

"Let's get you back in the apartment first. Then I'll get you some coffee," I said.

We brought him back into his building and up the stairs. His apartment door was open and unlocked.

"Hey, Don," said Vandyne. "You shouldn't leave your apartment door unlocked. Someone could come in and rip you off."

"I didn't mean to," said Don. "I just got scared and panicked."

The only things in his apartment were his sleeping bag, a carton of L&Ms, and a crystal radio set.

"Is this the same kit you had when we were kids?" I asked Don.

"I think so!" he said, coming to life. "I found it outside my door! It doesn't work!"

"I know someone who can probably fix it!" I said. "First, though, let me get you some coffee." Vandyne was about to say something to me, but I cut him off. "Don, this is my friend John. He was in Nam, too."

"I've heard you were in Nam," said Don, sitting down on his sleeping bag. "Heard you were a very big hero."

"Who told you that?" Vandyne asked.

I sprinted out the door to get that coffee back as soon as I could.

17

IT WAS LATE AFTERNOON WHEN I WALKED INTO THE TOY STORE.

The midget was nursing a pot of green tea at the counter, drinking directly out of the spout.

"Are you awake yet?" I asked him.

"I could shoot cans off a fence," he said, "if I had a machine gun and an unlimited amount of bullets."

"Now that's the kind of poetry a GI could love. I think cops would like it, too."

"There was a time when all educated Chinese men wrote poetry. It was a part of the imperial examinations."

"That started during the Tang dynasty, right?"

"No," said the midget slowly, his lips loosening into a thick and limp rubber band. "The exams existed in the Tang dynasty, but they started during the Sui dynasty, the shittiest forty years in China's history."

"That was a short dynasty, but what was so shitty about it?"

"Well, the economy was bad, the army was drafting young men to fight in an unpopular foreign war that was going badly, and the widely despised head of the state was basically forced out of office. Sound familiar?"

"Sounds like America! How did China recover from it? Maybe we can learn how to get America back on track."

"There was a military coup and the emperor and his entire family were slaughtered."

"Wow, we're not going to do that."

"But, hey, it led to the foundation of the Tang dynasty! Poems from that time have yet to be equaled!" He stopped to pick at something in his teeth. "That must have been a hell of a time to be alive," he said through his fingers.

"It must be exciting to have someone interested in your old poems. Between this and the documentary, you're a star! What are you doing here?"

"I'm here for the kids. There is no nobler cause that a business can address."

"I'm not so sure that the kids appreciate what you do for them."

"I'm kind of doing it for me, too. I didn't have a store like this when I was young. At the very least, it's a safe place for kids to hang out instead of waiting on the streets for trouble. So you mentioned this morning that you wanted to talk to me?"

"Irene had wanted to talk to Vandyne and me this morning before meeting you."

"Good night, Irene!"

"I had caught her in a compromising situation with someone and thought that she had wanted to explain herself a bit. But she wanted to talk about something else. Irene was one of the witnesses who found the two bodies a couple weeks ago. She had heard something that might prove helpful in the investigation.

"She mentioned the nickname 'Brother Five' for a snakehead. This name has come up a few times. I'm thinking it has to refer to something about the number five."

The midget slammed his hands on the table in shock. "No!" he said. "How in the whole wide world did you figure that out?"

"Anyway," I said, ignoring his mock surprise, "it still leaves me with three suspects, I think. 'Five' phonetically is the same as 'Ng.' There are five brushstrokes in 'Tin,' as in Mr. Tin at the Greater Chinese Association. And you know what? There are five stars on the Communist Chinese flag, so that could refer to Mr. Song of the Together Chinese Kinship."

"That's pretty weak, that last one on Mr. Song."

"So it's impossible?"

"I didn't say it was impossible," said the midget, tapping his fingers. "But Mr. Song is probably the least likely among your suspects."

"You haven't even met him, how would you know?"

"That's true, how could I possibly know? In fact, why are you even bothering to ask me?"

"I just, ah, wanted to know what you thought. Run a couple things by you. That's all." The midget was the last person in the world I wanted to annoy. "I'm sorry I questioned your abilities earlier. I'm just looking for your help on this."

He let out a small growl of disgust. "I was just playing around, Robert. Don't apologize for anything with me. It makes me feel like I've been manipulating you."

"But you know, you have so much insight into everything, don't you think you could be using your powers of intuition to help Chinatown?"

"Help do what?" he asked, not bothering to deny his abilities.

"Make life better in Chinatown! Right now you could help get rid of the snakeheads!"

"I could probably help stop the guys operating right now," he mused. "But do you know what would happen next? The entire smuggling routine would become even more ruthless and dangerous. Snakeheads would charge even more money and illegals would be even more miserable here."

"You're not going to try to stop me, though, are you?"

"What can I do to stop you? Maybe it's the Taoist part of me talking, but I wouldn't hold you back from anything. You have to explore your own feelings and do what you think is necessary."

"You're a Taoist?"

"Sometimes."

Paul came out from the storeroom in the back.

"Hey, Paul," I said. "Do you know anything about these things?" I pulled out parts of the crystal radio from my pockets.

He came over and put the parts on the counter. "It's a crystal radio," he said.

"Yes!" I said.

"So where's the crystal?"

"Oh. I don't know."

"You need a piece of galena or some equivalent mineral, like pyrite, or fool's gold."

"How does the crystal work in it?"

"Do you really want to know, Robert?" Paul asked.

"Honestly, no," I said. I turned to the midget and asked, "Do you sell crystals here?"

"I don't sell Age of Aquarius crap. Real radios use nine-volts."

"If you go to RadioShack," said Paul, "they might have the crystal, but they'll probably force you to buy the entire kit, too."

"This thing has a lot of nostalgic value for a friend of mine," I said. Don had told me it was the first thing that he had ever bought for himself. "Paul, can you go get the crystal for me? I'll cover for you here and pay for it."

"Why can't you get it yourself?"

"I don't know what to ask for and I'll probably fuck it up."

"Um, Robert?" said the midget. "We have kids in the store."

"I'm sorry, kids! I use bad language because I'm a bad person." One little boy brushed his cheek with a finger at me to show that I should be ashamed of myself. I took out my wallet and gave a five-dollar bill to Paul. "Get back here as soon as you can," I said.

"I'll try."

"What do I have to do here?"

"I was about to sweep the sidewalk in front, but you can do that now, Robert."

I groaned. The toy store's brush broom usually gave me blisters or splinters or both.

"Here," said the midget. "Put on this pair of work gloves. I don't want you to mess your hands up again. I don't have any Band-Aids left."

I went out and pushed the broom around, looking at scraps of paper that liked to gather on the roughest parts of the concrete. I was dimly aware that I was thinking about my father for some reason. Maybe because it was a manual-labor job, something he had thought that his son was above.

I found a stubborn glob of gum and lost a few bristles to it. I'd have to take a box cutter to it later.

Someone said, "Did you get a promotion or something?"

I looked up and saw Ng regarding me with a smirk. "You talking to me, Brother Five?" I asked him as nonchalantly as someone leaning on a broom can be.

"What a funny little name you keep calling me. How did you make it up?"

"I heard that was the handle that you go by when you're smuggling people."

"I heard they call you Officer Trespass."

"Since when?"

"Since this morning when you tried to force your way into my offices. They're not open to the public, especially when the contractors are at work."

"Your guys were playing music at a level that was unacceptable."

"Unacceptable to whom? Is it really so strange for men to be listening to music while they work?"

"It's weird for them to be playing lion dance music. They should be listening to Aerosmith or Lynyrd Skynyrd."

"I know what it is. You find it unusual when Chinese people enjoy their culture."

"I'll bet that at the end of the day those guys go home and work on their calligraphy. Meanwhile in our wonderful Chinese community kids are shooting each other down like dogs in the street."

"I'm doing something about it," Ng said, pointing a thumb at his chin. "I bring those kids together, teach them their own history, and give them something to be proud of. That's more than the NYPD has ever done. You take their pictures like they're in a zoo, and when you treat the youth like animals of course that's how they're going to act!"

"Well, see, the kids only look up to you because you're a part of the criminal underground. It's cool to be bad. Kids used to love Al Capone, too."

"I'll admit freely that our operations have an illegitimate past. But my family's business will be completely clean by the end of this year. Maybe even in time for the two parades in October, if everything goes well."

"When you're just another businessman in Chinatown, you might lose their respect."

"Maybe, but they're going to be different, too. They're going to be kids with a future."

I heard a light tap on the window. Out of the corner of my eye I saw the midget raise an eyebrow at me. I nodded my head just slightly and he nodded back.

"The lion dances are the first thing," Ng went on, ignoring the midget. "After that, when all the renovations are done, we're going to have Chinese history classes so our kids know where they've been and they can feel a sense of purpose. Also English classes because, frankly, they need to know it better to have a real future here."

The Greater China Association for years had been running Mandarin-language classes that some kids were forced to go to and, at least when I went there, they were as agonizing as regular school. The Chinese teachers were far meaner than any of the white ones.

The only thing we learned about Chinese history was that Communism was bad and that the KMT was going to launch an attack and reclaim the mainland. They cited how tiny Japan was able to beat gigantic Russia. Huge portraits of a grim Sun Yat-sen and a smug Chiang Kai-shek regarded us from the front of the room to show how serious the Greater China Association was about it. Of course, Together Chinese Kinship or any other group that openly supported the Communists was nonexistent at this point.

That was all okay, because none of us had taken what we were "learning" too seriously. Nearly all of us had been born in the United States, and we knew English well enough to get decent jobs anywhere else in the country. We also knew it well enough to read extremely unflattering things about Chiang Kai-shek in the American media.

These days, the kids who had just come over were screwed, because their English was terrible or nonexistent. The schools weren't equipped to do anything with them except put them in overcrowded and under-staffed English-as-a-second-language classes apparently designed to group resentful kids together and form them into gangs.

They weren't learning anything in school about America, much less reading, writing, and arithmetic. With both parents working dead-end jobs there wasn't anybody at home to tell them about Chinese history, much less make dinner. It was no wonder these kids didn't know what the hell was going on and didn't care.

"I'm also going to have guest speakers come in so they can see the breadth of this community that they belong to," said Ng. "Maybe you'd like to come in and talk sometime. I'm sure they'd like to hear from your perspective as someone who rose up from humble Chinatown roots."

"Don't forget Nam, though."

"I'm going to keep politics out of it, Robert. The KMT and Communists are already waging enough of their brainwashing war on our community. They both have their own systems of favoritism that have perverted modern Chinese culture. Our society needs to go back to the same system we had during the Tang dynasty, when the most qualified were elevated to the highest societal positions, not whoever had the most powerful friends and family.

"That idiot Mr. Tin is the head of the Greater China Association because his old man was one of Chiang Kai-shek's top supporters in Shanghai. That Mr. Song is the chairman of Together Chinese Kinship because his family sends money to the Communist secretary-general.

"These men have both led privileged lives. I have, too. But the difference between them and me is that I'm empowering the community, not just myself."

I looked at him and saw that he believed every word. I felt a little bad for him that Eddie Ding was going to put him away. What he said made sense and what he was doing was actually good for Chinatown.

The funny thing about it all was that if he had only held on to his family's crooked business operations instead of trying to sell them, he would have been safe. Trying to come clean was a dangerous business.

I sat at my desk picking at a tasteless rice bun. Eating it was like churning wet concrete until I drank enough coffee to break it up and, for some reason, swallow it.

"Ran out of peanut butter?" asked English.

"Yeah."

"Anyway, how about you go to 11 Pell Street. Actually got a complaint of a gunshot, kids running, last night. Responding officers found nothing and even the complainer wasn't sure which way the kids went. Complainer wouldn't come down to look through the Polaroid books."

"So I go down, make a token appearance, and thank the complainer for making a minimal effort."

"Basically."

My phone rang. I took another swish of coffee before picking up the receiver.

"Detective," I said.

"Robert?"

"Yes."

"This is Rose."

"How are you, Rose?"

"I'm all right," she said, although she sounded like she was treading water. "Robert, can you meet me for lunch today?"

"I guess so." I could tell that we were going to talk about Vandyne and that it wasn't going to be good.

We set up to meet at a Chock full o'Nuts at Broadway and Thirty-fifth. Their "heavenly" coffee was never as good as the Chinatown kind was, but it was different, and different was how I wanted my mouth to taste.

Rose was already waiting for me outside and we went in together.

"I hope you don't mind coming here. I like that they hired Jackie Robinson all those years ago as an executive, so I want to patronize them when I can."

"Chinese people love coming here now that they've brought back the 'no tipping' policy. They might not hang on much longer, though. That Rheingold deal killed them." A few years ago Chock full o'Nuts had bought the Brooklyn brewer to try to save it but ended up closing the plant anyway. I could have told them the product wasn't worth salvaging.

Beer.

I shook my head and rubbed my hands. Rose and I took seats on two stools on the outside curve of the winding counter.

An older black waitress in a hairnet came over.

"You two together?" she asked. The waitress had freckles across her cheeks. Clear plastic eyeglasses sat at the end of her nose and she looked at us over them.

"Yes," I said.

She cocked her head slightly. "You married?"

"She is," I said, smiling.

The waitress smiled back. She had the wrong idea, but Rose and I didn't bother to fix it.

I had never really fallen in love with the nutbread-and-cream-cheese sandwiches, so instead I got a ham sandwich with pea soup. Rose just had the soup.

I was stirring sugar into my coffee when Rose started with, "John hardly ever talks to me, anymore."

"He's been busy. We're both under a lot of pressure. Most of the squad is out dealing with the FALN bombing. We have to handle the rest."

"John never wants to talk. Never. Whatever I want to say, it's always the wrong thing and the wrong time. He just shuts me down."

"Rose, you guys are in couples therapy for help. I'm sure you can work everything out."

"Now he says he doesn't want to go anymore. He says he's done talking to people who don't get him."

"I get him, Rose."

"You're his friend, I know, but he's not getting what he needs by talking to another cop who's a veteran."

"Don't forget that I'm an alcoholic, too," I added.

"That doesn't matter, Robert."

I decided not to tell her that Vandyne had gone to one of the vets' rap sessions. Hearing about it for the first time from me could only make her feel worse.

"I think the having-a-kid thing is getting him down," I said.

"I know, that's why I don't talk about it anymore. We don't talk about a lot of things anymore. Just the other day when we went to see my sister, he said almost nothing—even at dinner."

"John told me about the visit. He said your sister's husband was sort of a condescending jerk."

"Condescending? Harry is a first-class wimp. He never stands up for himself. My sister walks all over him. She even made him do the dishes while we were having coffee."

"Harry's the doctor?"

"Yes."

"He's got all this fancy audio equipment that he shows off, too, right?"

"Turning on your stereo for music during dinner means you're showing it off?"

"He did it by remote control, right?"

"Actually, my sister turned it on. She was the one who wanted something playing to make dinner less awkward."

"I guess that's reasonable."

Rose touched a finger to her forehead and rubbed a spot over her left eye.

"Robert, I can't start over again." She closed her eyes and shook her head slowly. "I know so many people who are splitting up just when they were getting started."

"No, Rose, stop," I said. "Don't talk like this. Don't even think like this."

Our waitress picked this moment to come over and refill our coffees. She looked closely into Rose's eyes and then into mine.

"Thank you," I told the waitress. She nodded without a word and walked away.

Rose twisted her napkin in her lap. "Robert, he doesn't even look at me anymore."

Taking that as a cue, I turned to her and looked at her face full on. Rose kept her hair in a short perm around her face, a lopsided oval that was fuller at the bottom. Her nose was long and slightly pointy. It must have been kissed and nudged around a lot. Rose's gray eyes were dull like a sheet of steel on a cold winter day.

Her mouth was the tight curl in the center of a cinnamon roll.

"Can I ask you something as a man?" she said.

I nodded.

"Am I still pretty? Maybe I've been losing my looks." She was sobbing, one hand balanced on the counter, the other on my knee. "I don't know."

Our waitress was in the back and said something urgently to a younger black waitress who looked at us and shook her head sadly.

I rubbed Rose's right arm with my left hand. "Of course you're beautiful," I said. "Vandyne tells me all the time how beautiful you are."

"Does he really?"

"John thinks you're absolutely wonderful."

She took a handkerchief from her purse and dabbed her eyes with it. "He never tells me," she said. He never told me, either, but Rose didn't understand the guy code. Talking about how pretty your girl is or how much you love her could come off as just plain showing off. When in doubt, just talk about sports, the economy, or the war.

"There has to be a way to help John open up more to me," said Rose.

"There's a lot of stuff from Nam that all of us are still dealing with, and this job can be stressful as heck, too."

"I know, I know. I didn't want to say it, but I think that John may have a problem with my sister and her husband because of the race thing. Maybe not."

"He said that?"

"No, he didn't. But I think I see some resentment. Maybe I'm just imagining it. After all, he obviously didn't mention it to you and you're his best friend."

"He didn't even tell me that your sister was married to a white guy."

Rose turned to me suddenly. "Harry's not white."

"He's not?"

"He's Chinese! Chinese American!"

"Oh," I said. I was so surprised that Rose paid for the check before I could grab it.

We hadn't gotten far from the counter when our waitress called out, "Don't worry. I didn't see you two here. I won't tell nobody!"

"What do you know about getting into people's business?" I asked the midget. We were at the front counter of the toy store, eating noodles I had gotten from one of the sidewalk carts.

"Jesus," he said, noodles dangling from his mouth. He slurped them up quickly. "Just stay out of it," he said.

"You don't even know what it's about," I said.

"Is it between a man and a woman and is that man Vandyne and the woman his wife?"

"Who told you?"

"No one. You don't really know that many people, Robert. Well, not that many people in relationships."

"Well, what do you think I should do? I had lunch yesterday with Rose and she was telling me—"

"Stay out of it."

"I'm worried that—"

"Stay out of it!"

"She was telling me she was thinking of maybe getting divorced!"

"Robert, maybe she just had to say it to get it out of her system. Maybe Rose just needed someone to talk to."

"That's the problem. She says Vandyne doesn't talk to her anymore."

"This is something they have to resolve on their own. If there aren't

disagreements, then relationships get boring. Anyway, don't tell Vandyne unless he brings the matter up himself."

"It could be too late by then."

"If you say that you met his wife and knew about their problems,
you're not going to help. You're just going to piss him off and he'll talk
even less to his wife. He'll trust her less for sure." The midget shoved
another mouthful of noodles into his mouth.

"But maybe I can help."

"You already helped by listening to Rose."

"Vandyne doesn't need to know?"

"Look, Robert. You and I are fairly close, right?"

"Sure."

"How would you feel if I told you that Lonnie came to me and said
you don't pay enough attention to her?"

"She said that! Why the hell did she tell you?"

He stretched his greasy lips to the left in a wry smile.

"Now you get it?" he asked. "Keep your goddamned mouth shut and
keep your mind on your work! Find out who Brother Five is, already!"

"How?"

"Did you talk to everybody you possibly could?"

"Definitely!"

"Are you sure?"

"I am absolutely one hundred percent certain."

"You can't think of anybody else, right?"

"Do you think I'm an idiot or something? Believe me, there's nobody
else left for me to see!"

18

I CAME DOWN THE HOSPITAL CORRIDOR AND SAW THAT PEEPSHOW was on guard outside the gangster kid's room.

"Hey, Chow," said Peepshow. He had a copy of *Cracked Mazagine* opened on his lap. A brown paper bag was at his feet and the air smelled like orange peels.

"Geller," I said to Peepshow. I made the mistake of clasping his hand, which was sticky. "Quiet?"

"It's like I'm guarding nobody," he said. "What are you doing here?" he asked.

"Well, I . . ." I paused, distracted by seeing Peepshow licking his sticky palm. "I think the kid might have some information relevant to this case I'm working on."

"He's not supposed to have any visitors. I mean, none except for his lawyer."

"I have to see him, though. I'm sure it's okay. Chinese people have to look after each other."

"I guess there's no harm. You're not going in to kill him or anything, right?"

"That is the farthest thing in the universe from my mind!" I said, smiling.

I went in and kicked down the doorstop to give Peepshow a false sense that he was still protecting the kid, who was propped up in his bed, reading a book with one hand. It was a little dim in there. The only light was from his nightstand lamp. The ceiling fluorescent lights were off.

Eric watched me come in. He picked up his bed remote and lowered the head end until he was fully reclining. Then he snapped off his light and tossed the book aside.

"I'm sleeping," he said. "Besides, I got nothing to say to you."

I flipped a few switches and all the lights came on. Eric groaned and I pulled up a chair next to his bed.

"What are you reading here?" I asked. I picked up his book. It was a *MAD* magazine book of stupid cartoons. "Hey, you and Geller ought to get together," I said, pointing back at Peepshow. "You're at the same reading level—zero."

"Look!" Eric said. "I told the black cop everything that happened. I don't know who shot at me, but I can take care of it myself."

"I know what you said so far—pretty much nothing. But I know your name is Eric. My name is Robert."

"I knew that!" he spat.

I looked into his face. Eric was about eighteen years old or so, a pivotal age for gangster kids. Pretty soon he'd be killed, go to jail for a long time on an adult-sized sentence, or get serious about a girl and move far, far away.

"What are you looking at?" he demanded to know. His nose had been broken at some point and seemed to be growing a knuckle. He had scars on his forehead and his skin was oily and blotchy like a slice of pizza when the cheese and sauce slipped off. Eric's eyes were scared and childlike. I felt a little bad that this kid probably would be laid out on a slab in the next year.

"What do you want!" he yelled. It sounds meaner in Cantonese and it shocked me into dropping any sympathy for him.

"I am so sorry to bother you, but I was just wondering if there was any chance you know someone named 'Brother Five.'"

"A snakehead, right?"

"Yeah!"

"I did some freelance work for him."

"Your friends, too?"

"Maybe they did. I'm not sure."

"Can you remember for me, Eric?"

He rolled his eyes and turned his head away. "Hey, dumbfuck," he said. "I was shot. You shouldn't even be here, now."

"I know you were shot. I'm here because I was worried about you. As I am worried about all the Chinese youth."

"Well, I heard you live with a little boy. Do you fuck him up the ass?"

I scratched my right ear and stood up. I went to the door.

"Nighty night, child molester," Eric called after me.

I kicked up the doorstop and started to close the door.

"Geller," I said to Peepshow.

"Yeah?"

"I'm closing this door because there's a bad breeze coming through."

"Sure."

"Now might be a good time for you to go over to the vending machines. Why not have a coffee break?"

"Aw, I get it," he said, smiling. "You're trying to get me to go down and get you a cup of coffee, huh?"

"Guilty as charged," I said, laughing. "But hey, let me cover you, too." I gave him three dollar bills. "If you feel like it, have a cigarette down there in the lounge, as well. I'm not really in a rush."

"Sure, I'll take a break. Why not, I'm going to be here all friggin' night." Peepshow stood up. I moved to shut the door. "Hey, wait!" he said, pushing it open.

"What?"

"How do you want your coffee?"

"Let's keep it simple. I'll take it the same way you take it."

"That's a good idea. Who could screw that up?" I could only smile and laugh a little.

I got the door closed. I locked it and turned down the blinds covering the windowpane.

"Hey!" said Eric. "What are you doing?"

I went and stood over him. "Eric, I need to know what you know about Brother Five."

"I don't have to talk to you. My lawyer already said I was done."

He looked scared when I grabbed the nurse call controller and dropped it on the other side of the nightstand, out of his reach.

"If you don't start talking," I said, "I'm going to find some way to hurt you and then I'll tell everyone that you tried to go for my gun and I had to subdue you somehow."

"You're a rotten cop."

"You're a rotten kid. Let's not dwell on the personal, though. I got no beef with you, but I'm trying to catch Brother Five."

"Okay. I helped keep an eye on some human snakes that he thought needed watching. They might have been trying to plan an escape or go to the authorities."

"You basically just shadow them from the safe house to their jobs?"

"Yeah, like a cop."

"No, not like a cop! Like a two-bit Nazi in fake leather!"

He squirmed a little bit in bed. "He said that they agreed to the terms of being smuggled over. We watched them to keep them honest and make sure they didn't try to cheat him."

"Brother Five told you that?"

"Yes," he said. Suddenly he winced in regret. "I didn't mean to say that."

"That's all right because I already knew. I wanted to hear it from you. So what would you do if you saw someone trying to get away?"

"I saw two people talk to a lawyer."

"How do you know they were talking to a lawyer?"

"There's a lawyer who sits in the back of the shoe store. Like how you used to sit in the back of the toy store. Oh, we all knew about you!"

"It was never a secret and it's not like I was creeping around, doing something illegal. So what did you do when you saw the guys talking to a lawyer?"

"I told Brother Five."

"Let me guess—those two guys are the ones who got killed, right?"

He gave me a defiant look. "Yeah, they were. But I didn't do it! I wasn't involved."

"Who killed them?"

"It was three kids, all under sixteen, so they couldn't get put away if they were caught."

"Where are these three kids now?"

"They're gone."

"Gone where?"

"Boston? Philadelphia? Taiwan? I swear I don't know."

"You told Brother Five and he had these three kids kill those two guys."

"Yeah."

"What does Brother Five look like? Old? Young? Tall or short?"

"I don't know."

"What do you mean, you don't know?" I had a quick image in my head of pushing a pillow in his face.

"I just talked to his assistant. I only ever met his assistant."

"You have no idea what Brother Five looks like?"

"No!"

"What's Brother Five's real name?"

"I don't know!"

"What does the 'Five' stand for?" I was going to run through my guesses with him but decided to hold back.

"Who knows!" He crossed his arms.

"The assistant was the guy who paid your salaries, right?"

"Duh!"

"What does the assistant look like?"

"He's a guy in a suit. Shaggy hair and sunglasses."

"Where can I find him?"

"You don't find him. He finds you. You feel a tap on your shoulder and then he's right there. It's always a different place. He walks with a limp."

That shaggy hair and sunglasses sounded like a pretty obvious disguise. The limp could be faked. It was probably Brother Five himself.

"Why were you shot?"

He kept his mouth shut.

"Was it because you knew about the two murders?" I asked.

"I'll take care of it. Don't worry."

That was as far as Vandyne had gotten with the Pagoda incident and it was as far as Eric was going to let me get. I took a step to the door.

"When you're well enough to walk out of here, you should do yourself a favor and leave New York. Start your life over in the country somewhere."

He looked up at the ceiling. "My life is here," he said. "Besides, what kind of a man would I be if I left? I would look like a coward if I didn't stay and get my revenge."

I looked at Eric. He reminded me of another wayward Chinaboy running full tilt at a brick wall. But he wasn't as smart as Paul. How was he going to make it?

"Eric, you have a lot of chances in this life, a lot more than your parents. Now you want to throw it all away so a bunch of jerks in the pool hall respect you. Let me tell you something. These people who you think are your friends aren't going to stand by you when it counts. Plenty of guys like you have very lonely funerals, if they even get one."

He still wouldn't look at me, his eyes defiantly fixed on the fire sprinkler. Maybe I had gotten through to him. Maybe he'd see the light, eventually. At least he wasn't dumb enough to threaten me.

He ruined my hope for him by opening his mouth.

"If I hadn't taken a bullet, Robert, I could put you in the high dive for the East River Olympics."

I smiled. "Shows how much you know. Both China and Taiwan are boycotting the Olympics, dumbass!"

19

DURING A COMMERCIAL, I ASKED PAUL, "HEY, SO, HOW DID YOU DE-
cide to give up the gangster life?"

He sighed and slumped over like it was the thousandth time I had
asked him. "I was never a gang member, not one of the core members,"
he finally said. "I never had a gun."

"But you were headed down that path, weren't you?"

He shrugged. "Maybe."

"More like 'probably,' right?"

"Well, one potential scenario is that someone I knew well could have
been shot or shot somebody. That could have pushed me over the edge.
I would have had to become a soldier at that point. I would have felt that
sense of loyalty. But that day you came up to me and almost beat me up,
my friends ran away. It showed me that I was foolish to have a sense of
loyalty to them."

"I'm glad you learned that lesson before you took a bullet yourself."
I thought about the Chinatown guys I knew who had served in Nam.
They had tried to form some sort of Asian veterans group. I had showed

up at the meeting, but one of the guys had a picture from Nam of him tied up with the white soldiers sticking bayonets in his face. It really pissed me off.

He told me the picture had been a joke. I told him he was the joke and left. That seemed to have busted up the group. I felt bad about it now, because we were all Asian men who had been stuck in the U.S. military—the most anti-Asian outfit in the world. But maybe it was best that the group didn't last. Apart from talking to Vandyne about it, I was done with Nam. I didn't need more people to complain to. The less people talked about the war, the better.

I felt itchy all over my body and not sleepy at all.

That kid in the hospital was bugging me.

Who the fuck was Brother Five?

Just a few months ago I would have started drinking beer and fallen asleep sooner or later. Instead I drank a can of Coke and told Paul I was going for a walk. He turned off the TV and turned on the CB radio to talk to his imaginary friends.

When I got to the sidewalk, I took a left and walked west on East Broadway until I was by the bridge overpass where the bodies had been found. I looked at the barren patch of ground, more glass and scrap metal than soil. The crime scene tape had ripped, and the ends fluttered in the light breeze.

If my father hadn't kept up with his debt payments he could have ended up dead on this tiny lot of unwanted America, or kicked into a ditch in California. I thought of my father's young and smiling face and saw it turn twisted and ugly, caked with dirt.

I put my hands in my pockets and continued west. I walked by an over-rice joint. A group of about ten teens were sitting there. Even though their food was already on the table, they weren't eating. Their heads were bowed and their hands clasped in prayer.

Joining a Christian group was one way of staying out of trouble. The gangster kids thought of them as sissies and didn't bother to mess with them. Same with the Boy Scouts. I'll admit that at one point I had wanted to join the scouts, but my father told me it was just a scam to force you to buy the uniform and books.

A car honked at me. I turned and saw Winnie wave to me from her convertible. I walked into the street and came up to her side of the car.

"What are you doing here?" I asked.

"I like to drive around the city, but for some reason I keep coming back to Chinatown, even though I spend the weekdays here. I'm not sure why that is. Maybe everything looks more interesting from a car. Even you, Robert."

"Isn't it a little late for you to be out?"

"But it's Saturday night!" she whined. "Let's go for a drive!"

"I don't know if I have time."

"Well, you didn't look too busy, staring at people in a restaurant. They might think you're some kind of weirdo."

"Ordinarily, I would be out with my girlfriend. But she's studying for a test."

"So you're *not* doing anything. You look a little down, too. Get in the car. Come on, let me at least take you home. I'm wasting all this gas idling here right now. You brought me home before and now I have to return the favor."

I came around and got in. I justified it by thinking I would ask her about her brother, but she was the one who kicked off asking questions.

"Your girlfriend is studying on the weekend? She doesn't sound like a fun girl!"

"You should know by now that I'm not a fun guy. Just take me straight home. Let's make a U-turn here on East Broadway."

"Sheesh!" said Winnie, swinging the car around. "Any regular guy who got in a convertible with a cute girl wouldn't be so anxious to leave!"

Her right hand suddenly went for something and I followed it. She was only pulling down the hem of her skirt, which was bright red and short. It was tight against her black panty hose.

"You like my legs, huh?" she asked, her eyes still on the road.

"I like the color of your skirt, but in this country red means 'stop.'"

"So red doesn't do it for you, huh? What does?"

"Information about how your brother's smuggling people into this country from China."

"Humph! What makes you think he's doing such a thing?"

"Don't they call him Brother Five?"

"No, you're thinking about that book, *The Five Chinese Brothers.* One brother can swallow the ocean."

"That book was a piece of racist garbage! It stereotyped Chinese people as slant-eyed ching-chongs with mystical powers."

"It had a positive message, though. It's about brothers sticking up for each other and shows that justice ultimately prevails."

I tapped my hand against the outside of my door. "See that far corner there, on the right?" I asked. "You can let me out there."

"You seriously want to go home now?"

"Unless you have something more to tell me about your brother."

"I might have."

"In that case, I'll ride with you as long as you keep talking."

She checked herself in the rearview mirror. "Say, do you think I look all right tonight?"

"Your face isn't the problem," I said as a puzzled look came over her. "How does Andy Ng, your brother, make a living?"

"You already know my family is pretty well-off. I feel a little embarrassed to say this, but he really doesn't have to work if he doesn't want to."

"But he's restructuring the family business, because he's trying to clean it up instead of just taking the money and not asking questions."

"Is that a shot at me?" demanded Winnie.

"Not at all. We're talking about Andy. I can't really figure him out.

Does he care so much about his family name that he wants to get it out of the alleys and wash it off?"

"I guess you could see it that way. Or you could see it the way I see it."

"How's that?"

"He's trying to push out the criminal elements of the family so he can have sole power. We have a number of uncles who head up various lines of business. If Andy signed away territory rights to other families, our uncles would have to go straight, too, or go back to smashing parking meters for change."

It was the typical summer night in Chinatown—hot and smelly. Somehow being in a car and feeling a breeze made it worse than walking through it.

I regarded Winnie. This was where she came alive, in a car and hot and cruising for action. There were two minor things wrong with her, though. She slouched and she rubbed her nose too much.

Apart from that, with her hair waving in the night air, she could have been a love goddess who flew down from the moon in a convertible.

"What if these uncles," I said, "weren't exactly on board with the plan? What if they wanted to stop Andy?"

"They are trying to stop him! He's been warned many times! They even tried telling him he's walking into a setup."

"What does he say about it?" I asked casually.

"He says he knows what he's doing. Andy's cocky because he went to school in the U.S. He thinks he's smarter than everyone else in Hong Kong and Singapore. But he also says Americans are too lazy and stupid to catch on to him and that Vietnam was the start of the decline of the West and the rise of the East."

"Do you believe that?"

She glanced at me and sighed. "I believe some Americans don't know when an opportunity presents itself."

"I have a girlfriend, Winnie. We already do plenty together."

"I've slept with married men, Robert. They've told me they couldn't keep their hands off of me."

I crossed my arms and shook my head. I couldn't believe that someone so oblivious to racial and social politics was so active in sexual politics, and she probably had a lot of endorsements from powerful players.

"Winnie, are you this way because you were sent to an all-girl school? Or is it *why* you were sent there?"

"I went to a coed university. You've never heard of it, but trust me, it was a lot tougher academically than almost any American college. My senior thesis was about how insecure men try to marginalize aggressive women."

"Did you get an A?"

She moved her hands to one o'clock and eleven o'clock on the wheel and grabbed it tight. "I was thrown out of school," she said.

"I'm sorry."

"When my father found out, he had everything fixed and they granted me my degree. But they still refused to accept my thesis."

I was suddenly struck with insight into her character. This didn't happen too often, and I felt unsettled by it. Because her university wouldn't accept her thesis, Winnie was applying it in real life as a sexually assertive woman. Maybe being a secretary was also a part of the role-playing.

"That guy Brian still bothering you?" I asked.

"He's a total creep. He doesn't turn me on at all."

"It was your idea to go to where the bodies were found, right?"

"Yeah, it was. I was just trying to push him a little. He was scared as shit."

"I just thought of something, Winnie. Maybe you're really a snakehead. You only play at being innocent."

She chuckled. "It's actually a fantasy of mine to have male slaves at my beck and call. Sweaty, smelly, and miserable slaves."

"That's my cue to go home."

It didn't take too long to get back to my corner.

"Are you going to ask me up for some coffee?" she asked.

"I would ask you up, but I haven't vacuumed." I got out and shut the door.

"You and I could have a good time if you didn't have so many hang-ups," Winnie said. "You know, these seats recline all the way back."

I leaned over, rested my hands on the passenger door, and said, "That might make enough room for two guys with you in there at the same time."

Winnie tore the car away, nearly ripping my hands off at the wrists. I chuckled to myself, but I couldn't help but wonder where this girl was a year or two ago. I would have burned that crepe dress right off her.

20

I WAS DRINKING COFFEE WITH THE MIDGET AT THE TOY STORE.
His new air conditioner was working great, and it made the glass in his
window rattle loudly enough so that we could have a private conversation right in the open. If we had something important to talk about.

"Seems like it's brighter in here," I said. "Did you get new lights or
something?"

"Naw, I had a new ceiling put in," said the midget, drinking alter-
nately from a cup of coffee and a mug of hot water. "Asbestos tiles. They
were unbelievably cheap!"

"Asbestos! Are you nuts? You're going to give all the kids here cancer!"

"Were you born in the year of the chicken, Robert?"

"I'm a tiger."

"I don't think a real tiger would be scared of ceilings. Asbestos tiles
are safe. The fibers are sealed up. You'd have to grate them up and eat
them for them to be a problem."

"What about all the cancer lawsuits?"

"There are slip-and-fall lawsuits in the city. Are you going to stop walking on the sidewalks? Anyway, everything causes cancer. Coffee probably kills more people than asbestos. I'll bet that the halls of Maxwell House are haunted by ghosts. Maybe that's why so many people burn Hell Bank Notes in Maxwell House tins."

"Hey," I said, then paused to take in a breath. "Do you believe that we can contact spirits of the dead?"

"Are you trying to get in touch with your father?"

"Not really, because I don't know what I would say. This is a little creepy, but I feel his spirit in me."

"He was your father," said the midget as he shifted a little in his chair. "He is a part of you, genetically."

"We were never close, you know?"

"Of course I know. It's a typical Chinatown story. The men have to work such long hours or lose themselves to gambling, whoring, and drinking, the kids grow up without fathers. I think these boys want the action figures because they are hungry for male role models."

Just then my eyes fell upon a model of an alligator trying to eat a soldier. "What do the girls want?"

"You don't know by now?" the midget joked.

"C'mon, I'm not kidding around," I said. "I wasn't close with my father when he was alive, but I've been feeling anger from his spirit. And it's not directed at me, either. It's the snakeheads."

"Everybody hates them. But they're there because people are willing to do almost anything to come here. They make reliable workers who work overtime, never call in sick or go on vacation. Oh, and they'll never organize a union. But you know what, Robert? Picking off snakeheads isn't going to solve the issue. As long as Chinese in China think they can have a better life in America, they'll make deals with the devil to get here. Especially the Fukienese and Cantonese. Going abroad is in their blood."

"How do we stop them from thinking they need to come here by any means?"

"We can't. When their relatives send letters telling them of the hard life they're having here, they don't believe it. They just think all the complaining is meant to discourage others from coming in and getting their piece of the pie. It doesn't help that they send back money and gifts in that fine Chinese tradition of starving yourself to feed your family and friends."

"I get it. They see the money and it talks louder than the letter. They should send pictures of the calluses, cuts, and burn marks on their hands."

"How about a book of pictures about how hard life is here? About all the hardships." Then he smirked. "We'll put you on the cover. That'll turn off all the ladies."

"We'll use your picture to scare all the kids."

"My picture won't scare anybody. They'll think that life is a circus here. Trapeze artists, the human cannonball, and, of course, a midget act. Popcorn and peanuts. They won't know they'll be shoveling up all the elephant shit."

"It's probably a union job. My father would have been better off shoveling shit."

"Your father and every other Chinaman."

"My father wasn't just another Chinaman."

"He was the same as all Chinamen in the sense that he worked long and hard at a job he wasn't guaranteed to have the next day. He had the same slouch. He didn't talk very much to anybody in his family, but when he ran into another man in the street they could talk so loud and so long, you'd have to pull him away or you'd never eat. I'll also bet he snored like a garbage truck."

"Jesus, he could shake pantry doors open," I said, smiling. "But you didn't actually know my dad, did you?"

The midget shrugged. "The story of men in Chinatown is the story of struggle—the struggle against the same things, unfortunately. The guys who made it out of the cycle, from what I saw, didn't get out until their kids finished college and sent back money." The midget looked up at me, raising an eyebrow. "I guess your dad had it all riding on you. He was treading water, waiting for his son to come back with a lifeboat."

"He wasn't struggling to keep his head up, you know? He gambled away money and spent a good chunk on prostitutes, too!"

"Robert," said the midget in a soothing voice, "don't you know by now that the duty of a Chinese son is to overlook the shortcomings of his parents?"

"What are the other duties of a son?"

"Having more sons to continue the line."

"That's it?"

"You say that like it's easy to raise kids. You don't know how hard it is dealing with a smaller version of yourself."

I was about to say something when the midget jumped up and pointed his finger at me.

"No! Don't you dare say it!" he said, smiling with his mouth open.

I couldn't say anything because I was laughing too hard at the thought of it.

21

I STOPPED CONDUCTING MY "COMMUNITY SESSIONS" IN THE BACK of the midget's toy store. It wasn't fair for me to be bringing people's problems into a place trying to conduct business. Apart from being dangerous—if more human snakes came in, snakeheads would surely take a serious interest in the place—it was just plain bad feng shui.

I did miss doing it, though. It was a nice way to wrap up the day, fielding questions and feeling like I was making an immediate difference for the better.

One day I fought the temptation to go to the store or a bar by going to a late-night over-rice place on Division Street that nobody ever went to. I half suspected the place was a front. I ordered some steamed chicken buns and read through the newspapers.

Usually the three newspapers would run wildly divergent editorials that made readers think they were reading about Chinese people in three different parallel universes.

But today they all said the same thing: Ethnic Chinese in newly united Vietnam were catching hell.

Chinese allegedly had collaborated with American forces during the war. They were branded as bloodsuckers for controlling Vietnam's economy and not spending any money where they made it. Vietnamese— with a newfound confidence from winning the war—were marching into Chinatowns and confiscating property, raping women, and conducting summary executions.

It sounded like the Vietnamese had picked up some things from the Americans.

Ethnic Chinese refugees, some who had been in Vietnam for three or four generations, were trickling into China, Hong Kong, and Taiwan. More people had wanted to leave, but the Vietnamese government charged ridiculous "exit fees" to exploit people on the way out.

I thought about the snakeheads, who exploited Chinese on their way into America.

Chinamen were exploited around the world whether they wanted to stay put or go anywhere. How would my father have done if he had never left Canton? I wouldn't have been born, but maybe that was the upside to it. He couldn't have known that his own people were going to screw him over so badly and that I would grow up to let him down so hard.

I felt mad again, but the only thing I could do about it right now was chew each bite of the chicken buns well before swallowing.

A young woman came in and ordered some buns to go. When she saw me, she came over and sat at my table. Her purse made a funny clunking sound when she put it on the empty chair next to her. She had on way too much makeup and perfume.

"Stephanie," I said. "Does your dad know you're out this late?"

"It's not even ten P.M.!"

"You're not twenty-one yet, are you?"

"I'm nineteen, okay? I'm old enough to drink!"

"We're not talking about a question of age. It's just not safe for you as a woman to be out this late by yourself. You also shouldn't be wearing a blouse that I can see your bra through."

"Well, why are you looking?"

"You're basically shoving it in my face."

"I know you can't help yourself," she said, lying back in her chair to stretch her blouse tighter against her body. "You're a man. I'm a woman. It's a natural reaction."

"You're asking for trouble, Stephanie."

"But I feel very safe with you, Robert." She leaned across the table and tilted her head at an angle.

"Do you feel safe because I'm a cop or because you've got a gun in your purse?"

She jerked back and crossed her arms. "You have no right to search through my purse!"

"I don't have to. It's as obvious as your bra."

"It's not mine, okay?"

"I know. You're just holding it for your wannabe-gangster boyfriend, right?"

"I don't have a boyfriend. It's my father's gun. I took it so I could protect myself. There are gunshots all the time!"

"Because chumps like you are arming themselves. Do you even know how to shoot a gun?"

"It's not hard. Switch the safety off and pull the trigger."

I shook my head. This was why Chinese kids shot bystanders more often than the intended targets. They never aimed carefully, never kept their wrists straight, and fired their Saturday night specials with one hand without bracing with the other hand. I heard about a punk who broke his own nose when he punched himself in the face as the gun kicked back.

I looked hard at Stephanie.

"Look, little girl," I said. "Don't you know that—statistically—if you carry a gun, you're more likely to get shot?"

"But at least I get to shoot back!"

"Why does your dad even have a gun, Stephanie? Is it because he's involved with human smuggling and needs to protect himself?"

"He meets with a lot of illegals, but he's not the one bringing them over. He only has the gun because he gets death threats from the anti-Communists!"

"You ever hear anyone call him Brother Five?"

"No. He doesn't even have any brothers."

"I see. In any case, I'm going to have to take that gun, Stephanie."

"What! No, please don't! My father will kill me!"

"He won't do it with this gun, at least." I opened up a cloth napkin and pushed it to her. "Take the gun out, put it under this, and slide it back to me."

She sighed and followed my instructions. It was a .45 automatic. I took out the clip and put it under my right thigh. I wrapped the gun in the napkin and put it under my right elbow.

"You're lucky I'm not charging you with unlawful possession of a firearm. If your father wants his gun back, tell him to come see me. Of course, I'll need to see his gun permit as well. He has one, right?"

"Of course he does. Anyway, everybody knows you guys are on the side of the KMT!"

"No we're not! If you were Chiang Kai-shek I'd still take your gun."

"You always have representatives at the KMT events. Your captain even went to the Greater China Association's New Year's banquet."

"He did?"

"Oh yeah."

"That's not surprising. We send representatives to all the major events in Chinatown."

"Almost all of those are aligned with the KMT, because they've been here longer and they scare people with their anti-Communist propaganda. Mainland China associations are smaller, but we're growing quickly. In a decade we'll be a real political force."

"What do you care, Stephanie? You won't be in Chinatown by that point."

"Who the hell are you to question my political conviction? I intend to be here after law school and for sure my father will be in Chinatown. By then, the U.S. will have full diplomatic ties with China—not with Taiwan or the KMT!"

"No way. That would be a slap in the face to everyone who fought Communism in Vietnam."

"Vietnam was a huge mistake, Robert. America deserved to lose."

"So men deserved to die?"

"You told me yourself," Stephanie said, getting up. "If you carry a gun, you're more likely to get shot."

I hate it when people turn around what you said to them. They should really come up with their own shit.

I saw Paul back at the apartment.

"Robert, what were you doing with that girl in the restaurant?" he asked. "I was walking by, but you looked too busy to say 'Hi' to me."

"I didn't go there to meet her or anything. I was there and she happened to show up."

"A girl who looks like that only shows up when she's called."

"Stephanie's a decent girl. She goes to Yale. She just likes to dress provocatively."

"For what?"

"Some women try to control men with their sex appeal."

"Does it work?"

"Let me ask you something. If that girl had come up to you and asked you to buy her dinner, would you do it?"

"It depends on what I would get in return."

"Whoa, tiger! You might be getting a lot more than you bargained for!" I showed him the empty gun. "Look at this. Some girls are loaded with more than looks."

* * *

Early the next day Stephanie's dad, Mr. Song, came into the detective squad office and conferred briefly with English. The only words I picked up were "lawyer," "illegal search," and "jerk."

Then English came over to me. "Let's just make this easy on everybody. Just give him his piece back."

"He's got a CCW?" I asked, already opening my middle drawer for Song's automatic.

"Yeah, yeah."

"But his daughter doesn't."

"She took it without my knowledge!" said Mr. Song, stepping over to my desk. "Sometimes she's very irresponsible."

I gave him back his automatic and the bullet clip.

"Mr. Song," I said, walking downstairs with him. "I'm sorry I inconvenienced you. Could I take you to lunch to make up for it? I'd like to talk to you about some personal things, too."

"Well, okay, but not in this part of town," he grumbled.

He took me to a place on Catherine Street that I'd never been to. It wasn't a fancy joint, but Mr. Song got the royal treatment on the way in and the cooks came out to shake his hand. He didn't bother to introduce me and nobody asked him who I was.

They gave us a seat in the back booth close to a burbling fish tank filled with floating shadows. The gasping, doomed faces of the fish emerged from the murky water when they crowded directly against the glass.

"You're very popular here," I said in English.

"I've helped a lot of people and solved a lot of problems," said Mr. Song.

"Tell me about the death threats you've gotten."

"I've been getting them for years," he said, enjoying a long nervous laugh. "This is not news to you guys or the police commissioner. That's how I got the license to carry."

"What's happened lately?"

"Just the usual. Every few months, we get a call from a pay phone. Saying, you know, 'Die!'"

"Who's making these calls?"

"I don't know, but I'm sure they're KMT backers."

"Maybe they're snakeheads."

"Why would snakeheads threaten me? I help the illegal immigrants when they run into immigration trouble. Unintentionally I help preserve the snakeheads' reputations of getting people over here safely."

I shifted a little bit in my seat.

"Mr. Song," I said, "can you tell me exactly how these people are brought into Chinatown?"

"I'm going to get a Coke. It cuts through the grease. You want one?" he asked. I didn't. He made a single hand gesture to a waiter and a can appeared instantly.

"Okay, Robert," said Mr. Song, "the story of the illegal Chinese has changed dramatically. Earlier this century, people came with fake documentation, saying they were the sons of Chinese already here. People already here would sell the fake documents and the so-called paper sons would come over. Naturally, the price was pretty steep and usually took a few years to repay."

"Oh," I said, "that's very interesting."

"With that method, the worst that could happen is that you ended up being detained for a while by the American authorities and questioned constantly to see if you were lying or not. Your life was not in danger and your actual transit was safe and comfortable on a passenger ship.

"Now, the typical story is that the snakeheads bring people over en masse in freighter holds to Mexico and sneak them across the border into the U.S. A few people die on the way over, and because these ships don't have sanitary facilities to accommodate all these people they ride the entire time in their own diseased filth."

"That's terrible. Why do they come up through Mexico? Wouldn't it be easier to just land in the U.S.?"

"Ah! It seems like it, but there's always a chance they'll get caught by the U.S. Coast Guard. Landing in Mexico is much easier. Then once at the Mexican-U.S. border there are already-established smuggling routes and guides. Once they are brought across, it's usually a long ride in the back of a truck to New York, or wherever the final destination is. The snakehead himself finances everything, bribes the right people, but is usually pretty far removed from the operations. The human snakes only meet the minor figures in the smuggling hierarchy."

"They might not know who the snakehead is?"

"They know who the little snakeheads are, the ones who recruited them in China, but not the big one."

"How much does it cost now? I've read that it's ten thousand."

"That's about right. One thousand as a down payment and the rest is due after arriving. The illegals are under the impression the debt can be paid off gradually, but the less scrupulous snakeheads—and there are more of them now—demand immediate payment when they arrive. The human snakes will be held prisoner in a safe house until the balance is paid."

"How are they supposed to get the money?"

"Two ways," Mr. Song said. "If their own families and friends in China can't scrape up enough, they have to go to a loan shark in their village and wire the money over. The callous snakehead is not in the business of sitting back and making money from high-interest-rate loans. It's pretty much a cash-on-the-barrel-now deal."

"How do you help the human snakes?"

"They are here illegally and we try to get them a legal status. Political asylum is a pretty safe bet, usually, especially if they're Christian. The Communists officially ban all religions."

"Is that why there are so many Fukienese churches? So the people can go to them and pretend to be Christian in order to stay in this country?"

Mr. Song looked at me and frowned deeply. "A lot of Americans who go to church pretend to adhere to Christian beliefs," he said.

Just then two dishes and two bowls of soup swung in. I saw the dreaded orange patch of a cooked shrimp.

"I really should have said this sooner," I said, "but I'm allergic to seafood."

"You're allergic to seafood! There's shrimp paste in everything!"

"I know. I didn't remember that Fukienese cooking was like that until just now."

"Jesus, what kind of Chinamen are we? They already know I can't have alcohol and now you can't eat seafood! Don't you know that wine and shrimp paste are the two pillars of Fukienese cooking?"

"Well, more for you to eat right here. Don't worry about me, I can get something later."

"No, that's not right. Let's just get you something now."

He called a waiter over and they talked in Fukienese. The waiter was shocked, and when he looked at me his face said, "Why the hell did you guys come here to eat?"

When the waiter left, Mr. Song said, "I just got you some beef chow fun."

"Can't go wrong with that," I said.

"Tell my daughter. She's a vegetarian."

"Your daughter's a little out of control."

"She has to learn and life is the greatest teacher." He sighed and turned to me. "She never listens to me, anyway. I give her a hard time about who she hangs out with, she comes back at me with a cheap shot about being an alcoholic."

"Please, Mr. Song, start eating. Don't wait for me."

"No, if we abandon our manners, we're animals."

"We're just rude people, not animals."

"I was an animal before I got dried out," said Mr. Song firmly but quietly. "I don't even remember the night my wife left me, but Stephanie told me I had hit her. I'm very ashamed about it."

"Hey, you know, I used to think the best time to have a beer was right after having a beer."

He made a sound in his throat and gave a tight smile. My chow fun hit the table and we finally started to eat.

"How did you get involved with Together Chinese Kinship?" I asked.

"My family is Fukienese, but we have been in Taiwan for a few generations. Fukienese people have very tight family connections, I think because Fujian Province is cut off from the rest of China by mountains. It's almost easier to take a boat across the strait to Taiwan than to get to other mainland provinces. Culturally we're very self-sufficient and eager to travel.

"I came here from Taiwan to study as a Japanese citizen, because at the time the island was a colony."

"I know that," I said.

"So I came here and got my law degree. After World War Two I got my American citizenship and started working at a corporate law firm. I brought over my parents from Taiwan and they reconnected with many of their old friends here in New York. They all started a Fukienese friendship organization in the late fifties—and of course, they didn't choose to have a political stance at this time.

"You know what they say, whenever a Chinese group is launched, within a year some people will defect and start up a rival group. Then we had all these little groups. But they still had many common interests. A few years before when China was finally admitted to the U.N. and Taiwan was ejected, all the groups came together to form an umbrella organization, Together Chinese Kinship. Because I was a prominent lawyer at the time, I was made chairman."

"What sort of lawyer were you?"

"Did you remember the farm-fertilizer business sale by Mobil Chemical? I had a hand in that."

"I would never put my hand in fertilizer."

"That's very funny, but just for your information, it was a very big deal. Very big. Anyway, to continue my story, immediately after the association started, boy, the Greater China Association and their constituents really came after us. They were already biased against Fukienese, but now they organized boycotts of Fukienese restaurants. Just a few years ago they demanded that I remove the Chinese flag from our office building. Which is ridiculous, because it was already flying at the United Nations. They demonized me, too. I've seen posters with my picture that say: 'Number One Chinese Communist Criminal!' I've never even been to the mainland, so they don't even know what they're talking about!"

"But you would go if you had the chance to, right?"

"Who wouldn't want to see China? All that history and culture staring you in the face?"

"Then why do these Fukienese want to get out so badly that they're willing to pay snakeheads?"

"Well, that's different," said Mr. Song. "They want a chunk of the prosperity that America offers to hard workers."

"And China doesn't offer that?"

"China offers equality without as much potential upside. These people are willing to endure serious hardships for a better life, like the original American colonial settlers."

"Don't you worry that you might be helping criminals who are mixed in with the human snakes?"

"I would say that they would fit in nicely among the original American colonists. Anyway, you guys are effectively allowing gambling, prostitution, and extortion in Chinatown."

"We're not allowing it. We just need more people to come forward and meet us halfway. Nobody will do it."

"Because they're cowards. The KMT sanctions those activities and has all the dissenters scared like sheep. When the KMT set about to conquer the hearts and minds of the people, that meant threatening to shoot people in their chests and heads if they didn't toe the line."

"But there's no gambling in Communist Chinatown, right?" I asked with an eyebrow raised.

"It's not as bad as the other parts," Mr. Song conceded. "We can't afford as many tables."

"So that's why the groups in Together Chinese Kinship have turned to smuggling as a source of revenue. Right, Brother Five?"

He put down his chopsticks and wiped his mouth with a napkin. Mr. Song seemed like a man who kept eating until just the bones were left, broken and with the marrow sucked out. To him, this break in eating was the most annoying thing in the world.

"I see what you're getting at, Robert. As I've said before, it's not the Fukienese who are the snakeheads. Yes, maybe at the local level in China there are Fukienese little snakeheads recruiting human snakes, but the big snakeheads are not Fukienese. It's either Taiwanese or Hong Kong people. They are the ones with the money and the ships. We try to bring our people over in the legal and safe way—through sponsorship!"

He crossed his arms and waited for me to say something.

"Mr. Song, I don't see how you can be so sure that you know what all your members are up to at all times. Believe me, it's not up to you to police your own people."

"I know for sure that no Fukienese are involved at the top," he said. Mr. Song picked up his chopsticks again. "A Fukienese would not put another Fukienese through such a horrible, life-threatening experience! Those other people—they don't care!

"They wouldn't even hire Fukienese to work in their restaurants until they had those labor problems this year! They know Fukienese will tolerate worse conditions than a Cantonese would! Go ask that Tin fellow about the smuggling! He knows all about it!"

"What makes you so sure he does?"

"Because he has the means to keep tabs on nearly everything that happens in Chinatown!"

I thought of Irene. "Oh, I wouldn't be too sure of that!" I said. "I think he's got a blind spot under his belt." I continued eating as Mr. Song looked at me carefully, trying to decide if I'd been drinking or not.

That night was an unusual one for me because I was at home reading a book, or, more accurately, trying to read a book.

"I've never noticed how dim it is in the apartment," I said to Paul. "This forty-watt ceiling bulb isn't cutting it."

"You told me to get used to it," said Paul. He was on the floor, reading *The New York Times*. "So I got used to it."

"Maybe I need a floor lamp in here. This isn't bright enough for you to study by."

"You've already destroyed my eyes enough so that it doesn't matter anymore."

"After you go blind, I'll buy the newspaper on tape for you."

"You'll probably end up getting the wrong day, too." He leaned out on one elbow and looked at me. "Are you able to get through that or do you need a dictionary?"

"I'm fine without a dictionary," I said casually. I had already spent more time reading the glossary in the back than the actual text to *The Pentagon Papers*. "What are you doing with this book, anyway, Paul?"

"I was in the Asian history section and this caught my eye."

"I mean, why did you even want to pick this up?"

"Robert, the Vietnam War was the first time America was defeated in battle! A whole nation realized that it wasn't invincible and even as it turned two hundred years old it was time for some soul-searching!"

"Well, not for me," I said. I closed the book and tossed it to the floor next to Paul. "I was there. I don't need to read about it, man. Just burn the thing."

"Brilliant and well argued," said Paul.

The phone rang. We both looked at the windup clock on top of the TV.

"Should be safe, by your calculations," said Paul.

"I don't know. I don't like the tone of that ring."

He shook his head.

"Look," I said. "I'm getting the phone, all right?" I got up and went to the bedroom.

"Hello," I said as pleasantly as I could into the receiver.

There was a brief pause before a gruff voice told me, "You're playing a dangerous game."

"Are you threatening me, Mr. Tin?"

"When I trust the care of my son to somebody, I expect that person to know the difference between right and wrong and the difference between freedom and communism! I heard you were seen dining with the head of Together Chinese Kinship!"

"Do you want me to call the New York State Office of Mental Health? I'm sure they can take great care of Don."

"No, no. Don't. Please."

"You're one to talk about right and wrong, Mr. Tin," I said, feeling that I was gaining the moral high ground. "How about I call Irene's husband?"

"I don't care if you do," he sniffed. "I've been very good friends with both of them for years."

"I think you're somewhat closer to Irene, though."

"Hmph." He had called to blow off steam at me, but I had doused him with cold water.

"Mr. Tin, why do restaurants overseen by your association employ illegal immigrants?"

"What! First of all, the Greater China Association does not 'oversee' anybody. We are pro-business advocates for our members, who all affirm that they stand for a free and democratic China."

"I know for a fact that restaurants run by members of the Greater China Association employ illegal Fukienese immigrants!" I bluffed. "Particularly Willie Gee and Jade Palace!"

"Yes," started Mr. Tin. "I have noticed Fukienese working there, but they are not illegals. Mr. Gee is one of our more upstanding members. I am sure he would not engage in illegal activities."

"Mr. Tin, I think we need to talk in person."

"You think it's a good idea for me to be seen entertaining someone who doesn't think he's above consorting with Communists?"

"Hey, at least I wasn't out with a white girl!"

22

MR. TIN PICKED ME UP IN FRONT OF MY APARTMENT IN HIS CHAUF-
feured black four-door Continental.

As soon as I got in the back with him, Mr. Tin scooted over and
slammed down the divider cushion.

"You used to steal the emblems from cars like these, right?" he said.
"Because you were in that deviant group, the Continentals?"

"It was a long time ago. I was young and stupid."

"You know something? You haven't been acting much smarter these
days." He told the driver to take the scenic route around Chinatown
and slid the privacy window closed. "Look at you, Robert. You used to
vandalize cars and now you're a cop."

"I used to kill people, too, and burn their villages down."

"But that was in the name of doing the greater good. We can't be
gentle in the face of communism!"

"What's so bad about communism?"

He made a funny sound in his throat, but it turned out that Mr. Tin
was one of those guys whose laugh sounded like he was choking.

"Robert, let me be the first to tell you that communism is a beautiful idea. It really is. Everybody being treated the same and sharing equally. But it's an idea that doesn't work in practice.

"Let's say you were working in a kitchen and you gave everyone coming through one half bowl of rice because there was a shortage that season. Then you see your mother and father in line. Are you going to give them only half a bowl of rice or just a little bit more?"

"I might give them both a little bit less than half a bowl."

"I'm serious, Robert! What kind of animal would be able to give his parents only half a bowl? And what about the rest of your family and your friends? What if your girlfriend, the bakery girl, came up to you saying she was hungry? Could you give her just half a bowl?"

"Well, if she really needed something to eat, she would just steal some pastries from work."

"That's exactly my point! Communism leads to theft and other crime!"

We were stuck at a light near Grand Street. A group of dishwashers and other kitchen staff in grubby uniforms were squatting on the sidewalk and smoking. It seemed like a short break from a long night.

"Look at our people," said Mr. Tin. He shook his head and breathed in noisily through his teeth. "Living these broken-up lives on the broken-up sidewalk. The Chinese people have a noble and illustrious history, but here we're just the lowliest of the lowly. Our ancestors endured war after war in the hope that we would someday have a united and strong country. All we have to show for it are these guys, a Communist mainland, and a democratic and free China on just one pissant island."

He seemed genuinely sad.

"Our ancestors also didn't expect their children's children to work twelve to fourteen hours a day and get paid below minimum wage," I said.

"Our ancestors aren't responsible for everything," he suddenly snapped. "They did what they could, but one always controls one's destiny to a certain degree. If these workers don't like their jobs, they could quit and get better jobs. No, they *should* quit and get better jobs!"

"The problem is that the restaurant owners get together and fix the wages. They also blacklist the 'troublemakers'—you know, the guys who try to organize unions."

"They should blacklist them! Do you know what unions would do to Chinatown!"

"Make people happy?"

"Nobody would be happy! The wages would be raised! Then the menu prices would have to be raised! Then the customers wouldn't come anymore! Then the restaurant closes! A lose-lose situation for everybody!"

"Couldn't the wages be increased without hurting the restaurant?"

"When you let the unions in, the sky's the limit! Every year, they want a percentage increase higher than the inflation rate. So what does that mean? Customers are subject to inflation, too! If you give wage increases higher than the inflation rate, tourists end up paying more percentage-wise when the check comes. The white people aren't stupid. When the prices go too high, they'll find somewhere else to eat. Look at how the Japanese are destroying our unionized car industry! Unions and communism are a one-two punch to the face of humanity."

He had thrown me off-track by talking about inflation. I didn't know much about economics, and Paul wasn't here for me to pick his brain.

"Mr. Tin, let's just talk about what we're here for. Let's talk about illegals working here and who's bringing them over."

He sighed and pulled out a silver case from his vest pocket. He picked out a cigarette and slipped the case back. He powered the window down a crack and lit up from a Bicentennial Zippo. "You don't mind, do you?" he asked, smoke coming out his nose.

"I don't care."

"From my standpoint, those illegal immigrants are heroes. We should welcome them as survivors from unfair systems. The Fukienese illegals are escaping from the misery of communism. The Hong Kong illegals are fleeing the tyranny of colonialism. They should be allowed to come here and work as much as they want."

"I think a lot of them are working much more than they want and more than they ever thought they would."

"That's exactly what I'm talking about!" said Mr. Tin, missing my point completely. "They can make more money here than they ever dreamed! They climb the ladder! America always rewards hard work!"

"So you would knowingly hire illegal Fukienese?"

"Sure I would! Not only that, I would hire as many as I could! There's more than enough work available! That's the best thing about China-town. There's work if you want it. Not like the rest of America, which is headed to almost double-digit unemployment! That's what unions have done to this country! Chinese people could do it the right way!"

I had a vision of coast-to-coast sweatshops and over-rice restaurants with outposts of the Greater China Association in every town. I saw people soaked in sweat even during their brief sleeping hours.

"You know what?" Mr. Tin asked. "I would go get the ethnic Chi-nese from Vietnam and bring them here! Get all of them jobs here!"

"The same way that your association helps smuggle in Fukienese?"

"Oh, I see! You're trying to trap me by my own words, huh?"

"Anyone ever call you Brother Five, Mr. Tin?"

"Of course not! What's the meaning of this?"

"The Fukienese don't have the money or the ships to bring people over. So it figures that the more established, um, capitalist Chinese do."

"Even though I'm sure our members do have necessary materials and desire to be snakeheads, they do not have the political capital. How are we going to be able to land ships in China? Do you know how much scrutiny a Taiwanese ship gets in Hong Kong? On top of all that, do you think a decent person would feel safe being at sea with a shipload of Communists? They could mutiny and kill the crew! My only view of it is that once they are already here, once the illegals have a foot on dry land, then we should help them and give them jobs."

"That's against the law."

"Listen, Robert. A lot of people employ illegals without even knowing. Most of them have paperwork that looks legitimate! How are they supposed to know? You were born here. That's easy to see. Now if you looked at a legal immigrant next to an illegal, how can you tell the difference? They look the same. They both don't know English too well."

"I guess you can tell which is which by the way one guy will work for half of what the other guy will."

"It's competition! You have to allow people to pick and choose how much they are willing to work for and, overall, what they want to do with their lives!"

"Mr. Tin, if only you had given the same freedom to Don, he might be all right now."

"I had everything set up for him!" he exploded. "I had the right school, the right girl, and the right job!"

"You wouldn't let him choose anything for himself! You keep talking about how great freedom is, but you never let your son have his!"

"Robert, don't be offended, but you must realize that Don was meant for a higher rung in society than you and everybody you know. There are more restrictions at higher levels of society and, yes, there is conversely a lower level of personal freedoms. That is the price one pays for being a leader!

"Don could be an important businessman right this very second! Don made the biggest mistake in his life by signing up for the army!"

"It might have been a mistake. But if you don't let people make mistakes, you don't allow them to learn to live their lives."

"Where did your father come from?" he asked.

"Why does it matter?"

"I'm curious."

"He was from a small Toisanese-speaking town in Canton—Toisan."

"There are only small towns in Canton, because it's one of the country's poorest provinces!"

"Guangzhou is a city."

"Ha! You call that a city? Do you know where I'm from? My family's from Shanghai. We were the top class of the elite! Even the white people had to defer to us! Look at you, Robert. You don't even know Mandarin."

"I know enough."

"How come you don't speak Toisanese? Didn't your father speak Toisanese to you?"

"My parents figured that since we were in America I should only know Cantonese. With all the Hong Kong people coming in, it seemed like the way to go."

"I know Toisanese, also, Robert. In fact, it's a requirement for the leader of the Greater China Association to know the dialect in order to fully embrace the people of traditional Chinatown. The people who were here before all the Cantonese speakers streamed in from Hong Kong.

"Your girlfriend, Robert. She's a Hong Kong girl, right?"

"She's an American girl."

"Ha, you're joking with me. Yes, she is a very pretty girl! Better watch her closely!"

"Mr. Tin, I thought you had a taste for white women."

He sucked in the smile on his face. "I told you that you're playing a dangerous game, Robert, and you're not even waiting for your turn."

I looked out the window. We were looping back to my neighborhood. I noticed that Tin's driver had something under his shirt that stuck up the fabric at the shoulders like owl tufts.

"Is this car bulletproof?" I asked.

"Yes. Why do you ask?"

"Your driver's wearing a bulletproof vest."

"He's armed, too." Mr. Tin lit up another cigarette. "That Song guy isn't the only one who gets death threats!"

"Before I forget, let me give this to you." I emptied my pockets of Don's radio set and gave the parts to Mr. Tin. "I got a new crystal for it, but I was too scared to give it back to Don. I thought he could hurt himself with it. But it was nice of you to try to give it back to him."

Mr. Tin nodded and fell silent.

When I came back to the apartment, Paul surprised me by saying, "I was worried about you!"

"But Mom, I'm a big boy now," I said, taking off my shoes.

"Seriously, Robert. Don't get into a car with any of the association guys—KMT or Communist! It's bad news!"

"I can protect myself, Paul. I'm a big boy with a big gun." I patted the revolver on my back to reassure myself.

"Look, Robert. You know those associations hire gangs on a freelance basis to guard gambling halls and prostitution houses."

"Of course I know! You think you know more about it than me?"

"Well, what happens if the gang is unhappy about the amount it was paid? Do you want to be sitting in the car when there's a hail of bullets? Even if there isn't gunfire, do you want to be a passenger in a car that's photographed as it idles outside a massage parlor?"

"Don't tell me how to do my job! I was interviewing someone regarding my case!" I sulked off to the fridge. A year ago I would have been popping open a beer. Now I pulled out a can of Yoo-Hoo. "Want one?" I asked Paul as I propped the door open.

He shook his head. "Weren't you the one who warned me about getting too close to associations when I was working at the gambling joint?" he asked.

"That's different, Paul, and you know it. You're just a kid that they would take advantage of. They wouldn't try to mess with me."

"How do you think Internal Affairs would feel about you associating with them?"

"I've got nothing to hide. I'm not scared of anything." I took a good swig of Yoo-Hoo and swallowed it. "Also, you just keep your mouth shut. If anyone asks, say you don't know where I was at."

"That's exactly what I did."

"What do you mean, what you did?"

"That's what I did when the guy from Internal Affairs called."

"When did this happen?"

"I went by the guidelines you drew up, Robert. I answered the phone seventeen minutes after the hour. Here's his number." He handed me a piece of paper.

"What did he say?"

"He said he wanted to talk to you and that he was from Internal Affairs."

I examined the phone number. Manhattan. What did I expect to glean from that?

"Why the fuck are they calling me?" I asked the scrawled phone number.

"I don't know," Paul answered. "Are you going to call him back?"

"Of course I will." I leaned against the wall. "How did he sound? Angry, happy?"

"Sounded casual. Like he had something on you."

What was it all about? I hadn't taken any gifts or money. I hadn't even gotten any free meals.

I came around and pounded the counter.

"Dammit!" I yelled. "If this is about getting free meals and taking those red envelopes at the grand openings I used to go to—"

"You took money, Robert? How could you?"

"It was bad luck not to take the money!"

"Looks like it's brought you some bad luck."

"Of course that fucking rat was all casual! Taking money in envelopes sounds bad, but that's completely outside of the cultural context! Those Internal Affairs assholes get promotions based on busting cops for bullshit like this!"

"You didn't spend the money, did you?"

"I did. A fool and his money are soon parted, right?"

"Does the fool go to jail after?"

"I'm not going to jail, Paul. Worse comes to worst, I'm going to get roped into Internal Affairs. That's how they build up the department. They figure it takes a crook to catch a crook."

"You're a crook?"

"No! Shit, I'm going to call this guy and tell him that giving token amounts of money is a part of Chinese culture and trying to nail me on it is racist!"

I marched over to the phone and spun the dial, making angry flicks with my index finger. Waiting for the dial to reset with each number only made me madder. My jaw tightened and my left hand squeezed the handset hard.

But when I heard the phone ringing, my hands shook in fear. I tried to swallow, but no moisture was there. I contemplated life in the hated rat squad.

After four rings a man lazily asked, "Hello?"

My anger came back full force. "Eddie, you son of a bitch! You had me shitting my pants!"

23

I WAS AMAZED AT EDDIE'S ABILITY TO CRACK HIMSELF UP.

"Oh, man, if you could have only heard your voice!" he said, breaking into another long laugh. "It was genuine anger and relief, with a hint of amusement."

We were sitting in a back booth in Junior's, the Brooklyn diner at the east end of the Manhattan Bridge, which ran over the East River. The west end of the bridge was Canal Street in Chinatown.

"I guarantee you, there was no amusement," I said. "Don't joke about Internal Affairs, man! I don't know how it is in San Francisco, but here that department is staffed by backstabbers and snitches."

"We don't have any crooked cops out there, so I don't know what it's like."

We were both halfway through beef-brisket sandwiches.

"Make sure you save room for cheesecake," I said.

"I don't like cheesecake."

"It's good here."

"I should say that dairy doesn't like me."

"Along with everyone else."

"Only bad guys don't like me."

"Yeah, speaking of which, how is it going with Ng?"

Eddie took a bite from his sandwich and talked with his mouth full. "Going good. Trusting dumbfuck is negotiating an offer with me. Got a lot of stuff on him."

"Jesus, Eddie, you eat like a dog! It's gross watching you."

"I've been out in New York City too long! I can't wait to get done and get back to being human again. Go down to SoCal for the beach. To hell with this place."

I coughed into my hand and took a drink of water. I didn't think I had much pride in my city, but at the same time I didn't like to hear people put it down.

"You know," I told Eddie, "you have to at least appreciate the lifestyle just a little bit. Think about it. You don't need a car, so you don't need to worry about parking or traffic jams or paying insurance every month."

"But then you walk around in the dingy streets like a freaking maggot crawling through trash at the bottom of a garbage bin. Chinatown's even worse. I hate walking around there, hate eating there. Shit, I just hate *being* there."

"They don't have street cleaning there because the streets are too narrow for the sanitation trucks with the brushes to get through."

"I'm not talking about that. I'm talking about the people, man. They just disgust me."

"You're talking about the restaurant guy who wouldn't file a complaint?"

"Yeah, I mean, that's a part of it, but it's mostly people who are just resigned to go day to day with their crummy jobs. I actually empathize more with the gang kids and even guys like Ng who are trying to make something out of themselves. These other people live life on their knees, waiting tables, washing dishes, working at bakery counters. . . ."

"Hey! You're making fun of people who live honest and productive lives! Are you really a cop?"

"Jesus, calm down, man! Yes, I know I'm a cop. I'm busting that Ng guy, right? I'm just not making the same mistake that you are, Robert."

"What mistake am I making?"

"You know, you think you're one of them."

"Oh, you're not Chinese, now?"

"You and I were both born here. They are immigrants from China, Hong Kong, or Taiwan. We are different from them."

"You mean you think you're better than them."

"Yeah, you're right. I do think I'm better, but you know what? They think I'm better than them, too. They might make fun of us behind our backs, but is there one of them who wouldn't trade places with either of us?"

I ate without saying anything.

"I guess I hit a soft spot with you, Robert," Eddie said. "You were born in Chinatown, so you have warm and fuzzy memories associated with it."

"No I don't. I spent my childhood thinking I was stuck here, so I joined a gang and fought other kids and did petty crimes. I wasn't sure what to do with my life, and when the draft came I welcomed it. I thought it was a way to serve my country and that it was a career for me."

"You really bought into the bullshit, didn't you?"

"I did."

"That whole patriotic thing was crap. Thinking that you're serving your country or the cause of freedom is an illusion." Then Eddie leaned in on me. "So is thinking that people in Chinatown are your people. Robert, you're going to transfer out at some point, so just save the ones that you can. Get Lonnie out of there. Get Paul out, too."

"They know how to take care of themselves."

"Can they dodge a stray bullet? Or can you rush there in time to catch it with your teeth?"

"It's not completely safe, yes, but there are worse neighborhoods in the city."

"Well then, tell me again why the hell you live out here. Dude, if you want to get really serious about this whole thing called life, move on out to California. I can find you a spot on the job. It pays more, too. Course, going out that far would probably mean that you and Lonnie get married first."

"Now that's a trip we're not ready for yet. When are you getting married?"

"I am in no rush at all. My old man didn't get married until he was forty-four."

"Unlucky age."

"He had me and he's still healthy, so how unlucky could he be?"

A waiter came by and cleared our plates. I ordered a slice of cheesecake with a strawberry topping. It came back instantly.

"You can have some strawberries and the graham-cracker crust," I said.

Eddie picked out a strawberry and popped it into the side of his mouth. "You're so generous," he said. "Will you let me lick your plate when you're done?"

"The fork, too," I said. "Hey, ah, Eddie, I was wondering something. You ever hear anybody call Ng Brother Five?"

"No."

"Does the number five mean anything in triad culture?"

"Not by itself. Triad titles start with the number four."

"Isn't the number four bad luck?"

"You're thinking of mainstream Chinese culture, with 'four' sounding like 'death.' In triad culture, 'four' represents the four directions and four seas. I'm sure they also love the association with 'death,' as well, to both scare off the general public and reinforce to triad members how seriously they should take their oaths."

"So 'Brother Five' would be a nickname from outside the triad."

"Almost definitely. Maybe it comes from *The Amazing Chan and the Chan Clan.*"

"Eddie, how is it that you were able to come off as a triad member and not an outsider?"

"I have a master's degree in Chinese studies, Robert. My thesis was on subculture and criminality. I also have source material. You're not the only ABC who can read characters, you know. Besides, I have some acting chops."

"Yeah, but the triad tradition is just so intricate. I understand that you have to kind of live it and be steeped in it. There's no way you can really just sort of book-learn it."

"Robert, I didn't think I'd have to demystify Chinese stuff for you! There isn't anything too arcane or strange in our culture that can't be learned and understood."

"Telly Savalas couldn't have gone undercover in a triad, no matter what kind of wig he had."

"Yeah, the lollipop would have given him away. That's really not a triad thing to do."

"Are you telling me," I asked slowly, "that you have no triad connections in your family whatsoever? Because I know that even if I studied triad culture for years, they would have tripped me up on something." I took a bite of cheesecake and pushed it around my molars.

"I've got a great memory and I'm a fast learner."

"I know you're really smart, Eddie. I can see it in your humor, which really pushes the envelope, by the way. I think you could do stand-up. Anyway, I'm thinking that a guy who has a master's in Chinese studies instead of a medical, law, or engineering degree must come from a pretty comfortable family rather than strivers. Not to mention that you're a cop now. Not to mention that Ng probably did some checking up on you and your lineage back in the old country. What line of business is your family in?"

Eddie popped another strawberry in his mouth and folded his arms behind his head.

When he was ready, he said, "Robert, my family runs a legitimate import-export business. The industry is more arcane than any triad cultural references and you definitely can't bullshit your way through it."

"How come you didn't join the family business?"

"I didn't want to be sitting in an office pushing a pen around and punching numbers into a calculator, man. But after hanging out with Ng, it seems a lot more exciting, now. I have to see if my dad's been keeping two sets of books, too."

"Would you bust him on tax evasion?"

"If he is, I'm sure it's on such a small scale compared with Ng. It's in line with the typical fudging."

"Does your father smuggle people into the country, too?"

"Big-time. How do you think *I* got into this country? In fact, I'm out here to set up another leg to our smuggling network. By the way, want to buy some heroin?"

"Can it, Eddie."

"Seriously, Robert, smuggling hasn't been the focus of my investigation of Ng, but I haven't seen anything linking him to it."

"Nothing even remotely suspicious?"

"Wet footprints in his office? Thumping sounds coming from his car trunk? A ledger book recording monthly debt payments?"

"Sure. I'll take any of them."

"I've got nothing for you on that front. But he's been talking about cleaning up the family business, and his rivals within the family aren't going to like it. So I wouldn't be surprised to see some heavyweight do something about it."

"Why would they even care?"

Eddie shrugged. Despite earlier remarks that he was lactose intolerant, he stuck a forkful of cheesecake in his mouth and swallowed quickly. He sipped some water to clear his mouth.

"Ng might bring some of their dirty laundry to light," he said. "They're also probably mad that one of their own could break the oaths of secrecy and go legit. Maybe they're jealous that he's going to be able to live a life without having to check over his shoulder all the time. At least until I put him in jail."

"What kind of sentence do you get for tax evasion?"

"Al Capone got six and a half years in Club Fed. Ng'll get less."

"Why are we even bothering with him if he's only getting a light sentence?"

"This case is going to make the government a shitload of money—probably tens of millions of dollars! New York City's going to get its share. The Feds are gonna get their share. We don't need to put this guy in the slammer as much as we need his money. There's no big payoff to catching a murderer. But a tax evader? You hit the jackpot!"

"We're just going after Ng basically for the money? Are we just a bunch of thugs? There are worse people we could nail." I had a vision of Willie Gee in prison garb, ladling out gruel to bikers with swastika tattoos.

"You break the law," said Eddie, "we poke a hole in your money sack and you take a few pokes up your ass in the big house." He took another big bite of my cheesecake.

"Why are we cracking down on someone trying to go straight?"

"We're helping him go straight even faster!"

The check came and I took care of it after a token protest.

"I'll give you a ride back to Manhattan in my car," Eddie offered.

"I never turn down a free ride," I said.

"Oh, it ain't free. You're going to be paying big-time!" he said, smiling. "I told you—dairy doesn't like me!"

24

I WAS SLEEPING WHEN THE PHONE RANG. I WOKE UP SLOWLY, GROP-
ing in the dark, feeling annoyed and thirsty.

"Okay," I said into the receiver.

"Hey," said Vandyne, "I really hate to bother you, but can I come
over?"

"Sure," I said. "I'll see you soon."

I struggled to hang up the phone. I came out of my bedroom and
shook Paul awake. I told him to go sleep in the bed. I folded up the Cas-
tro Convertible so Vandyne and I could sit on it. I filled up a teapot with
cold water and put it on the stove to boil.

When my old partner calls me up and wants to come over, I don't ask
why. I say, "Yes." If he asked me to jump, I wouldn't even ask, "How
high?" I would just start jumping and hope it was good enough.

I would never question anything he asked of me. I knew he would
do the same for me. We trusted each other with our lives. Maybe our
souls, too.

When Vandyne came up, I saw that he was in bad shape. His face was puffy and his eyes were red. He sat down on the couch and wiped his mouth.

"What is that smell in here?" he asked. "Onions?"

"That's from the Make-a-Better Burger mix. We had 'em for dinner."

"I didn't know you cooked."

"I don't. Paul did. He's a smart kid, but if he had to, he could definitely fall back on flipping burgers."

"Rose left me," Vandyne said. "She's gone."

"Jesus!" I said.

"She didn't even say much on the way out. Just that she was at the end of the line with me, that we've lost touch with each other, and that I don't talk to her anymore."

"What did you say?"

"I didn't know what to say! I was in shock! So by being quiet, I only proved her right."

I moved to the counter and made a cup of Brim and a cup of Folgers. I brought them to the coffee table by the sofa and sat down next to Vandyne.

"The Brim's on the left, if you want decaf," I said.

"I'm not going to sleep anyway," he muttered, taking the Folgers. Damn, I thought. Now I was stuck with the Brim.

"How were things going?" I asked. "I mean, I never heard you say you and Rose were having a bad time."

"Deep down, somewhere, I knew there was something gone wrong. I didn't realize that what I was feeling doesn't just affect me. It affects everybody around me."

He drank his coffee. I took a sip of Brim. It was so bad it tasted like it was something good for my body.

Vandyne put down his cup and covered his eyes with his hands.

"If only somebody could have warned me," he moaned. "If there was just some way I could have gotten a telegram that my marriage was in trouble. Just something."

I put the Brim on the coffee table and tried to crack my wrist bones. "Maybe there was just no way of knowing," I said. "It was one of those things meant to happen. You know?"

"Yeah, maybe, partner. Maybe it was." He propped up his head in his hands and stared at nothing.

"This is probably just a temporary thing. You guys just need time away from each other."

"She did go to her sister's place. That's not too far away. Just embarrassing that they know we're having problems. Now that jerk knows everything."

"You mean your sister-in-law's husband, right?"

"Yeah. That one."

"You never told me he was Chinese, you know?"

Vandyne sat up. "I didn't think it mattered," he said, sounding defensive.

"If it doesn't matter, then why didn't you just tell me?"

"So if I have a problem with someone Chinese, I have to check in with you?"

"Of course! I might know the guy and straighten him out!"

"Believe me, you don't know this guy. Anyway, I don't think of you as Chinese."

"I'm not Chinese? You mean I'm not Chinese enough?"

"Naw, I see you as a brother." He held up a hand. "As my brother."

I nodded.

Vandyne crossed his arms and tilted his head. "Hey," he said. "How did you know Harry is Chinese?"

I took a long, deep breath, but it didn't give me enough time to think of something to say.

"You talked to Rose, right?" he asked.

"I did."

"Dammit, Chow! You held back on me!"

"Vandyne, I didn't know how serious it was! I thought maybe you guys were just having a small problem or something. She didn't say she was going to leave you and everything." I didn't remember her saying that, anyway.

"You talked to her today?"

"No, no! About a few days ago. You have to remember, we got together as two people who care about you."

"You got together with her! You saw her in person!"

"Yeah. For lunch."

"I bet she made you go to Chock full o'Nuts."

"We did go there."

He leaned over and balanced his elbows on his knees. "Oh, hell, I can't blame you, Chow. It wouldn't have made a difference if you had told me or not. I still wouldn't have known what to do. It's all my fault. The whole thing."

"What are you going to do now?"

"Just let her cool off for a few days before trying to contact her."

"She told you where she was going to stay. It probably means she wants you to go get her back."

"That could be it."

"She says you haven't been communicating much, so you should probably talk her ear off. Soon. Maybe send her flowers at work?"

"That's a good idea."

"Oh, and make sure you tell her how beautiful she is!"

"Hey," said Paul from the hallway. "How come I never get tips on women from you, Robert?"

"How come you never get any women?" I asked. "Why are you spying on us?"

"Your phone rang. It's Eddie."

I got up and went to the bedroom.

"Eddie," I said into the receiver.

"Robert. I got a little piece of information for you."

"What?"

"You know the bodies of those two illegals?"

"I can't forget."

"Well, turns out that they had a detour on the way to the potter's field. Mr. Tin paid for having them shipped to China."

"Tin? From the Greater China Association?"

"Yeah, him!"

"What's he trying to pull?"

"I don't know, but it's an expensive distraction, if that's what it is."

"Thanks for the info. I'll check in with him in the morning."

"I'm sorry to call so late with maybe not so important information. I didn't know I'd be waking up a kid."

"That's all right. He doesn't care."

"Okay, then."

"Hey, Eddie. Offhand, what would you say is a good way to get a woman back? I got a friend whose wife—"

"Vandyne?"

"What! Um, no! Not him!"

"Has to be! You don't have any other friends!"

"Shit."

"Anyway, my advice is don't try too hard. Women get annoyed when you try too hard. They complain that men aren't attentive enough, but they are creatures that love to fight and win your attention. So it pays to ignore them a little. In fact, Vandyne should probably err on the side of coming off as not caring."

"She left because she felt like he didn't care."

"Then I think he should err on the side of trying too hard. All women are different. You have to respect their individuality."

"Thanks for the advice."

"Don't mention it. Hey, if it doesn't work out, then tell him to come visit me in San Fran. I know a lot of fine women who have it together. Maybe you, too? That is, if things don't work out with Lonnie. I mean you said you guys probably aren't getting married, right?"

"I didn't say that, I meant just not real soon."

"So maybe you want to play the field some more on the side?"

"I'm set, Eddie."

"Hey, I'm sorry again for waking up Paul. Sometimes I forget you have a kid over there when I call on the later side."

"He can handle it. He's more like a roommate."

"Sounds young on the phone. Anyway, are you busy tomorrow?"

"Depends. What's going on? You got some fine women you want Vandyne to meet?"

"No. We're busting in on Ng. Want to come watch?"

"What time?"

"Twenty-two hundred. Oh, and don't tell anyone but Vandyne."

"Yeah, see you. And thanks." I hung up. I had mixed feelings about Ng. Locking him up somehow didn't feel right.

I came back to the living room. The burger smell was pretty strong. Then I saw that it was because Paul was making more Make-a-Better Burgers.

"Oh, Chow, I asked Paul if there were some left over. I didn't mean to make him cook some new ones. I haven't eaten dinner."

"I'm hungry again," said Paul. "How about you, Robert?"

"I could eat one," I said. I went over to the couch and picked up the Brim and drank it quickly in big gulps. I hated it, but I also hated wasting things, and I figured the onion taste from the burger would make everything better anyway.

25

VANDYNE AND I CRAWLED NORTH ON MULBERRY STREET AND pulled in behind a box truck that was parked on the sidewalk against the funeral home. It was about midnight and the streets in Chinatown were dead quiet. Our radios were off.

"This is it," I said. "This is the end of the line for Ng."

"I still remember when you almost believed he was going to save the youth of Chinatown," said Vandyne, stretching his arms behind his head.

"Just goes to show you, man. Everybody has an ulterior motive."

"How long do you think he'll get?"

"Eddie said Al Capone only got six and a half years and that Ng will get less. Funny thing is Capone got his start right on this block, when this used to be Five Points."

"He murders all those people, bootlegs enough liquor to fill the Great Lakes, and yet he gets busted on something stupid—tax evasion."

"Criminals spend so much time planning out their crimes, they never think about how they're going to hide all that money. Once they grab the money they think they've won already."

Vandyne looked down at his hands.

"Say, Chow, you ever have one of those integrity tests?"

"No. Not yet. You?"

"Yeah. Tried to get me about a year ago. I was ticketing a car, not too far from here, on the other side of the park. The window was open and a book was sitting in the front seat. *Gone with the Wind*. I won't forget that. There was a five-dollar bill sticking out, like a bookmark. I was going to leave a note and turn the book in to the station before someone else reached in and stole it."

"But you were going to keep the five bucks?"

"I swear, I was going to turn the whole thing in. But before I picked up the book, I stopped. I thought about what a racist book it was and that I didn't want to help somebody who was getting their kicks reading it. I mean that bill was more than halfway through."

"Of course, it was an integrity test. The lousy five bucks should have tipped you off that it was Internal Affairs trying to catch you. They're way too cheap to even leave a twenty-dollar bill in there!"

"You know, partner, if I had picked that book up—just picked it up— they were going to swoop in on me right there. Then you and I would be having a very different conversation right now. I'd be asking you about what restaurants you liked to go to for free food and I'd be wearing a wire."

"It's a good thing you trusted your commitment to racial justice," I said, crossing my arms. "So if it were *Manchild in the Promised Land* sitting there, you'd be done, right?"

"I'd be Manchild Wearing a Wire."

"It doesn't make any sense for Internal Affairs to recruit the crooked cops that get busted, but I guess no one would volunteer to join."

"And a sore cop would want to trap another one."

"Five puny dollars. What kind of integrity test is that? Finding money and not picking it up is an intelligence test. An integrity test is when it's life versus death."

Vandyne grunted, but I wasn't sure if he agreed or not. I think he was annoyed at the memory of being baited.

I looked around. The streets and sidewalks looked dirty in the spots under streetlights. I looked up Park Street and wondered when I would see the Department of the Treasury agents swoop in.

Suddenly, sounds of a lion dance came thundering above.

"It's Ng's last hurrah," I said.

"Be on the lookout for him sneaking out in a lion costume," said Vandyne.

"He'll be the lion holding the briefcase."

A man dashed out of the building entrance next to the funeral home. It was Don. He ran up to the box truck and slammed his hands against the sides.

"Jesus," said Vandyne.

"I'm going to get him the hell out of there before Don fucks everything up!"

I jumped out and grabbed Don's right arm.

I said to him through clenched teeth, "Don, you've got to go back to your apartment!"

"The men are coming!" he yelled. "The men behind the walls!"

I twisted his arm behind him to a degree that should have bent him over in pain, but he remained as wild and squirming as ever. Don knocked my radio to the ground. I managed to drag him to the vestibule of his building through the wide-open door. All four of his limbs were going crazy. I didn't know how much longer I could hold out.

Don broke away from me but ran inside instead of out in the street. I shut the door behind me and crouched down slightly, ready to tackle him under his center of gravity.

I wasn't sure where Don had picked up the sledgehammer, but it had me reconsidering which side of the door I wanted to be on.

He held it in two hands, casually walking in a circle by the first flight of stairs and looking up at the ceiling.

"Careful with that, Don," I said. "Sledgehammers can hurt people."

"Don't you hear them, Robert?" he asked. "They're coming!"

He turned and slammed the sledgehammer against the wall.

Wow, Don, I thought. You can kiss your security deposit good-bye and then some. Your dad is going to freak out and somehow blame it on me.

Pow! Pow! He was swinging away at the walls Daddy had always tried to put up around him to keep him safe. Dust from pulverized brick, plaster, and paint swirled ghostlike around him. The sledgehammer struck again and again. This probably would mean years of institutionalization for Don. He was too much of a threat to himself and others to live on his own now.

I fingered the leather holster of my service revolver. I was becoming afraid that I might have to use it if he came at me. Maybe I should walk away, barricade the door from the outside, and call an ambulance.

I thought I heard a cry come from the wall. Was he waking up the dead from the funeral home next door? A hole was opening up. When it was about the size of a face, Don stepped back.

Strangely sober, he said, "Robert, take a look."

I walked over, waving my hand through the dust in the air. I looked into the hole and saw a confused Chinese man looking back at me. I shook my head to make sure it wasn't a mirror I was looking into. He turned to somebody and said something in Fukienese.

"There really are people back there!" I said.

I looked at Don. He was sitting on the stairs, wiping his brow and panting.

"Gimme that," I said, pointing to the sledgehammer. He handed it over and I swung away at the wall around the hole.

Bricks crumbled away like cookies. Soon the hole was a few feet wide. Through the dusty air I saw a line of Chinese men staring back at me. I dug my thumb into my holster, stretched out the leather, and pulled out my gun. The men backed away. There was some light in there, enough to see around.

I turned to Don and said, "Go get Vandyne." He nodded, then went upstairs. "Out front, Don!" I yelled at him. Maybe he was running to the roof. I cursed him.

If I left now, these men, obviously illegals, might run away. I had to take a chance that Vandyne would come out and check on me for backup.

I ducked and stepped through the hole. I found myself in an alley that ran from the funeral home to the courtyard of the condemned rear-tenement building. At one point the alley had been crudely bricked up, but it was all knocked down and hollowed out now. Someone had even installed a lightbulb at the corner of the alley where it turned. I counted fifteen smelly men, all in their twenties and thirties. They wore dirty tank tops and slacks and seemed too dispirited and tired to be any trouble.

"What's going on here?" I asked in Cantonese and then in Mandarin.

"We are victims," said one man in Mandarin. With his unkempt hair, glasses, wide nose, and miserable expression, he looked oddly like Woody Allen. "They make us move from city to city every few months. We were living in the safe house," Woody moped, pointing to the rear tenement. "Then someone just told us we had to get back into the truck right away."

"How do you get into the truck?"

"This tunnel goes to the loading dock of the funeral home. This is how we got in. But there's nobody here to open the truck, so we're stuck here."

"You guys are human snakes, right?" Woody nodded. "Who is the snakehead?"

"We call him Brother Five."

I walked to the courtyard end of the tunnel and looked up. I saw the lights on at Beautiful Hong Kong's offices. I heard shouting and figured that the Treasury agents and Eddie had made their move already.

Then I noticed a shadow scampering down the remnants of a fire escape. It dropped to the ground, fell over, and then started running across the courtyard.

I backed into the tunnel and crouched down.

"Be quiet, everybody," I said.

Ng came into the tunnel, out of breath. "Truck driver. Ran away," he gasped. "I'll take you out."

I stood up and pointed my gun at his chest.

"Have you checked the tank?" I asked. "You're running on empty, Brother Five!"

"Robert!" he said, opening his arms. With a surprising dash of energy he rushed me, and I couldn't get my gun around fast enough to clobber him on the head. We both hit the ground. My sap dug into my thigh. I sure could have used it now, especially since I dropped my gun. Ng was punching at my face, hitting every other time. There was so much silt in the air it was hard to see and breathe.

I reached around desperately with my right hand and came up with half a brick. I slammed it against Ng's head twice. He rolled off of me. I got up and recovered my revolver.

"You're a snakehead, Ng! I should just shoot you right now!"

He was on all fours, breathing hard. Some blood was leaking out from his head around his ear.

"Listen, Robert," he said. "I gave these people better lives!"

"You made them into slaves!"

"They make more money now than they ever would have in China." He switched to Mandarin so some of the men could understand. "Yes, these people have suffered, but in the long run they will be much better off than if they had stayed in China. They will remember me for helping them."

"They might remember you on visiting day, but don't count on it."

"Hey, all of you! I know a lot of you are unhappy now, but I told you exactly what you would be doing! Did I lie about anything? I've been protecting you from unpatriotic Chinese like this man here!"

"It's very patriotic to exploit your fellow Chinese, isn't it, Ng?"

"Look, Robert! I want to show you something. Don't shoot, okay?" He reached into his back pocket with his thumb and index finger and slowly drew out a thin, stubby knife. Ng tossed it aside.

"See that?" he asked. "I could have stabbed you, Robert, but I didn't! You are still a brother to me. You're just confused right now." He looked at the hole that Don and I had made in the side of the tunnel.

"You're confused, Ng! You fuck over people from China and find some way to justify it!" Blood was rushing through my ears. "What about those two you had killed, Ng? Did you really need their money so bad?"

"I didn't know they were going to be killed!" he said. "I contracted a gang to just scare them. They got carried away!"

"They were tortured and killed! Animals don't get treated like that!"

"I paid good money to their families! I settled the score!"

"I'm going to settle the score right now!" I flipped the safety off my revolver.

"Robert, you know I'm not the worst one out there," Ng said softly, trying the calm-talk technique. "If you get rid of me, some cold-blooded bastard will take my place. Someone who doesn't have the interests of the people at heart."

Shouting from the courtyard grew louder. They were looking for Ng.

"I'm going out that hole, Robert," he said. "You're going to let me through."

I stepped over to block it.

"No way, Ng."

He was still on all fours but crawled closer to the hole on his belly.

"Think about your own illegal-alien father, Robert," he said. "How much worse would his life have been in China?"

"He might still be alive, Ng!"

"It was what he chose, Robert." Ng rubbed his head and rose shakily to his feet. "Now I have to go. So step aside, brother." I thought I saw him reach into his back pocket.

I shot him.

26

WHEN I PULLED THE TRIGGER I IMMEDIATELY SAW MYSELF STAND-
ing in a clearing in a jungle, surrounded by smoke and fire.

The recoil from the shot bounced my wrist back like right after I
had slapped an old papa-san or mama-san.

I watched men running away into the courtyard, screaming. I turned
my head and saw Vandyne peering at me through a broken patch of green
bamboo.

I pointed at Ng's crumpled body and said, "Mere Gook Rule, Vandyne." That was how we used to justify killings.

But Ng hadn't died. I had shot him in the upper arm and the bullet had
passed through without even hitting bone.

He was charged with violating several federal and state income-tax
laws. We were still waiting for an indictment for conspiracy to smuggle
aliens.

The big problem—for me in particular—was that Ng was suing the

NYPD and looking to indict me for attempted murder and reckless endangerment.

"Shooting an unarmed man!" thundered the Brow, the C.O. of the Fifth. "Have you completely lost your already-feeble mind, Officer Chow! Or do you people find that to be acceptable conduct?" I was in a meeting in his office, which meant one of two things—trouble or big trouble.

"Sir, he could have been reaching for a knife!"

"He says he took it out and put it down first!"

"I don't remember that. I'm a little confused about it." I didn't dare mention my father or the Vietnam flashback.

"If you're indicted, you'll have to hire your own defense lawyer, Officer Chow! The department won't stand for a dissolute character!" He stomped his foot and raised his broken eyebrow at me.

"He was smuggling people into this country and I stopped him."

"That will make a wondrous opening statement! Why, the jury will be leaping out of their seats—to hang you! If I had had any say in it, I would never have allowed you to take on investigative assignments. This incident proves me right!" He stomped again to emphasize his point.

"Sir, I do have Lefty in my corner. Of course, you knew him better as Jewey Jew Jew."

The Brow broke into a hideous smile and his blue eyes sparkled. "Ah, yes! Well, we'll see how Lefty feels about you after the witnesses are finished with their statements upstairs!"

"We have witnesses?" I asked, shocked that any Chinese—much less illegals—would make statements about anything.

"They're upstairs with English right now," he said, his smile breaking into rapturous joy as he sensed my fear. "They were quite anxious to be witnesses, as a matter of fact."

"They're willing to take the sworn word of illegal immigrants against a police officer?" I said.

"I sympathize with you, Officer Chow. Surely the worst of The Finest are more reputable than scum that floated over and washed up on our shores. But this matter is out of my hands. You're at the mercy of the liberals now."

I took a deep breath.

"May I leave, sir?" I asked.

"Dismissed in disgrace," he said.

I left and shut the door behind me. I looked up and saw English coming down the stairs. I went up to him.

"How's it looking?" I asked.

He smiled. "These three guys say they saw him coming at you with a knife."

I recognized two men coming down the stairs as being human snakes. The third one, who was still talking with the pretty community interpreter, was the guy who looked like Woody Allen.

"What's going to happen to them?" I asked English.

"It's up to the INS now," he said.

"Does testifying help them in any way?"

"It actually probably hurts them. They already had a consultation with a lawyer, but they still testified that they were smuggled here and weren't facing persecution in China. With statements like that, sooner or later they're going to be deported."

I couldn't believe these Fukienese guys were sticking their necks out for a Cantonese guy, and I say that because I was sure that they didn't see me as an American. Either way, I had little in common with any of them and they only stood to lose by helping me out.

The three men shook my hand and I got a lump in my throat.

"Don't worry about us," Woody whispered to me. "When we get back to China, we'll pay a fine, but we'll try coming again until we make it."

The indictment never came down for me, and Ng's suit against the NYPD was dismissed. Unfortunately, there wasn't enough time to get an indictment against Ng on conspiracy to smuggle aliens.

Ng had been recovering in Columbia Presbyterian Hospital under a fake name and switched rooms daily, but that didn't prevent unknown assailants from shooting Ng and two armed guards to death. The hospital's staff hadn't heard anything unusual but told the New York *Daily News* that Ng had had many laughs with several different Oriental visitors.

The D.A.'s office had tried to find Eric, the kid who had been in the hospital, as a potential witness against Ng while he was alive, but nobody was at the street address Eric had given and no one had seen him since he had been discharged.

I found her on the sidewalk outside her Midtown apartment, watching movers roll out furniture into a trailer truck.

"Winnie, I'm sorry about your brother."

"Officer Chow!" she cried, and grabbed my arm. "Oh, I'm feeling so many different emotions, I don't know what to say to you. I'm mad at you for shooting my brother, but I knew he wasn't a good man. Still, I never knew it would all end like this!"

"It's a little tough for me to believe that you had no hand in what happened to Andy."

"I'm a girl. I don't know anything."

"But you must have *heard* a lot."

Her expression shriveled up a bit and I got an idea of what her mom looked like.

"Look here, Officer Chow. I've been cleared of any wrongdoing by agencies of your federal government. I'm even negotiating a settlement for paying the back taxes on Beautiful Hong Kong."

"I see you're on the run, though, like a common criminal."

"I'm leaving because this country disgusts me. I think the main problem is that you have too many different people and cultures in America. You people don't even know who you are, mixing in with everybody."

"'You people'? You mean Chinese Americans?"

"Of course! The Chinese people of Singapore separated from the dark-skinned people of Malaysia and we've never been happier, because Chinese people are strongest when we stick together!"

"We do have a lot of problems in America—I'll give you that. But our country is made from people who came here from other parts of the world for better opportunity here. We don't always get it right the first time, but we believe that everybody here is equal. I'll bet you've never seen so many different people as in the streets of New York."

"This is an ugly, smelly city and it makes me sick."

"Hey," I said. "You can badmouth America, but shut up about New York."

That only hardened her up even more. "I'm sorry I'm not in a good mood, Officer Chow," she spat, "but I have to go back to Singapore to bury my dead brother."

"Just a second, Winnie. Tell me you knew he was Brother Five."

She looked at me hard with glaring eyes that could burn ants on the sidewalk. "You have no decency whatsoever," she said, crossing her arms. "I didn't love Singapore when I was growing up, but now I see how much better it is than America."

"What are you going to do there, Winnie?"

"Well, *somebody* has to head the family business."

I stopped to see Mr. Tin at the Greater China Association's office, but I was held at the reception desk. He came down instead of letting me up.

"Mr. Tin, how is Don? The last time I saw him he was in the ambulance—"

He broke in on me. "You son of a bitch! I trusted you to look after my son and he ends up in the emergency room!"

"He was examined and released!"

"I've sent Don to live in a good Shanghainese community in London. It was a mistake to ever let him live among the lowly Cantonese!"

"You're keeping Don from getting the help that he needs, Mr. Tin."

"It's my business, not yours!"

"Why did you pay to have those two bodies sent back to China?"

"It was a decent thing to do, so of course you wouldn't understand why, Robert! Historically, the final duty of any association to their members was to send bodies back to China for an honorable burial in the family cemetery. I wanted to see those two men treated with respect after what they had to endure here."

"Thanks for clearing that up, Mr. Tin."

"Stop calling me Tin! My name is T'ien, you peasant! If you ever bother me again, you're going to end up worse off than a dead dog with three legs!"

To confirm that I had ruined my reputation in all quarters of Chinatown, I went next to Together Chinese Kinship's office. Mr. Song jumped out of his chair and charged me, stopping just short of my nose.

"You son of a bitch!" he yelled. "You got me roped into this snakehead bullshit! All the Chinese newspapers have hanged me along with the Fukienese community on the editorial pages! Even the Communist paper is distancing itself from me!"

"You didn't break any laws, Mr. Song. You're not being charged with any crimes whatsoever."

"My reputation was torn apart by being investigated by the INS!"

"They said they didn't find anything! You're clean!"

"But they were here! Now everybody thinks I'm good at hiding things—and smuggling people!"

I heard footsteps overhead and glanced up the staircase.

"Don't bother looking for Stephanie!" Mr. Song said. "I sent her back to Connecticut already to keep her out of reach from you!"

"Me? What are you talking about?"

"I saw you looking at her! Like a dog drooling after meat!"

* * *

I met Izzy for a sandwich at Katz's on Houston Street.

After I told him about everything, he said, "It's tough."

"Looking back," I said, "maybe I should have given you a call while this was all going on."

"Why?" Izzy was the kind of guy who liked to grunt while eating, and his grunts were louder than his voice.

"So you could have advised me. I mean, I got a zero on your test, so I obviously need some help."

"I would have listened," he said, wiping his mouth. "Don't know if I could have helped."

"Well, from what I've told you, is there anything I could have done better?"

"Different, sure. But not better."

"Things could have been way better! The guy didn't have to die!"

"But you're okay. That's not bad."

"Do you think you guys'll find the guys who killed Ng?" I was referring to Izzy's Manhattan South crew.

"Naw. Nobody talks. No media pressure. Have to nail FALN first, anyway."

I squeezed mustard on one side of my plate and thumped out some ketchup on the other side for my fries.

"Izzy, everybody in Chinatown hates me now."

"The leaders hate you. Not the people." He smiled. "You helped the people and the leaders resent it."

"I've basically tried to do the right thing, but I'm worried that I might be making everything worse."

Izzy shook his head and sipped from his can of black-cherry soda. "You're young."

I took Vandyne to Penn Station to catch a train to Philly.

"How long are you going to stay out there?" I asked.

"Few days, I guess. Been a while since I've had time for my momma. Rose knows where to reach me, so she can if she wants to."

"How's that going?"

He threw up his hands. "You tell me. You haven't talked to Rose, have you, partner?"

"Naw. Chock full o'Nuts was the last time."

"It's all right if you do."

We slapped hands hard and hugged.

I didn't get to see Eddie before he went back to San Francisco, but I promised to visit him sometime. He told me on the phone that he had found the guy who knew my dad from the association days. The former association hall was now cut up into a mixed-use building and my father's old friend sold slippers on the ground floor. Eddie sent my father's articles by Express Mail. The old man had everything in a locked box, and out of respect Eddie hadn't gone through the contents.

The FALN thing was still going on, so I had the squad room to myself when the package came in.

I took out my keys and cut the packing tape. Eddie had put some San Francisco Chinatown postcards on top. It looked less crowded and spread out than New York. On the back of a picture of Miss Chinatown 1975 he had written MY GIRLFRIEND!

Under a layer of crumpled newspapers I found the box. It was disappointingly light. A key was taped to the plastic handle.

I unlocked it and opened the lid. There wasn't much inside. On top was a copy of an unevenly folded certificate of identity issued to Chinese people from the Department of Labor. The picture attached to it was the same one my mother and I had burned money to. The certificate identified my father by the ridiculous name of Ah Chin Fong. It was his paper name plus a stray character.

A scrap of paper recorded everything he had eaten in a particular week. Pork in shrimp sauce, preserved bean curd, and pickles figured in many entries. This was probably why he hated pork in shrimp sauce, preserved bean curd, and pickles by the time I was around.

Under that was some sheet music that featured pictures of Al Jolson on the covers. I wasn't aware that he had performed outside of black-face.

At the bottom was what I thought was a diary. As I flipped through the pages, it became apparent that the book was a ledger.

I turned it sideways to read the columns. It was undoubtedly my father's handwriting, and while it was mostly numbers, small notations left no doubt as to what the book recorded.

"Paper identity $2,000, boat travel $200," was the column head for most of the entries. The names of the people were written in code—"long fingers," "old duck," "Mr. Brown"—and apparently they paid weekly increments of five to ten dollars.

Most had a black line drawn through with my father's seal stamped at the ends of the entries, running pages and years down the line. Several accounts were ominously cut short.

I shut the book and pushed it into my bottom drawer and kicked it shut. I braced myself on my desktop with slippery, sweaty hands. My father had been a precursor to snakeheads like Ng. He must have made huge amounts of money, but I was at a loss to explain why my family, when I grew up, was barely scraping by.

My phone rang. Lonnie told me the Presswire interview went great and that she thought she had the job. I don't remember what I said.

27

September 9, 1976

IT WAS LONNIE'S LAST DAY AT THE BAKERY AND A TON OF PEOPLE
had turned out to see her off. She struggled to hand me a box of moon
cakes to bring to my mother's house for the Mid-Autumn Festival. It
was so crowded I could feel other people's heartbeats.

"Robert, it's crazy!" she shouted.

"You're going to miss this!" I yelled back.

"Yes, but I'm ready for a change!"

The cash register was invisible under taped red envelopes that were
stuffed with five- or ten-dollar bills. Most of the envelopes had scribbled
notes on them reading: "Good luck, Lonnie!"

The bakery was getting a little too pushy and we only managed to
touch fingertips before I had to go.

I stopped by the toy store, but it was also packed. The door wouldn't
even shut.

I banged on the glass and waved to Paul and the midget. Paul gave
me the thumbs-up. The midget nodded at me.

* * *

My mother greeted me at the door in a Hawaiian blouse.

"Where did you get that from, Mom?" I asked as I stepped in.

"I went to Hawaii a few months ago. Didn't I tell you?"

"I don't remember you saying. I would have remembered. Did you go by yourself?"

"I went with a friend from work."

"Man or woman?"

"Robert, what are you thinking? Of course a woman! Just a girls' trip!"

I brought the moon cakes to the kitchen and undid the red plastic tie.

"Mom, do you think of your husband often?"

"What kind of question is that?"

"He was a real swell guy, wasn't he?"

"Don't slander your father on a holiday . . . or any other day!"

"I didn't tell you, Mom, but I got ahold of some of Dad's old stuff from San Francisco."

She smiled as wide as she could, but there was fear in her eyes.

"That's wonderful!" she said. "How did you manage to find it?"

"I have a friend who works in the police department out there."

She swallowed. "What sort of things did you find?"

"I found some sheet music and a funny little book in there."

"Was it Al Jolson's music?"

"Yes."

"Oh. He had always wanted to learn how to play Jolson's songs. He liked that it was happy music. Never got around to it. Never got the piano, either."

"You know what was in that book, Mom?"

"I don't know."

"It was a record of people making payments to the association. People who were illegally brought in."

"Are you sure?"

"I have the book in my desk *down in the squad room at the police station!*"

"Burn it!" she yelled. "He should have destroyed it years ago. But he needed it in case future disputes came up. He was always scared the authorities would find it. He just never imagined that it would be his own son."

"Dad was sneaking people into the country and exploiting them, wasn't he?"

"It was a complicated situation, Robert. People in the association had a number of paper slots to bring in fake sons from China. The association helped to broker between buyers and sellers. Your father made sure that once the paper son was through payments were kept up."

"What happened if they didn't have the money?"

"Then your father would let them pay late or they would provide goods in place of that."

"What happened if they couldn't do that?"

"Sometimes your father would even make the payment for them."

"What about after that?"

"I don't know! A lot of things could have happened!"

"Did he have people killed, Mom?"

"He made sure that everybody paid off their debts!"

"But some people couldn't pull it off, right?"

"Almost everybody did!"

"That's still not everybody! You told me that a dead Chinese body would just get rolled into a ditch and buried, no questions asked!"

"Robert!"

"Did he shoot people, stab them, or strangle them?"

"I don't have to listen to this!"

"How many people did Dad turn into ghosts?"

"Your! Father! Did! The! Best! He! Could!" she yelled, her face as red as a lit paper lantern.

We were both furious and ready to bite each other's heads off. I pointed at the box of moon cakes.

"Mom," I said as calmly as I could muster. "That box of cakes was a present from Lonnie and it's not going to waste. Now put some tea on and we're going to sit down and eat them all and have a happy Mid-Autumn Festival!"

"All right, Robert."

My mother told me most of my dad's story in a detached, matter-of-fact sort of way as we ate slices of moon cakes. I was sure she was still leaving stuff out.

Nobody eats moon cakes because they taste good. In fact, I couldn't tell the difference among the date, red-bean, and lotus-seed fillings. It was all dense and impossible to chew and swallow without some hot tea to help it down.

Some of the cakes have a hard-boiled egg yolk in the center that represents the moon. Why you'd want to eat the moon, I don't know. I could have asked my mother, but I wasn't going to interrupt her for that.

My father's pathetic little tale would have made a great holiday wire-service story for Lonnie. Yet I didn't quite know how to tell her—or anybody else—about all this.

He had made his association rich out west by exploiting the illegals. The elders were so impressed they sent him off to New York with a chunk of money and a deed to their San Francisco building to secure a loan for a building on Mott Street. It was going to be the association's East Coast headquarters.

The New York associations had gotten wind that a potential competitor was planning on setting up shop in town, but instead of simply shooting my father, they killed him with flattery.

"A big shot from California!" they called him. "A king from the West!"

They brought him out to eat and set him up with tabs at the bars. He also had generous accounts in the gambling dens and beds at the brothels.

My father's sweet ride in New York didn't last long. Soon he had lost everything in the gambling dens—even the deed to the San Francisco association's office. Somebody flew out there and took it over, establishing a West Coast office for one of the New York associations.

On top of that, my father had worked himself heavily into debt. Someone took pity on him and got him two jobs washing dishes and waiting tables to work off the debt. He was still in debt fifteen years later when World War II rolled around. He enlisted in the segregated navy and served food and coffee on an aircraft carrier for two years.

After his discharge, he flew to Hong Kong and got my mother under the War Brides Act.

When they got to New York, they found that his debt had continued to accrue interest while he had been away. He was almost back to where he had started.

My mother did all she could to prop him up. Working for Americans. Cooking and cleaning. Giving him a son. The debts were eventually paid off, but the sour man who was left was beyond redemption. He was already pickled by the poisonous choices he'd made in life.

My father was a snakehead who couldn't handle his own bite.

On the subway ride back to Chinatown I looked around at the twisting lines of the spray-painted ceilings, walls, and seats. I had the whole car to myself, which wasn't really a luxury. The subway car jerked around and sometimes the lights went out. I felt like a lone crayon bouncing around inside a marked-up box.

Getting out of the Canal Street station, I heard a raucous celebration up on the surface world complete with screaming, fireworks, and loud drumming. Mid-Autumn Festival was usually fairly restrained, with people choking down moon cakes with their unfortunate friends and family.

I came up the stairs and found the streets so crowded that all I could see at first was black hair and raised hands.

"Mao's dead! Mao's dead!" the crowd yelled.

The Greater China Association was shooting off alternating rounds of fireworks and firecrackers. I struggled to walk down Mott Street.

Above me people were leaning out of windows, shaking KMT flags like they had bugs on them.

"You see that?" an old man said to the grandson on his shoulders. "That's the real flag of China! It's going to be flying in Beijing before I die! The Communists are finished!"

I brushed off burned scraps of firecracker paper from my head and shoulders.

I made my way through crowded pro-KMT Chinatown and through the empty blocks of lit windows in pro-Communist Chinatown to get to the place that I call home.

Acknowledgments

FIRST OF ALL, I WISH TORRENTIAL RAINS OF LOVE UPON MY UNI-versal partner and first reader, Cindy Cheung.

Sunyoung Lee, you are wonderful in every way.

My agent Kirby Kim, you're the man!

My editor Diana Szu, you're the woman!

All respect to clans and extensions of Kaya, Cheng, Cheung, Kim, Lin, and Liu.

Detective Yu Sing Yee, NYPD (retired), and Detective Thomas Ong, NYPD (retired), thank you for letting me bust in on you again.

The Asian/Pacific/American Institute at New York University granted me access to their archives. You are awesome and beautiful people: Jack Tchen, Laura Chen-Schultz, Alexandra Chang, and I-Ting Emily Chu.

Heavy bows and respectable gifts to Wanda Cheung, Chez Ong, Corky Lee, Molly Cain, Mayumi Takada, Neela Banerjee, Chris Bowe, Harvey Dong, Karen Maeda Allman, Sarah Onufer, and Eugene Shih.

Epigraph from *Xunzi: Basic Writings,* translated by Burton Watson.

www.edlinforpresident.com
www.myspace.com/edlinforpresident
www.facebook.com/edlinforpresident
www.twitter.com/robertchow